Published by Winsor Bleu Editions
www.miriamnesset.com

See the website for other books by Miriam Nesset
www.miriamnesset.com

Book design by Miriam Nesset
Cover art by Linda Windell
www.mStarStudio.com

Printed by Walch Printing
Portland, Maine
U.S.A.

For my daughter, Alison…

with thanks to Ginger Lawson for the inspiration, Raphaelle Goodrich for French translations, Alison Rowe, Donna Saywright and Ginger Lawson for first reads, Paul Pouliot, Sag8mo of the Cowasuck Band of the Pennacook-Abenaki People for Abenaki/Cowasuck translations, Regina Schaare-Denio for access to her extensive library, Joan Martinez for technical assistance, and Cpt. Phineas Sprague, Jr. for nautical advice.

Sea Smoke is a novel, a work of fiction. References to historical circumstances, locales, events or people are fictitious. While some place names may in reality exist, they are not necessarily accurate in their juxtaposition, geographic location or description.

Sea Smoke

A Novel

By

Miriam Nesset

The ocean disentangles the netted mind.

Everything loosens and comes back to itself.

—Anam Cara

— CHAPTER ONE —

Where are they now? What lands and skies
Paint pictures in their friendly eyes?
What hope deludes, what promise cheers,
What pleasant voices fill their ears?
Two are beyond the salt sea waves,
And three already in their graves.
Perchance the living still may look
Into the pages of this book,
And see the days of long ago
Floating and fleeting to and fro,
As in the well-remembered brook
They saw the inverted landscape gleam,
And their own faces like a dream
Look up upon them from below.

From *Finale* by Longfellow

A freshened wind breezed across the deck of *Mordonn*. Captain Penberthy stood at the starboard rail staring at the figurehead—a scantily clad sea nymph astride a dolphin. Turning, he looked across the water toward Penwith and the low bank of clouds to the west, thankful for the promise of good weather at last. It was the change for which he'd been waiting. Gentle waves ruffled against the wooden hull moored in the harbor—the restless ship surging at anchor as though impatient to be at sea again. To southward, the sun cast its early fall light on the calm and serene waters of Mount's Bay in the distance. Moving aft, his thoughts on the tide and wind, he made ready to alert his mates they'd be leaving in the morning on the tide.

The last ship to arrive in the harbor from America, across the western sea, had carried dreadful news of pirates. Captain Spargo, with his ship *Pygenmys Kolonn*, had happened upon the galleon *Grysel*, floating in doldrums. She appeared to be abandoned, and his first thought had been to put a boarding crew on her and sail her back to England as salvage. After giving orders to stand off, back sail then heave to, he had sent a boat with three men over to assess the possibility of claiming it. They soon returned with the ship's log to report a ghastly scene. The entire crew had been murdered and the captain, long dead as well, lashed with warp to the mainmast. The helm had been tied off by slipping a becket over a spoke. With no further interest in the ship, Captain Spargo had ordered *Grysel* scuttled as a mercy.

"Ennis, assemble the ship's company," Penberthy instructed, regaining the quarterdeck.

Ennis was the only seaman aboard who had sailed with him before, and Penberthy was happy to have him as part of his crew.

"All hands on deck," Ennis roared with negligent ease, resting his hand on the binnacle box next to the helm.

Penberthy listened as a seaman standing at the forecastle caught the order and passed it on. Soon the command, relayed from man to man then deck to deck, echoed throughout the ship. The captain suspected it was not indifference but a hangover that dulled Ennis' usual good nature and alertness. He'd taken shore leave with the crew the night before, going to a tavern in port.

Gorran Ennis, a jolly soul with laughing eyes—strong as an ox but slight of build and bandy-legged. As a mate, he would oversee the crew. Through years of experience, he had become proficient in a wide variety of navigational duties, but he would never be a captain. He hadn't the disposition necessary nor had he enough peace within. This would probably be his last sea voyage for he was ready to *bite the anchor*. Now a wizened old tar with reddish hair and whiskers streaked with gray, his face was imprinted with years of weather extremes at sea—his character as colorful as the scarf banded round his head. His hair was in a queue and, like most of the other sailors he wore a blue and white striped shirt with a bateau neckline, baggy pants, and black, salt-stained half boots.

The crew emerged from the forecastle to join the men of the first dog watch, standing in disorderly fashion before the captain to receive their instructions. Penberthy ran a tight ship and frowned in seeing their lack of formality and impertinence warranting correction. Most of the men were very green, chattels to the captain to be paid when the voyage was completed. In addition to the seamen and captain, the ship would carry a bosun, purser, carpenter, doctor, cook, blacksmith, and sail master. Several of the men, the cook among them, were coastwise seamen inexperienced in deep waters. Others had been tried offshore but not in the North Atlantic. All had great interest in sailing to America, more than willing to put their "X" on a labor contract.

Life aboard a ship could be harsh, dangerous, and filled with great challenges. It offered little more to men than the opportunity to know their strength and spend their pay in a new port. Overall, seamen were a restless breed—a motley crew full of grievances, imagined or otherwise. Most accepted their lot in life, but only a few without grumbling. Meals on the ship were mediocre at best—the staple, salted meat too tough to chew. While food stores were fresh when they set out, eventually weevils would appear in the biscuits, water barrels often afloat with scum. The berthing area, with only small gratings for ventilation and light was, in good weather dark, stifling, damp, and thick with the smell of the bilge. Hammocks were mildewed. In bad weather, below deck was soaking wet. Drowning and injury were constant considerations. Penberthy saw his task not so much to ease their complaints and worries but to create an environment of strict discipline that would deter laggards and silence any thoughts of resistance that might evolve into mutiny.

"My responsibility is to see this ship, crew, and cargo safely to Boston," Penberthy began. "I haven't been impressed with how you step to or respond to orders from the mates. This will change immediately. God help the man that crosses me or the mates on this ship. Is that clear? I'll not have it! I will more than welcome the opportunity to make an example of the first man that chooses to do so. Understood? When any order is given, you will carry it out without question as though the very devil is chasing you. Show some pride in your efforts. Load the last of the fresh stores aboard, check the rigging one last time, then get some rest. There will be no shore leave. In the morning, ready your stations and look alive when the call is given to roll out. We make sail with the turn of the tide. Hands dismissed."

"Aye, aye, Captain," the drone of voices returned.

Having been told off, the crew scattered to their common duties with backward glances. They would be leaving on a day that, according to traditional lore, was bad luck—the concern obvious on their faces. Penberthy was aware of the sea myths regarding when to leave, who and what should or should not be aboard, and other nonsense, but refused to entertain silly notions that might interfere with the voyage schedule or captaining of his ship.

"Smithie, have their knives been blunted?"

"Aye, Sir, yesterday."

"Very well, proceed to your post."

"Ennis, split the first dog watch while the stores be loaded. Pick two replacements to take the last split and second dog watch. Set Chegwin to deck lookout."

"Aye, Aye, Sir," Ennis returned.

While not many of the crew had engaged in criminal activity, most had unsavory pasts. Some bragged about it, others remained tight-lipped regarding their former lives, only their demeanor exposing them. Penberthy had hired them at their word that they would work hard and could get along, and he planned to hold them to it. There would be no donnybrooks aboard his ship. Being a seaman was not for the delicate of mind. It required strength and discipline as living conditions deteriorated, was exhausting, and often a trial of boredom. The men had been busy since hiring on, readying the ship for departure, mending the sails and rigging, painting, and caulking. They first loaded cargo at the wharf then, once the ship had exceeded a safe draft at the berth, in the harbor where it was anchored. At sea there would be chores to do, routines to follow, and watches. They were at the mercy of the weather and Penberthy's ability to anticipate and avoid dangerous situations.

Only Ennis had made the trip to America before. Though prone to exaggeration, he had disavowed tales of the Sargasso Sea swallowing ships whole or terrifying sea serpents and mermen, instead talking about a New England coastline replete with sea obstructions—capes, points, islands, and headlands chiseled from the shore. He told of wild currents and extreme tidal waters in the Gulf of Maine that eroded headlands—at high tide filling bays and swallowing capes and islands, at low tide marooning ships becalmed on the flats.

He had experienced impressment first hand—a continued practice despite the repeal decades earlier of The Jefferson Embargo that had been enacted in part to stop it. The embargo, passed by the United States Congress in 1807 in response to Napoleon's dominance at sea with England, sought to avoid war by refusing to trade with Europe. Instead of achieving its intent, it crippled sea trade and commerce, drove up prices, left seamen without work, and contributed to events leading to the War of 1812. Improvement then normalcy had resumed in the decades since its repeal a year after enactment, but international trade had been slow to recover. It was not only British sailors that were impressed, but also those who appeared British. Ennis delighted in filling the ears of the crew with the possibility of their ending up in the Royal Navy.

On his last trip to America ten years earlier, he had gotten injured when cargo being offloaded in Boston fell on him. Unable to return to England with his shipmates, the only way he could find to get back was to sign onto an east bound Yankee ship that needed crew. The ship was soon intercepted at sea by the captain of a British vessel. He had been happy to be back in British hands but, having spent so much time and energy in avoidance of service, not so happy about being pressed into what turned out to be three years in the Royal Navy. Feeling that a man who had survived all he had deserved special attention, he felt obligated to impart his wisdom from years at sea—an endless source for tall tales and sea myths that kept his fellow crewmen entertained and appropriately in awe.

As a hired transport of the merchant fleet, *Mordonn* would have legal protection against impressment. Penberthy had been warned that many of the seamen going with him to America would not return—jumping ship and forfeiting their pay to remain. Loyalty to King William IV prevented him from any interest, other than curiosity, in the States. He was well aware that for the second leg of his voyage he might face difficulties in hiring a crew and be forced to take on incompetents or afterguards as seamen in order to get back to England. Still, he remained eager to go and for the opportunity at last of seeing Boston. Warnings regarding extreme tides, winds, and currents along the coast in the Gulf of Maine didn't bother him. It was hard to imagine anything more hazardous than conditions in An Mor Keltek, the Irish Sea, off Cornwall's northwest coast, Lands' End to the south or the Western Approaches. *All coastlines have their dangers and must be cautiously approached*, he concluded.

Scarlet streaked across the dimming sun in the western sky. With abstract attention, listening to the soft wash of the sea against the hull and the hum of the wind through the rigging, Penberthy watched the men hauling stores aboard for the voyage. His mind was fully occupied with plans and preparations. The crew was allowed little by way of dunnage. They got most of their clothes from the slop chest—cast offs from seamen previously on the ship. Concerned instead for enough food and water, he had planned carefully to insure their supplies would last well past the long trip of about a month to the New World. Food stores had been calculated to the man and, even though they could probably count on rain water, hogsheads of water, along with puncheons of rum and ale, were loaded. In addition to food stores there were spare sails, bolts of sail cloth, and endless coils of rope.

Several men were busy hoisting barrels of grain, salted meat, dried peas and beans, liquor, and water aboard with parbuckles from tenders on the port side of the ship. Others lugged the stores. Smitts, the purser, supervised the hauling and storing of goods, barking orders as the men climbed up and down the ladders between decks in a continuous flow to the galley, chandlery or hold. Fresh stores of raw vegetables and fruit were the last loaded.

Mordonn's mission, backed by wealthy Pensans merchant Carne Pender, and captained by Lanyon Penberthy, was to deliver its cargo of textiles, hardware, pig iron, and china to Boston. All total, over two hundred ton burthen had been laded, most of it secured in the hold, to await the captain and favorable winds.

Waiting patiently on the stone quay the day he'd come aboard a week earlier, Penberthy, in the traditional waistcoat, breeches, and tricorn hat, had followed the progress of the men rowing toward him—watching as they made fast along the wharf and tied up. One of the crew took his satchel and the captain made ready to step into the gig. Before he could get aboard, the seaman assisting him diverted his attention to a young lady walking toward them from the landward end of the wharf. Penberthy soon recognized her as Lamorna, his wife's younger sister. She held a small bundle in her arms, her head covered with the hood of a blue wool cape. In silence, she stood before him staring up into his eyes.

"Lamorna, what are you doing here?"

"I'm coming with you," she answered. "I have all my belongings with me."

"No, that canna be," he sternly responded.

Lamorna's mother had died giving birth to her. Her sister, Kayna, twelve years older, had virtually raised her and been a surrogate mother by all accounts. Their father, a fisherman often at sea, and Lamorna lived with Kayna and Lanyon once they were married. Lamorna had been devastated by the loss of her father, then sister. And so, despite his debilitating grief, Lanyon had kept her with him. Rosen Hendey, his housekeeper, saw to them both.

"Does Mrs. Hendey know you're here?" he asked, taking her arm and steering her away from the men.

"I can be an indentured servant like those who have gone before to America," she importuned, ignoring his question.

"No!"

"You must give me that chance. I have no one, nothing to keep me here. I don't want to stay here," she argued, in tears.

"What about that gray cat of Kayna's?" he asked, motioning to the cat that had suddenly appeared to stand next to her. "Who is to care for Morrigan?"

"With nine lives to live, I should think a cat could fend for itself," Lamorna offered, doggedly swiping away her tears.

Her response had surprised him. Being gone so much, he'd never paid much attention to Kayna's cat. But Lamorna had taken immediate and irrevocable custody of Morrigan upon Kayna's death, caring for it far more than her words indicated. They were so joined as to be nearly inseparable. Lanyon understood Lamorna's plight and desire to leave all too well, but he also saw in her a tendency to attach herself to anyone that would allow it. *And why wouldn't she*, his thoughts defended, *given such losses for a young girl.* She had grown close to Mrs. Hendey but had absolutely adhered to him since Kayna's death, despairing each time he left to go to sea. Looking at her, acknowledging that she had no one close in his absence, he felt great compassion. But taking her would present a whole series of difficulties and provide no end of additional responsibilities.

"The ship is no place for a young lady. T'is a merchant ship with cargo bound for America I'm responsible for, not a passenger ship."

Standing before her, drying her tears with his handkerchief, he noted, and not for the first time, how little like her sister she was—only a child, really. Kayna had been sensible and patient. Lamorna never did anything in halves. She was tow-headed with cerulean blue eyes, more similar to him than to her sister who was dark-haired with deep brown eyes. Kayna had been full-figured, womanly, a mother, while Lamorna was tall, wiry, wraithlike. He doubted she could make half a shadow. The differences between sisters was a mercy. Had they been more similar it would have been unbearable for him to have taken Lamorna into his care.

"Why do you so want to go to America when I and Mrs. Hendey are here?"

"There's no longer anything for me here," she reticently replied.

"Do not say I am nothing. I care for you as a sister, Lamorna."

"But you're not here—not often."

"T'is my work, Lamorna. My livelihood is with the sea."

"Then let me go with you."

He read the challenge and bravado in her eyes, but there was no way to accommodate her. Despite the burden of it, her welfare continued to be foremost in his considerations as he searched his mind for a solution.

"Soon after I return from America," he finally sighed and earnestly spoke, "I will be making another voyage there next spring, captaining a ship with passengers. I promise to include you if you still want to go. I'll even pay your passage."

"Do you so promise? Promise to take me with you?" Lamorna questioned, after a long pause.

"Yes, I do. Meanwhile, you must stay in my house with Mrs. Hendey. Now go! I have a ship to captain."

Brusquely turning on her heels, Lamorna followed the stone wharf toward town, her woolen skirt billowing with each stride. Loneliness and abandonment were not foreign emotions to him, and he felt great sadness as he watched her figure grow smaller. All things considered, he felt satisfied that he'd done the best by her he could. It was hard to believe she was nearing the same age Kayna had been when they'd married. He thought of Lamorna as being much younger. Instead of following her mistress, the gray cat remained behind, staring eerily up at him for a time before disappearing over the edge of the wharf. Sealing his promise to his sister-in-law with a nod of his head, Lanyon boarded the waiting launch.

His thoughts had remained scattered as the rhythm of the oars carried him out to the ship. He'd been on board before and knew the ship to be old, with well-worn decks. But it was freshly painted, the sails were new, and it appeared to be seaworthy. Once he'd climbed the boarding cleats and slipped through the gangway to step out onto the deck, Ennis had welcomed him with an earnest and firm handshake.

"Right foot first, Captain," Ennis blurted, winking. "Haul up t' gig and lash it to a cabin, as t' longboats has been, men," he roared.

Penberthy, taking his satchel from a crewman, had then proceeded to his cabin. Though he'd come aboard that day, shortly after the cargo had been loaded, it would be another week before favorable winds obliged them enough to set sail. The week had gone slowly, none more eager to leave than the captain.

Once the goods in the hold were unloaded at the docks in Boston, typical stores of fish oil, furs, livestock, agricultural surplus, oak barrel staves, casks, hoops and shingles, tar, turpentine, and rope would be hauled aboard and brought back to England. Since they were getting a late start, their anticipated arrival in Boston mid-October, it would be late November before their cargo could be loaded for the second leg of the voyage.

"I'll be in my quarters," Penberthy instructed Ennis, leaving him on the quarterdeck.

"A moonlit night bodes well fer weathah tomorra," Ennis informatively offered, sounding relieved as he pointed to the eastern sky where a silver blaze of moon breached the horizon. "By the time we git t' America, we'll be seein' t' Hunter's Moon."

Without comment, Penberthy went to his cabin. He found the old pagan ways and superstitions distracting, if not annoying but, knowing it was useless, made no effort to free the men of their notions. In his quarters, setting their course with charts, dividers, and parallel rules, he reassured himself it would make the best use of the immediate weather. Confident of good weather three days out, he wasn't worried but chewed on it a while. How the ship handled was an extension of him. Though a seasoned deep -water captain, he'd not been in charge of a vessel bound for North America. As a ship's mate he had made a few voyages to the West Indies and was therefore more familiar with Atlantic waters off the northern coast of South America. Once he'd become a captain, merchants had hired him to take cargoes, usually quintals of fish, to Spain and Portugal, then lade cargo from The Azores or Canary Islands. There, in ports, he'd seen the brigs that had come from New England crewed by Yankees, wishing he would be assigned the challenge of a route there. Now he was to get his chance.

His years of sailing provided confidence but, knowing how eagerly the sea waited to expose errors and take advantage of misfortunes, venturing into unfamiliar waters always resurrected prudent concern. And so, he was glad for the experience of Ennis. The safety and responsibility of the ship's company, as well as the cargo, weighed heavily with the captain, and he was earnest in his determination to run a secure and well-organized ship. Vowing to keep a firm hand on the crew and shape them up, he extinguished the lantern and retired to his berth.

It was a restless night with visions of pirates tramping tormented seas, blustering gales, and water funnels tearing at his mind. The more he tried to sleep the more awake he remained. He recognized his concerns as the last calling of the land—normal worries with which every captain had to make peace. Reviewing his training, he thought about his years of apprenticeship as a cadet officer—the authoritative bosun who had driven him harder than most, his navigation and seamanship studies, and exam to become second mate. He had enjoyed learning about celestial navigation, ship stability, and cargo, always longing for the day he'd captain his own ship. Once the anchor was aboard, he knew well there would be no time for imagination. He could only take each moment as it came, trying to identify and avoid all perils.

The plan, this voyage, was to cross the English Channel and enter the North Atlantic. Then, evading the brutal winter waters of the northern route, they would head south, catch the Northeast Trades and sail between the Mid-Atlantic Ridge and the continent. Well east of the Azores, they would skirt Madeira, turn west toward Bermuda and, from there, north to Boston. The ship was a three-masted full-rigged vessel with square-cut sails. She was one hundred five feet long, twenty-eight at the beam, with a rounded bow, and three decks. Having lower castles and being narrower across the beam than many of her sisters, she was somewhat faster—an advantage at sea he'd experienced when the ship he captained had been pursued by freebooters on his last trip to the West Indies.

Though he was a capable captain, early on his superiors had told him he was too easily distracted and inclined to daydream. Years at sea had allowed him to explore his weaknesses and know who he was, freely admitting a tendency to resurrect the past and drift, consciously guarding against it.

He slept only briefly, dreaming of his innocent, free-roaming days as a young lad before being pressed into service. Long before daybreak he was up and dressed. Seeing him moving about, the first mate called out the crew as the captain went up the cabin gangway onto the deck. The heavy ship, moored in the calm harbor, rolled rhythmically as it floated on the water. The anchor cable, pulled straight and taut with unfavorable winds, went slack in turns as the wind pushed the ship's stern against the tide. He was impatient to be underway. Watching from the quarterdeck, he assured himself the wind held strong, silently uttering a prayer for a safe voyage. It was more a mantra than anything specifically devout.

He was not a religious man. It would have been an unlikely choice given all that had befallen him. Surrounded by loss, except for his years with Kayna, to date he had tallied mostly misery in life—unable to understand what immutable laws of the Universe had visited grief on him.

Though of a stable psychology, experiencing only sporadic episodes of mercy or blessing had produced in him a complex but very limited gratitude. Early in life he'd concluded that if God was in the details, He would get no reverence from him.

"Ennis, it is time. The tide has turned."

At the order, the men scrambled from the forecastle onto the deck to stand before their captain. The sun was just breaking the horizon to the east—the western sky still a mystery.

"Men, t'is a long voyage we're about," Penberthy pronounced, ignoring furtive glances, "so be sharp at your duties and at all times ready when summoned as we go. Your respect and obedience is expected. Ennis give the order to raise anchor and prepare sail."

"Rig the capstan," Ennis ordered from the waist.

Five seamen grabbed the capstan bars, shoved them into the barrel's holes then heaved them round. One foot at a time the hawser slowly rose from the water, popping as the pawls lifted and dropped. When the elbows and feet became organized and the slack was out of the cable, one of the crew quietly started the anchor chantey. Others soon picked up the song and rhythm.

"Stamp around the caps'n, make some noise boys, and sing again that dear olde sweet refrain."

Once the anchor was pulled, the men struggled to fake the heavy, wet, six-inch thick cable onto the cable tier. Penberthy watched the activity, his mind focused on the voyage ahead.

"To the sheets and halyards," Ennis roared.

There was great excitement in anticipation of getting the ship to sail and the men scurried to their various tasks. Climbing like monkeys, part of the crew went aloft. High amid the rigging, the braces were pulled, the yards swung into place. With an inexperienced crew, getting underway went less smoothly than expected. In time, amid curses and orders, *Mordonn* glided gracefully toward the harbor entrance. Small lighters flitted about in the bustling harbor, taking goods and stores to the waiting ships or from ships to the wharf. Men shouting, sea chanteys reverberating, and the clanking of capstan pawls on other shipboards could be heard across the growing span of water. Once in Mount's Bay, the courses snapped into place, full canvas was spread and, under all the sail she could carry, *Mordonn*, shuddering, took to the vast emptiness that was the sea. It was Friday, September thirteenth—a date and day of little concern to none but the most foolishly superstitious.

"Steady as she goes," Ennis instructed the helmsman. "You'd make an eel seasick following your course. Steer to west' so'west."

Penberthy found most aspects of being aboard a ship aesthetically pleasing—the massive pine masts thirty-six inches in diameter thrusting a hundred feet skyward, the immense spars, yards, and booms supporting the sails, the rhythmic sound of the bow wake as the huge mass of vessel pushed through the water, the musical creaking of the rigging under tension, the vibration of the straining sails, the acrid smell of salt water. The familiar mixture of salt water, hemp, and wood smells were comforting to him, as was the smoothness of the quarterdeck rail he firmly grasped. Watching the helmsman, he thought of his earlier days as a seaman at the helm. With a tight grip around the spokes, he had experienced for the first time the satisfying harmony between man, machine, and nature. He never tired of watching the men at their tasks in getting underway as the sails filled then became taut, driving the immense ship forward. The smell of pitch and tar, however, was something he'd never gotten used to. To him it was noxious, nauseating, for some inexplicable reason.

His mind wandered to the time several years ago when Kayna had come aboard one of the ships he captained while it was tied up at the quay. He often thought of her perspective regarding ships. Standing on the quarterdeck, she had described the bow of the ship as very masculine—the stem that aggressively cut through the water, the samson post as the strongest part of the ship, the dark, dank, abyss-like crew quarters below the weather deck with only small gratings for light and air.

"Even though the captain's quarters are aft, it feels very feminine to me," she said. "It's like the ship is androgynous. The masculine signifies the operation or function of the ship, while her movement, especially while sailing, is very feminine. Here in the center of the ship, the heart, is where the two energies merge. I've not sailed with you but, when I see ships leaving the harbor, their huge milky sails look like spreading angel's wings, making the ship come to life and urging it to sea."

Surreptitiously wiping his eyes with his sleeve, Penberthy refocused his thoughts to the present. There was great anticipation in setting sail—a dramatic event signaling their departure from the harbor after so much preparation—the culmination of much planning and organizing. Their destination was fixed each time they set out, but all knew the voyage to be uncertain. The sea with its mysterious ways would always prevail, having them at her mercy, whether beneficent or cruel. The life of a captain was lonely, but the sea had become a solace and his only constant, despite its sweeping fluctuations.

He looked toward Pensans, unaware it would be for the last time. The cobbled streets, all leading to the waterfront, were lined with brick commercial buildings housing businesses associated with the seaport—prevalent among them, the taverns frequented by sailors in port. Most houses were simple, growing more modest the farther they were situated from the harbor. His was tucked into an alley between Quay and Chapel Streets, not visible from either the ship or harbor. For a moment his thoughts turned to Lamorna, wondering how she was faring and hoping she believed his heartfelt promise to her.

Pensans had become his home only recently. Though away from it far more than not, he liked it well enough, mostly for its convenience. Porthusek, where he'd grown up, was a sheltered harbor tucked in at Lobber Point on the rugged and wild northwest coast of Cornwall. The town, built up in close proximity to the sea, seemed to merge with it at high tide. The sea had been all he'd ever known—the desire to be a seaman compelling, strong, and unrelenting from the beginning of his memory. When returned from service in the Royal Navy, he'd worked on the docks. As a young adult he became a seaman, learning how to reef and steer a ship, the parts of the ship, directions, how to box a compass, and read the weather. Once he'd worked his way up from chore boy to captain's apprentice, he was put in charge of shipping and transshipping commodities like wood, stone, and pottery produced in the town or region to other coastal ports, but the lure had been to captain larger ships transporting cargoes to the Continent and America. The tiny Porthusek harbor was a port-of-call for fishing boats. Larger vessels could only be moored in deeper water far from shore, making loading and unloading cumbersome and unprofitable. He'd talked his wife into moving to Pensans where he could work on ships coming into port from Europe or America. In time he'd made repeated trips in charge of crews to continental ports, as well as the West Indies, gaining the confidence of captains as well as owners. Eventually he'd been given the responsibility of captaining a merchant ship.

Kayna had never liked Pensans, a known den for wreckers. She was afraid to be out and about in the village with the rough, bawdy crews on shore leave from aboard ships in port. Early in their married life she had come to the wharf to meet him when receiving news his ship was entering the harbor. After a couple of drunken sailors stumbling out of a pub had made improper advances, she waited at their home. Always longing to be back in quiet Porthusek with friends and family, she had endured— tending her herb gardens, weaving, sewing, and managing their home and two children, with Lamorna as company in his frequent absences. Their love and passion had remained strong through seven years of marriage. Never had there been a day when one look into her deep brown eyes couldn't dispel any disagreements or stresses between them. He'd grown convinced her death had been punishment for some unknown sin. Seeing no way to ever again be happy, his heart in chains, he'd adopted an unapproachable demeanor.

Though formidable by nature, he'd become unrelenting following Kayna's death. It had made him a better captain, more focused and less prone to daydreaming and mental wanderings. Crews were afraid of him, and that was often to his advantage, but sometimes he appeared cold and heartless, and that did not serve him well. Behind his back there had been some derision—crewmen plotting against him. Learning of it, he'd softened to a degree, claiming experience as his teacher and becoming more amenable at face value, despite the great sorrow he carried within.

The loss of his children had been devastating in itself, but he was gone so much to sea that little Gwennap, three, and son, Tremayne, five, had been near strangers to him. As their father, he felt their loss at some level of consciousness, but not their physical absence. It was his Kayna for whom he mourned. His heart ached to breaking every time he thought of her and their life together—the ghost of the lost days they now would never spend always hovering. His childhood, like so many of the time, had not been easy, hardening him to the world. Kayna had softened his hard edges, opened his heart, given him something to exist for, work for, and a purpose to life. She'd always been such an integral part of everything he did, everything he knew, that without her he didn't know how to live, often didn't care to live, envisioning a death at sea.

They'd been married in the Quaker Meeting House in Porthusek on May Day when she was seventeen and he twenty. Neither had ever entertained the idea of being with anyone else or considered living anywhere else on earth until the opportunities in Pensans. Times had grown hard in Porthusek since they'd left. Its isolation and good source of water had protected it from cholera epidemics, unlike other parts of England. They'd heard of the terrible symptoms associated with the disease—retching, achy limbs, and extreme thirst—counting themselves lucky to have escaped its ravages. Porthusek was not so fortunate with influenza. It was suspected that immigrants brought it with them across the Irish Sea. He couldn't know, when

Kayna returned to Porthusek to care for her ailing father early that spring, that it would also claim her and their two children.

He and Kayna had grown up together. Like most children of Porthusek, they'd roamed the steep hills surrounding the village, watched boats coming and going in the harbor, the flux and reflux of the sea, from high atop the rocky cliffs of Bodmin Moor. Running freely through the narrow streets, they'd squeezed between slate-fronted or whitewashed cottages so close together no adult could pass. Toward the uppermost part of the village they'd set small carved wooden boats in one of the streams before running down to the harbor to watch them race to the sea. Sometimes they helped fishermen land their trip of fish or sat, quayside, watching crews unload. Their days together had seemed eternal, their lives before them a limitless expanse of time.

In Porthusek, the semidiurnal tide rolled in, then out. The extremes flooded the harbor at high tide, settled boats in the marl at ebb. With the foaming waves of the ephemeral tides, the fog held fast—a seemingly inseparable sea partner that drifted in and out, creating its distortions and illusions, concealing its secrets. There was something about the sea that had called to him and, though he hadn't wanted to be a fisherman like his father, he'd often wondered if it was his voice he heard in his mind and heart.

All aspects of being on the water fascinated him, contriving to give him a feeling of comfort and belonging not felt while on dry land. According to some of the books he'd read, *mar* meant mother as well as the sea, a plausible explanation for the nurturing he felt while on board a ship. Though voyages were long and often the seas rough and dangerous, he couldn't imagine a life spent away from it. The contentedness felt while on the water, despite netted emotions, provided a sense of calm and order—like he was part of the ship or the ship an integral part of him.

As a lad he'd been pressed into naval service. Tresco Penberthy, his father, had been lost at sea when

Lanyon was only eight. They had been a poor family, though able to manage on a fisherman's profit. In time it would prove impossible for his widowed mother to feed her three hungry children. When a captain of the Royal Navy came around with a press gang looking for men and boys to complement his ship, *The H.M.S. Kolonn*, Lanyon, aged twelve, was pushed to the fore by his mother to stand in front of the sober and responsible man in uniform towering over him. Brass buttons too numerous to count stared him in the face—his timid eyes reflected in their shine. Without even the opportunity to say good-bye, he followed along behind the captain down Kernow Street to the docks where he was rowed out to board the naval ship anchored in deeper waters.

Conditions were novel, adjustments difficult, and the lot of a chore boy not a happy one. Theirs were the menial tasks of cleaning out the pens of the livestock or chicken coops and all other order of things distasteful and low. Most of the boys he served with came from poor families, often guilty of petty crimes—vagabonds all. Lanyon didn't fit in well. Early on he learned not to reveal anything personal that might draw ridicule. It was his secret goal to become a sailor someday—topman, if possible, so he could tend the rigging. At first he'd thought he might strive for a commission in the navy, but his years at sea, often in battle, left him without a desire for more.

In the service of the Royal Navy he was under the command of Admiral Seacat who ventured west into Atlantic waters to engage the French in battles for supremacy. Rarely did Lanyon see the light of day. Confined to the dark, damp, and smelly bowels of the ship, most of the time he was homesick and in active misery. Sometimes after sunset he'd sneak up on deck to gaze at the starry night and dream of being home, back in Porthusek. A moot point, as he was to discover. In his absence his mother had died, and he was never to learn what had happened to his brothers, assuming they, like him, had gone to sea. He was envious of the midshipmen, *snotties* they called them, boys his age but from wealthy families, being trained to become officers. When able to, he listened in as they learned their lessons in navigation and astronomy from the ship's schoolmaster.

The bosun, a ponderous man with only one eye, had supervised the seamen, assigning duties and seeing that they obeyed all orders. When Lanyon wasn't ankle-deep in pig, cow or chicken ordure, he was assigned to the purser to clean up the stores or as gofer to the cook, who was lame. The bosun was also in charge of punishment. Under his oppressive hand, a sailor had been keel-hauled for being in the admiral's quarters without permission. It took witnessing only one flogging of a jack-tar, forty lashes with the cat-o'-nine-tails, for Lanyon to do as he was told without question—content in being insignificant enough to be overlooked.

Though he'd often rued his fate in being pressed into service at such a young age, he acknowledged his rare luck in having been assigned to the center squadron of the fleet, in the flagship *H.M.S. Courage* with the admiral. He was a son of the sea for three years. As cabin boy in the wooden prison of the lowest deck of the ship, unless they took on water or the hull was blasted through during exchanges, he would avoid mortal danger or witness wounded ships, aflame, butt-sprung and sunk with all aboard. During battles he ran gunpowder from the gunroom to the gunners, ducking and cringing at the percussive cannon firings—the smell of gunpowder choking him. For a young lad he had plenty of salt but nothing could snuff out the memories that lingered—blood flying so freely he'd tasted it, filth beyond reason, the stench of burning flesh, the sounds of men moaning in agony or screaming as the ship's surgeon cut off a limb—and after each battle, the burials of the dead at sea, sewn into their hammocks.

Before he had left, though he was only twelve and she nine, he and Kayna had pledged their eternal love, vowing always to be together. Upon his return, he found her waiting, and it was as though they'd never been apart. *Soul Partners*, she called them. Holding him tightly around the middle, she had made the haunting pronouncement that often waved through his thoughts.

"Hear the song sparrow singing in the distance? It's telling us our forever can start now that we're together again."

So much for forever, he scoffed within, remembering her words.

He had worked hard on the docks with the sole purpose of earning enough money to allow them to be married. When he became a seaman she was happy that he was able to do what he wanted. Despite misgivings, she supported his decision to move them to Pensans. It was hard enough returning to their home in Pensans each time he came from the sea but, though there were many fond remembrances of his years in Porthusek, he had never returned—the tragic memories by association too difficult to bear. Their marriage had been happy, even blissful. But all things positive in his life had been obliterated with Kayna's death. While dreaming of her haunting image, as he often did, he felt happily reconnected. Upon awakening, his devastating sense of loss again crushed him.

Mordonn was supposed to have left mid-summer but it had turned to September before a crew could be garnered, the cargo loaded, and the weather cooperative enough to set sail. He would like to have had a more tried crew, as he usually did when going to sea, but the men he'd found would have to do. With the threat of pirates, crews had become more difficult to commission. Master mates and experienced seamen were often recruited, plucked from merchant ships to serve in the Royal Navy. It had taken him two months to get his crew together, using great promise, even some subversion, to do so. He hoped their lack of experience would not be an issue in the challenges sure to come while on this voyage.

At the taffrail, he watched Pensans fade in the distance as they made their way through the English Channel and passed Lands' End under a vaulting blue sky. The Isles of Scilly would soon appear in the distance over the starboard bow to the north. Avoiding the tricky waters of the Western Approaches, they would drop south into the gemmy Atlantic Ocean. Though he was dispassionate about Cornwall, it felt good to leave. Each time he sailed from port it was with renewed hope that the sad memories could finally be expunged, and he would return a happier man—that somehow the bounding main would heal him, and his heart efface the ache of such losses. Looking seaward, he watched the sails straining toward the horizon, endeavoring to allow the past to recede with the shoreline so he could once and for all put his exhausting grief behind him.

The crew seemed eager for the adventure of sailing west but with an air of concern for where fate and the voyage might be taking them. It was a palpable fear, easily assigned to the always-present element of danger. Despite some crew comradery, being surrounded by only the lonely sea for weeks or months at a time was extremely isolating. Under full sail, they passed ships working their way toward the harbor, knowing they would be the last seen for some time and hoping for their own fortuitous return.

"Fair weather iffen it don't breeze on," Chegwin optimistically predicted, as he stood watch at the port rail.

Mordonn was beamy for a ship its size and rode the waves well. *True to her name*, Penberthy acknowledged, translating the Gaelic carved on the transom's fashion piece to English in his mind—*Sea Waves*. Following the figurehead at the bow, helmsman Awbrey steered the ship off a westerly wind. She scudded smoothly over the water—her square sails furled and gleaming. They soon swept through the Channel. One more ship passed across the prow a mile out, then they were alone on the open sea.

There was no land dividing the Channel from the Atlantic Ocean so it was difficult to know when the transition had been made. Only the rhythm of the ship provided clues. Ennis instructed Awbrey to steer south, southwest, and they bore off the wind. The crew settled into their duties and routines. During the last minutes of daylight, Penberthy felt the ship ease into the rolling waves that signified they were at last in deep water. As night came on, the silver water reflecting a bright, low-hanging gibbous moon, the crew went to their berths convinced of fair weather and forgetting concerns. Penberthy stayed topside until very late, standing on the quarterdeck as clouds covered the silvery moon, and they headed into the mysterious blackness.

"Be on your toes," he instructed Ennis. "I'll be in my quarters."

Hearing the bells, clanging in pairs to call the first watch, he stepped into his cabin. It had been a flawless, smooth day of sailing as they streamed south. At his desk in the master's quarters, he opened the log book. Pushing aside the crew registry and list of stores, he made his entry then prepared to retire for the night. He laid his clothes over the desk chair as he undressed, carefully positioning his vest so his letter from Kayna wouldn't fall out of the pocket. Years ago, as he was about to go to sea for the first time, she had handed him two small leather pouches.

"This one contains a letter proclaiming my eternal love for you," she had whispered. "You must carry it with you in your vest pocket, closest to your heart, at all times. And, this pouch, if you so choose it, might hold a letter from you that I may carry with me always, to have and cherish during the times we're apart."

She had made the pouches from fine leather, carefully bound with tiny, delicate stitches—each packet just the right size to hold a folded letter and fit into a pocket. The day he'd first read her letter, tears had formed in his eyes to know such love, and did still, each time he read her words. Her letter had inspired him to write his own, which he had handed her at the dock before first setting sail. Though he did not have a way with words like she, he hoped they expressed all his burgeoning heart knew. After her death he had tried to find his letter among her things to claim as a small consolation, but it was not to be found.

Glancing out the stern windows, he saw the constellation of Cygnus, the Swan, flying south—a reminder of his beloved. Kayna knew all about the sea, the woodlands, flora, fauna, the moors, and sky, often sharing her extensive knowledge with him as they stood together on Bodmin Moor. She had told him that the night sky was filled with birds, Pegasus among them. The Swan was of particular importance to her because just to the right of it was Lyra, with Vega, its brightest star. Patiently he had humored her, attentive as she mapped glistening lights in the dark heavens—feigning interest, as well as the ability to actually see the flying horse, Swan or any other obscure constellations, when it was only the celestial spheres of her beautiful eyes he cared about.

Crossing the rough cabin floor, he made ready to climb into his berth. Pulling back the coverlet, a sleek gray cat crawled nonchalantly from beneath it, startling him. He thought it a figment of his imagination as he struggled with the reality of what he saw before him.

"How on earth did you get aboard?" he asked aloud, impulsively reaching toward the cat.

The cat purred in response, rubbing up against his hand. The captain was too surprised to be angry, too uncertain he was actually seeing the cat to do more than react. On closer inspection, he realized it was Morrigan, Kayna's cat. He'd seen other cats as light gray as the fog, but none with one blue eye and the other dun-colored.

"Of all the trips at sea I've been on, why have you chosen this one, Morri? Shame upon you! Lamorna will surely be distraught at your absence."

There was no way they could return to Pensans, nothing to be done but continue on the voyage with the cat aboard. *It won't be the first cat aboard a ship*, he excused. To save face with the men, he decided to behave as though the cat was part of the plan rather than a dreadful mistake. *Most won't know the cat is known to me*, he concluded, as he crawled into the berth and lay down. The cat curled up next to him and went immediately to sleep, as did he. With the ship comfortably shifting and rocking in moderate waves, it was his first good sleep in several nights, and he dreamed well.

He and Kayna, as small children, run up the sloping hill through tall spring grasses. As young lovers, they walk hand in hand to a rocky outcropping on Bodmin Moor to stare out over the sea. Kayna's dark blue dress billows with the sea breeze. Her eyes are dark and myste-rious. "Only the elementals endure," she tells him. "Their energy can be changed but not erased. Did you know this rock was long, long ago made by fire?" The breeze fresh-ens as they sit beneath an oak tree on the heath amid bracken and fragrant broom. When he turns to her, she is no longer a child but the mother of his children. She is singing and knitting a blue sweater that he intuits must be for him. Prompting her to put down her knitting, he leans into her with a kiss full on the lips and feels his body re-spond. "It sorrows me to leave you alone again, but I must sail the seas because that is what I do. Sailing to America will afford us opportunities not now available. Though we will be apart for a time, I will only love you more." A mild salty breeze tosses Kayna's black hair as she turns to face Lanyon, looking at him with eternal, smoky eyes. "We will always be together no matter what may happen. We've always been together, Soul partners connected in body, mind, and spirit that cannot be sepa-rated by time, distance or circumstance. Always remem-ber that." She stands, then walks away from him. At the crest of the moor she turns to look at him, shape-shifting first into a young girl then an old woman, a crone. Walk-ing slowly, she disappears into the gathering mist. "Kayna, don't leave me," he calls after her. Left sitting on the moor, the familiar ache of her absence spreads over him, and he starts to cry. A black crow swoops down to stand before him. He shoos it away. Then Kayna's cat, Morrigan appears from the fog to stand at his side, rub-bing against him and staring into his eyes.

"Kayna," he called out, as he awakened from the realistic dream—jumping in surprise to find Morrigan staring him in the face. Wishing it could be his Kayna, he got up and, searching his vest, found the pocket contain-ing her letter. With clumsy hands, he removed and unfold-ed it. The letter was almost torn through at the creases. Grease and salt stained the paper, the ink was smudged, the print unreadable in places. Having long ago memo-rized the letter, he read again her precious words.

My Dearest Love,

A love that is full of splendor but only for the present can die, and so is fleeting. But a love like ours that is greater than personal desire can be set free, transcending into eternity. Do not let a struggle within or grief or tragedy keep you from believing in our eternal love. Do not let your heart be a captive of love, nor your devotion destroy you. The mind, in torment, circles in descending spirals when love of self is absent. Become a part of eternal love by turning it inward. Our thoughts must be ever expansive and free. First comes self-love which, through grace and hope, conducts us in an upward spiral to enkindle eternal love. Eternal love is not an earthly love that shrinks into fear and regret, but a love that grows and multiplies, manifesting all we desire and shining back on us all. We are bound together by a love that cannot be measured in time because it belongs to eternity, and eternity has no time. Our eternal love cannot be eclipsed by distance because eternity knows no distance. Though we are not together, nothing can separate us or weaken our eternal love. Trust your intuition, knowing it represents the merging of your Soul with the Universe. Listen to the cawing of the crow and the purring of the cat. Look always to the silver moon and I'll be there.

Your Forever and One True Love

Staring at Morrigan looking devotedly up at him, Lanyon wondered how Kayna could know her profound words would provide his only comfort—winning again his heart, soothing his restless Soul, softening his course nature. Though grateful to still have her words, he remained convinced that nothing could heal his heart nor compensate the loss. Wiping tears from his eyes, he folded the letter, replaced it in the leather pouch, put it in his vest pocket, and got dressed.

It would be a long voyage, and he made no attempt to conceal the presence of the cat, letting her roam freely about the decks as though she belonged there. She shadowed him wherever he went during the day. At night they slept in his berth. Humored by the presence of a cat on board, which the crew knew to be a sign of good luck, they immediately took her in. In recognition of her gray coat, they called her *ghost cat*, spoiling her with food, petting, and holding her—laughing at her mismatched eyes and dexterousness as she walked along the railing, daintily stepping over each belaying pin. Only Coltrane, the cook, saddled with the responsibility of feeding and cleaning up after the cat, had any problem with her being on board.

It didn't take long for the weather to turn on them. As the Portugal Current drew them nearer to the coast of France, the sun burned off cool morning air, but it gradually grew cloudy. The Bay of Biscay, known for its violent weather extremes, was a tricky stretch of water. Under a cheerless sky, the canvas rustled and the ship creaked and groaned as it rose and fell with each opaque wave. Dampness hung in the air. Low gray clouds signified the approach of rain and unstable weather. Penberthy, who had been in his quarters keeping a watchful eye on the barometer, felt the ship slowly respond to changing weather and emerged to assess the situation.

"Wind before rain, drop sails and sail again—rain before wind, topsails in," Ennis quipped, as the captain joined him on the quarterdeck.

Lightning began slashing through the bank of dark clouds, then they emptied. Rain and chop foretold a wet and nasty squall advancing. It wasn't long before strong winds forced the swells into spray. Huge waves slapped against the hull. Pelted by rain and waves, the men on watch became drenched, carefully moving across the wet deck to their duties as the ship rolled and surfed in a following sea.

"Shorten sail, Ennis."

Visibility was greatly hampered but, from the quarterdeck, the captain watched his crew attempt to furl the sails. Himself clinging to standing rigging, the topman urged the men to reef the topsails. Through great effort they completed the task then slid safely down the tarry backstays to the deck.

"Head off the wind," Ennis boomed.

As evening approached and they struggled south, the waves built higher, increasing in intensity, and seas were rough. With each wave the bow reared up then tore down the back side, dipping deep into the troughs between swells. The crew held firmly to whatever they could as the tumbling sea continuously washed over the deck, soaking all in its path, slow to flush out the scuppers. The squall showed no abatement. Morrigan, on deck during the onset of the storm cowering beneath some coils of rope, was in hiding.

"Keep her steady," Ennis instructed the helmsman.

A few of the unseasoned crew became *mal de mar* with the extreme pitching of the ship, retching over the starboard rail. Staying on deck might have hastened their recovery, but they insisted on going below. Someone was sent to the cook for ginger, but it was too late to expect improvement. Some of the crewmen took pity on those who were seasick, unstringing their hammocks and moving them to the center of the berthing deck where the motion of the ship was less immoderate.

Around fourteen hundred hours the next day, the squall subsided as quickly as it had materialized. Winds completely died and the seas grew calm, but they'd experienced some damage. Water seeped through cracks in the decking on a regular basis but, with seas washing so continuously over the aging deck, it was much worse. Seams had opened up, the pitch pushed up into ridges between planking.

"Bosun Smith, have some men pull t' canvas on t' main mast an' alert t' sail master we'll need it mended," Ennis ordered. "Look o'er all quarters an' decks an report back t' me."

"The cargo in t' hold is shifted," Chegwin reported, climbing through the scuttle.

Ennis knew the uneven distribution of cargo could affect the ship's motion. In rough water, it would become a problem.

"Take five crewmen wit you t' restow t' cargo," he ordered. "Tell t' chippy t' check t' masts an' rails for degrading."

"We're leaking two decks down, below the water line," Smith reported minutes later.

"Can it be patched wit tar an' oakum?"

"I'll do my best."

"Set t'men to pumping an' resting in shifts. Morton, have t' men clear this raffle then square away an' relieve Awbrey at helm."

Listening to Ennis bark orders, Penberthy knew things were well in hand but was concerned about the damage. After telling Ennis to make a full report of the damages to him as soon as possible, he went to his cabin. The cat came out from hiding, rubbing up against his legs as he stepped into his quarters. *My Soul partner,* he averred with a pneumatic chuckle.

"T' men be pumping, Sir. T' damage haint so great but t' chippy haint got all 'ats needed t' fix things an' Coltrane says some of t' food stores got spoilt," Ennis reported that evening.

Some of the food, protected in wooden barrels or hogsheads, had become saturated with water in the storm. Hard tack, their staple, was a virtual loss.

"We'll tuck into Funchal for repairs and to freshen our stores of food and water. Alert the men."

Once Ennis had left his cabin, Penberthy sat on the edge of the bed, pondering their situation. Exhausted from a harrowing day, that could have ended in disaster, he lay down next to the cat, and slept.

Kayna stands on the steps of a cottage holding a bouquet of spring rose blooms. When she sees him in the distance, she calls to him, holding up a blue sweater she has knit for him. "Wear it well," she says, "it will keep you warm no matter what." She lays the sweater across the back of a chair, gets up, then walks toward the shore. When she comes closer, he can see that she is walking across water, like the waves are solid ground. She looks more beautiful than he has ever seen her before. Her indigo blue dress billows in the wind as she stretches out her arms to him. He tries to get to her, but the ship is sinking, and he can't reach her. "All will be well," she calls to him. "Do not fear because I will be with you."

The disturbing dream roused him from sleep. Aware he had slept later than usual, he quickly dressed and went up onto the deck, the dream continuing to occupy his mind. Striding to the quarterdeck, he joined Ennis and the helmsman. The men had pumped through the night, clearing the hold. Debris from the storm had been cleared but repairs were still needed.

The day did not grow brighter, nor did the next. Cargo was restowed, their supplies and stores in the galley and lazerette put back into place, rope and rigging scattered across the deck, faked. Dr. Soadey saw to the injured. With the storm behind them, the crew settled into daily routines and the days and knots ticked on.

By Sunday, in deeper water, some of the jack-tars fished with hand lines for tuna and horse mackerel off the port rail hoping to augment the evening meal. Morrigan was always at hand, ready to receive fish innards tossed her way, her stomach soon bulging to twice its usual size. It was a day of rest and, with no priest on board, no compulsion to worship. But, as was his custom, the captain read some inspirational literature and led the crew in meditation. Later, the men sang songs, played games of whist, boisterously skylarked, teased the cat or told stories. Ennis, who knew his sea lore, was always ready to chime in with another tale.

"Ya knows," he began. "Originally priests was taken onboard t' insure good weather an' t' keep the ship from fallin' int' t' hands of t' devil. If they ran int' a storm or had bad luck, t' priest was tossed overboard. In time, it got easier t' jest christen t' ship an' leave t' priest at home."

He often engaged the crew with romantic stories, most untrue, about New England—telling of men the size of giants that worked in the forests, lumbering, ships built to go faster than any seen in Europe, coastal monsters that lured ships to the shoals, Indians who raided and burned homes, raped women and girls, and sold the scalps of

Englishmen to their enemies, the French. In a confusion of facts, he talked of witches that could raise the dead, shape-shift into animals or birds, disappear and reappear at will or turn men into toads, full moons that bode danger, larger than seen elsewhere in the world, fog they called sea smoke, thick as your hand, mysteriously distorting solid and tangible realities and so dense it could only be cut with a sword.

Three days after the storm, Penberthy felt a ship more dramatically in motion as he awakened and knew the wind had freshened. Checking his barometer, he confirmed a reading of high pressure. On deck he found wispy clouds floating across the sky to the east, turned rosy by a rising sun.

"Speed?" the captain questioned Ennis.

"Six knots."

"Steady as she goes. We need to steer off the coast of Spain so keep a course south, southwest."

"Aye, Aye, Sir."

The bells sounded, signaling a change in watch. Awbrey replaced Dawkins at lookout, climbing the ratlines to the crow's nest.

Over the next week, a mild breeze pushed them south but ever so slowly. The weather was favorable and seas, bounding. Despite the sun drying things out, the ship dripped with damp. When a brisk breeze swept across the deck, the hatches were opened to help dry the ship out. There was work to be done, and Ennis kept the men busy chafing gear, holystoning the deck, re-roving or splicing lines and halyards, tarring rigging, rope rotations or patching and mending sails. Still, the men became restless. Morrigan had become a fixture, tolerated but mostly ignored, and she spent longer hours sleeping in the captain's quarters.

It was another Sunday—a sun-washed day. Penberthy gave the men leave to rest once their chores were finished. As the sky brightened, the men emerged from the forecastle, most occupying themselves with the mending and washing of clothes, haircuts, writing home and, with permission, filling their pannikins with ale. Morrigan stretched out on some faked rope and slept, soaking up the warm sunshine. Penberthy stood at the starboard rail watching schools of fish swim in the shade of the ship. As the day dragged on, several of the crew slept. Others lolled on deck, listening to another of Ennis' tales, while their clothes dried on the rails..

"Sailors first got tattoos cuz they thought it 'ud be a good luck charm an' a way t' identify 'em iffen they got lost or kilt. Course that ain't gonna be no problem here," he added, seeing the alarmed looks on the faces of his small, captive audience.

Penberthy smiled, noticing some barefoot sailors sitting next to the fore scuttle, drying their boots and stockings in the sun. Seamen's tattoos were well familiar to him but, though he'd heard of it, never before had he seen such obvious evidence of superstition. Several of the men had a tattoo of a pig on their right foot, a rooster on the left, for good luck. *I'd say it must have worked*, he spoke within, scanning the ship. *The squall damage could have been much worse. Or maybe the cat is good luck after all and it was Morri that allowed our good fortune.*

When the northeast winds picked up they made headway at last. With white waters churning off the bow, the ship laboriously cut deep waters—canvas flying. As seaman Derrick took his watch on the forward deck, he heard a blow. Looking over the starboard rail, he saw a shiny black back and fluked tail surface, recognizing the huge whale as a humpback.

"Humpback at starboard," he called to Chegwin, at watch in the crow's nest.

"Whale to starboard," Chegwin boomed.

By the time everyone crowded the rail, the whale was close enough for them to see the knobs on its lower jaw. When it breached, the tell-tale wavy edges of its enormous tail could be seen. It had to be forty feet long. Another stubby dorsal fin appeared, then a blow could be heard as a second whale surfaced, most likely its mate. They swam alongside the ship for some time, as though mistaking it for another whale, occasionally breaking the calm surface then gracefully diving deep into dark waters. The men clapped their hands in a rhythm they hoped would draw the whales closer and again to the surface. The huge mammals complied for a time, surfacing several times before joining the rest of their pod to continue their migration to warmer, sub-tropical waters. They could be seen for hours in the distance, spouting at predictable intervals. No sooner had the men returned to their duties when another call came, this time from Ennis.

"Dolphins," he yelled, looking over the port rail.

The crew on deck immediately shifted to the port rail to see the dolphins. All knew it meant they were near land, though the coast of Portugal was still very far away. Dolphins followed the ship all day, dipping and diving in the bow's wake.

At the starboard rail, Penberthy gazed westward toward the Azores, unseen over the expanse of sea. He had sailed there before. Several of the peaks were the tallest on earth, measured from the ocean floor, appearing blue from a great distance. Past the lush green and wild largest island of Sao Miguel lay the brown sandy beaches of Santa Maria. He had visited both islands, usually calling at the port of Vila Franca on Sao Miguel to pick up cargoes of brandy and wine. It was a thriving fishing village that reminded him of Porthusek, and he hoped not to have to go there again.

"We've good weatha luck, Captain," Ennis offered, joining him at the rail and jarring his thoughts. "*Mordonn* must have a gold coin nailt to t' keel."

Without comment Penberthy turned and went to his quarters, hoping for a good night's sleep and that, despite his foolish inclinations, Ennis' optimism would hold true for the entire voyage. Another restless night followed. When he slept, his dreams were of Kayna. By morning he was more exhausted than when he'd retired.

With the light of dawn the next day, a smir appeared on the eastern horizon. The men's spirits immediately lifted at the prospect of seeing land, vying with each other for the first glimpse of Madeira. As the bow broke the water, enormous schools of fish shimmied away from the ship with the pilot fish in the lead, then a Portuguese man-of-war was spotted. At the port rail, some of the men watched, hypnotized by sun's rays descending into the clear water to an unknown depth.

The wind fell light and the sails were shifted as the ship continued southward. None aboard could know where or how far *Mordonn* would take them nor that they were on a passage, not a voyage. It would be four more weeks, into the last days of October and six weeks from their departure from Pensans, before they would learn their fate.

— CHAPTER TWO —

And ever the fitful gusts between
A sound came from the land;
It was the sound of the trampling surf
On rocks and the hard sea-sand.

The breakers were right beneath her bows,
She drifted a dreary wreck,
And a whooping billow swept the crew
Like icicles from her deck.

From *The Wreck of the Hesperus* by Longfellow

The Northeast Trades held steady and soon they were near the Madeira Islands off the west coast of Morocco. On deck, Penberthy inhaled the air, noting its change from the tart and salty smell of the ocean to the heavy, sweet, seductive, and promising smell of land—a mixture of the scent of flowers, wood smoke, and cooking odors. Watching for signs, he spotted shore birds, then dislodged seaweed afloat on the water. Noticeable changes in climate were evident, more tepid and subtropical. Midmorning, the high sea cliffs of Madeira came into view. They could see the *levadas,* or aqueducts, running down from the mountains. The ship slipped past Porto Santo then tucked into Funchal, the largest port town on Madeira, nestled into the mouth of a ravine on the south coast. The sunny slopes rising from the town were ideal for viniculture, producing the coveted Madeira wine for which the islands were known. Because many English had settled in Funchal, the architecture felt familiar. Many of the houses had towers that enabled their owners to watch ships coming and going from the harbor. Penberthy had been to Funchal before, lading cargoes of sugar, fennel or *funcho,* and wine bound for England.

"We'll be two days in Funchal," Penberthy told Ennis. "There's work to be done loading fresh stores and making repairs. If the work is accomplished by tomorrow night, you can give the men shore leave, but make it clear that anyone not back on the ship by middle watch won't get on. We sail at sunup day after tomorrow."

The men worked hard. Fresh stores of water, fruits, and vegetables were loaded aboard. The sail master oversaw the mending of sails while the chippy made repairs to port and starboard rails and reinforced his material supply. Lashings, and the standing and running rigging were checked then rechecked. Coltrane saw to his cache of fresh food. Having given orders to Ennis, the captain occupied his time with reading charts and watching the tide. Morrigan, at his side, showed no interest in leaving his cabin or ship and Penberthy did not encourage her otherwise.

The second night, the mates remained on board but, having earned shore leave, the rest of the men recovered their land legs and headed for the taverns along the port road. They were a rowdy bunch but mindful of their duties. All were back on board by the designated time the next morning, save one—last seen carrying a rather buxom woman over his shoulder and heading down Rua da Pico da Cruz.

At sunup they left on a fair tide and moved back into Atlantic waters. Penberthy estimated they were about four hundred miles north of Tenerife in the Canaries, and three hundred miles from the coast of Africa. For centuries, traders on their way to the New World had stopped at La Palma or El Hierro in the Canaries en route to the West Indies. They, however, were headed for Bermuda. They would follow the Canary Current southwest, then swing west and skirt the top of the Northeast Trades, well south of the high pressure system that hovered over the center of the North Atlantic.

If the high pressure system did not move south, they would have an easy sail west. Otherwise, they would have to cross the Intertropical Convergence Zone, a barrier they'd need to get through in order to take the Trades across the Atlantic. For days they might be becalmed or experience rain, violent thunderstorms, variable winds, and awkward seas. It was a matter of luck.

Besides watching the barometer and skies to keep an eye on the weather, the captain took sightings with the morning stars, noon sun, and evening stars. He used a sextant to get bearings and monitor their position by measuring the distance or angle between the stars and horizon. Of particular importance, and requiring clear night skies, were the three stars, Vega, Altair, and Deneb, known as the Navigational Triangle.

Out of Funchal, they had a lovely sail for well over a week. It grew hot. When the sun was strong enough to soften the tar in the decking, it was pressed back into seams. Skies were clear and dispositions even. Then, a few days before they anticipated catching the Trades, the high pressure system moved south, colliding with a low front, and they were becalmed in the Horse Latitudes. Waters grew smooth, mirror-like, as the captain and his crew waited for the laggard wind. The ship was roly-poly, requiring few sail changes.

To maintain strict obedience, the captain had the men practice tacking maneuvers and going aloft. He demanded precision. Every sail change, every maneuver, was done in anticipation of the time when the ship, its cargo, and the lives of the men depended on seconds. *Never dog any maneuver* was his motto. Following orders, between practicing maneuvers, the crew holystoned the deck and neatened the ship, complaining about the difficulty in coiling rope that had dried stiff in the hot tropical sun.

When they weren't busy, they watched the sea life that abounded in the waters surrounding them. A school of tuna swam past, easily visible in the pellucid waters. Dolphins followed them for a time, and circling sharks were spotted off the starboard bow. Two mating sea turtles locked together, floated on the surface of the water for hours. Evenings, the captain spent more time in his cabin. Stroking Morrigan, always near, he found his mind drifting backward in time to the days he and Kayna had been together. Patting his vest pocket to make sure her letter was still there, he recalled her sweet smell, like the roses she so loved, her enchanting smile, and piercing, timeless eyes. It was a torture even to say he missed her, the words too hopelessly inadequate to express how he felt. Sometimes when he looked at Morrigan, staring up at him, the cat's eyes became dark and mysterious, and he saw Kayna's eyes in them. At such times, the reminder of his loss was more than he could bear, and he pushed the cat away. Always, Morrigan returned to again win his heart, jumping into his lap to be pet or curling up with him as he slept.

Thinking of Kayna, he went up on deck to watch the moon rise. Ennis, always at hand, joined him at the taffrail for a few moments.

"Iffen you kin see t' moon clearly, then twill rain soon—iffen you cain't then it already is," Ennis advised.

The next morning the barometer started dropping, and the ship was held in abeyance. At first the rain was moderate, but soon a series of nasty squalls surrounded them. When the storm quickly receded, the crew counted themselves among the lucky. Chegwin spotted a funnel-shaped column in the distance. It was not considered a threat, but an object of macabre interest, and the men clambered to the rail to watch. The water spout looked like a hand reaching down from the bank of dark cumulonimbus clouds, snatching up the sea. It tipped westward in a serpentine motion, silently writhing and swaggering across the horizon. When the sun dipped over the foreyard arm, with half the crew on deck, another spotting was made.

"Look at t' silver streaks," Dawkins shouted, pointing over the larboard rail at the arching horizontal stripes of light shining in the setting sun.

"They be flying fish," Awbrey pronounced, proud he knew.

A couple of the men crawled onto the bobstay to have a closer look while the rest rushed to larboard.

Watching them, Captain took note of his crew. On his last trip the crew had been irreverent, insolent more than not—malcontents who scuffled and complained about the food, captain, voyage, and everything else—toadies and lick-spittles who obeyed to his face but ridiculed and under-mined his authority behind his back. It was not the kind of crew to be counted on in a fix. He'd been all too glad to have gotten through their voyage without extreme diffi-culties and be rid of them, seeing to it that none of them had signed on for this trip. Most of his crew were novices, some edgy, and at times surly, but all good men. None were a disgrace to salt water and, as far as he could tell, there were no slackers or Jonahs among them. Staring at their tan, leathery faces, he hoped they would want to make the return trip of the voyage with him, even though he knew it couldn't be counted on.

The men showed signs of boredom and were as impatient for a change as he was—all eager to end the first leg of their voyage and be safely in port. In his cabin, Pen-berthy plotted their course with parallel rules then walked it off with dividers. Though known for his navigational skills and sailing knowledge, he didn't control the weather and hoped not to be tested. Experience had taught him that the weather and sea trumped all expertise, making a mockery of training. Climbing to the deck, he stood at the starboard rail for a time to study the sea and sky for infor-mation, finding nothing by way of encouragement. He could hear Ennis at the bow, in parley with some men.

"I kin tell ya how there come t' be figureheads on ships, why ships is called female an' t' first voyage its maiden voyage," he began, pointing to the stem where the figurehead was fastened.

"How is it you know so much?" Morton chal-lenged.

"I hear things an' I listen, unlike some known t' me. In ancient times when t' Romans, Greeks an' others first set sail, a virgin was sacrificed when a ship was launched t' allow safe passage across stormy waters ruled by powerful sea gods like Neptune or Poseidon. Her head was cut off an' attached t' t' bowsprit. When the head fell off int' t' ocean it meant t' gods were happy an' had accepted t' sacrifice. Then t' soul of t' virgin went int' t' ship."

"Aw c'mon. You knows that fer shur?"

"Swear t' gods," Ennis laughed.

Chuckling to himself, Penberthy climbed to the quarterdeck. Ennis, on his way to join him for instructions, stopped at the main mast, pulled out his dulled knife, and jabbed it with force into the southeast quarter of the spar.

"What are you doing, Ennis?"

"Trying t' conjure up t' wind, Sir."

"You need a sharp knife for that, I believe."

They were becalmed for two more days. The seas so placid there was not even enough movement on the water to make the ship creak. There seemed little else to do but take the weather in stride, but the men had even tired of watching glorious sunrises and sunsets. Immersed in the ocean's solitude, they had become morose. Morale was low, malaise increasing. In his quarters, the captain grew troubled about weather that seemed determined to impede their progress.

The following morning, a light wind came up from the southeast pushing them northeast, and he wondered if there was any chance Ennis' knife had influenced it. As the wind freshened, the sails were set, and the ship responded and came to life.

"A good wind, ain't it, Sir?" Ennis offered, taking credit for it. "Hope it don't git too good. I knowed of wind that 'ud blow t' breath right outta a man—suck it from his nostrils," he added, before turning from the scowl he saw forming on the captain's face to relay his orders.

For a time they sailed easily along. The ship slowly rolled in variable winds and modest waves. Several days later, Penberthy alternately paced and watched the barometer in his quarters. Subtle movements of the ship told him the weather was changing and not necessarily for the good. When the barometric pressure started dropping, he knew a depression approached. Skies were clear, but the wind started blowing like hell. Late afternoon, high cirrus clouds spread across the horizon, and swells began building. By midnight, rain pelted the ship. The wind took on a fierce edge, slicing at the sails. Vicious lightning lit up the sky as thunder rolled and rumbled. Briny waves washed continuously over the deck. Through the night *Mordonn* rode horrendous seas, battered by the storm.

It began to subside the next morning, but the ship was drenched with water and there was some additional damage. Of greatest concern was their food supply. Much of it had been ruined by violent waves relentlessly washing over the deck and seeping through every crack, crevice, and seam. They were again in light airs. Winds were from the southeast but had little strength.

A haze hung on the water and visibility was only moderate. The men kept busy cleaning up debris from the storm, and trying to fake saltwater-drenched rope. By late afternoon they were in clear weather and becalmed. Captain Penberthy, standing on the quarterdeck, had just fixed their position when he spotted topmasts peeking over the horizon.

"Ship off the starboard quarter, Sir," the lookout bellowed.

Penberthy raised his speaking trumpet, asking for the identification of the vessel, but the lookout had no further information.

"Can't see more than 'at t'is a brig, Sir."

The rosy intermittent light of a setting sun played with Captain's vision. An amorphous figure in the distance momentarily appeared, then disappeared as though erased. He kept vigil as the topmasts of a brig came into full view, the first ship seen in days. Through his spyglass he saw that the mizzen mast was rigged, and the sails on the two forward masts, reefed. The Union Jack flew off her ensign staff, and he assumed the ship to be friendly.

"Hoist the colors," he shouted to the first mate. It was his intention to let them know they were allies, comrades under the English flag.

He considered himself an expert at recognizing ships by the height of the bulwark and turn of sheer but soon saw his error in judgment. *I should have known that a peaceful ship sailing off even a modest wind would have all its sails set,* he chastised within. If a privateer, it would be carrying a *letter-of-marque* from its government. Pirates, however, rarely bothered to honor the universally accepted rules of engagement, attacking anything and everything with discretion. As he watched, behind the Union Jack on the main mast they raised not the *joile rouge* but the pirate's flag of no quarter. Thoughts of *Grysel* came to mind. They would all be murdered if captured. When the studding sails were run out he knew they'd been spotted. It became obvious the pirates' intention was to gain more speed, alter their course, and intercept *Mordonn*.

The ship was steered to north but, without much wind, they could make little progress, and were vulnerable to attack. *She'll not have us if I can help it,* Penberthy vowed. They could stand where they were and commission their carronades, but it would be an insignificant defense against the guns of a pirate ship. Noting high cumulonimbus clouds to the south where a weather system might include rain, possibly wind, he took their only chance, and a distant one. In the shade of those clouds, he hoped to find a breeze strong enough to drive them into the Trades, and make a run for it.

"She be haulin' for us iffen she catches any wind," Ennis croaked.

"All hands to the sails," Penberthy urged Ennis. "Steer south."

Though questioning the order, Ennis knew to say nothing. He gave the order. The ship became a flurry of activity as the crew went to work. All knew the barque, a rakish vessel, once at full sail could quickly overcome them even in a modest wind.

"Helmsman, haul off," Ennis shouted from the quarterdeck. "Head her southwest. Unfurl those sails, men. Run her as fast as she'll go."

The ship was slow to steer. With only a light

breeze to their back, they laboriously moved south. When clouds finally shadowed the water surface, the wind increased. Eventually they found variable pockets of stronger winds and it started to rain. The canvas luffed and threshed as the ship lurched and rolled, scudding the waves, heeling to port then starboard. Penberthy kept a watchful eye on their foe. By all estimates the pirate ship was not gaining on them, but they couldn't count on it lagging behind for long. As darkness came on, the situation appeared hopeless.

"We've hit the Trades," Ennis roared.

"We'll run silent," Captain advised. "Dowse the lantern hanging on the mainstay, and have the cook throw the galley fires overboard."

Through the night, pushed by following wind and seas from the east, the Trade Winds carried them. Without galley fires there would be no warm meal, but no one complained. The crew held their watches alert and listening, in a void of light. Penberthy stayed on deck. Seas were eerily calm and the ship sailed easily, suspended in the dimension of relative silence. Only the rhythmic rubbing and creaking of the rigging, and gentle swooshing of waves against the hull as it cut through the water, could be heard.

By daybreak, searching the interminable horizon and in all directions, they could see no sign of the pirates' barque.

"Be the pirates gone?" Dawkins inquired.

"They're no longer after us," Captain replied.

"All be good then, Sir."

All was not good. The geography of the Bermuda Islands was low, making them difficult to see from a distance. Because they were surrounded by extensive coral reefs and small islands, sailors relied on spotting Morgan's Cloud, the sea cloud that hovered over the lagoon in which the islands sat, to navigate safely into harbors. Penberthy could see no sign of the cloud. Verifying their position, he realized they'd missed Bermuda. The Trade Winds had pushed them north and east of the islands. If they took advantage of the wind, they could catch the Gulf Stream northwest of Bermuda in a couple of days then move north toward Boston. Since they were already behind schedule, and convinced they were only four or five days from their destination, Penberthy made the decision not to backtrack to Bermuda, lay over for fresh stores, and risk being intercepted by the pirates.

"Full sail," Ennis ordered at Penberthy's direction.

As the men went aloft, up the lines hand over hand, Penberthy watched the sails belly out. In gentle swells and with a full press of canvas, the ship ran free. Their first day off the Bermuda Islands, skies were clear and the Trades swept the ship easily along. That evening, under a bright moon, the ship gurgled along at five knots. At last they were making good time. Penberthy stayed on deck until he felt sure all was well then retired to his quarters to try and get some sleep. It was another restless night, and he slept little. In the early hours, just before dawn, he dreamed again of Kayna.

They are on board the ship as it tosses in turbulent waves. Looking to westward, Kayna goes to the port railing, pointing to a black crow flying in the distance. "There is where we'll be soon," she tells him. "Where?" he asks. "There!" she repeats, waving her hand over the scene before them. As he looks to where she is indicating, the waves become calm, the wind dies, the fog thins, and the sun comes out, revealing a distant island lush with spring green vegetation. "Will we get there safely?" he asks, turning to her. In the place where she had stood is only Morrigan, her gray cat. "We will get there and then our eternity will begin," Morrigan tells him.

Stirring with a jerk, he disturbed Morrigan sleeping at his side. He thought about the alarming dream as he dressed, and concluded he was spending too much time with the cat. It was early. He could hear the messmates in the galley having their breakfast as he stepped out onto the deck.

The day was overcast. Clouds were forming far to the south, but seas were gently rolling, the ship handling well. Late afternoon, they entered the warm waters of the Gulf Stream and steered north.

"Keep Dawkins on deck at watch, Ennis. Send the rest to their chores and continue north. I'll be in my quarters."

"Mr. Coltrane," he ordered the cook, as he passed the galley, "tea, if you please."

"Is things a'right? You seem worried, if I may say," the cook assessed, soon appearing in the captain's quarters. He swept the cat aside from beneath the small table with his foot and set the tray down.

"Everything's fine," Captain responded from his desk chair, acknowledging the cook's comment. "Don't you have things to do in the galley? You could have sent one of the men with my tea."

"I needs to tahk wit you so I come myself. I doona wish t' bother ya, Sir, but our stores of viands be very low. So much was damaged wit' water in 'at storm, and rats has gotten into t' flour."

"Do what you can. We'll not be long to our destination. Ration, if necessary," the captain offered, projecting a lack of concern. "I'll have my tea here at my desk, please. I need to get to work and you to the galley."

Sipping his tea, Penberthy studied their situation, going over what he knew in his mind. Distracted from his thoughts as his stomach growled, he looked up from the charts. Glancing toward his berth, he saw Kayna sitting on it, her black hair tossed by a mysterious breeze suddenly rustling through his quarters. Her clear dark eyes stared back at him as he rose, then, somnambulant, walked slowly toward her. At his berth he found only Morrigan perched at the edge. Leaning over, he pet the cat, and she immediately started purring.

"I've heard that solitude, monotony, long hours of hard work at sea, and lack of sleep can cause a man to see fetches," he told the cat. "Also poor diet," he added, rubbing his stomach as he returned to his desk.

Doing his best to ignore the hallucination, he focused on the food problems Coltrane had brought to his attention. Their stores were indeed very low. They'd had little more than fish and beans for nearly a fortnight, and he questioned his decision not to double back to Bermuda for provisions. His stomach ached and burned from lack of proper nourishment. He could only imagine what the men experienced. *Noticeably absent are the greens necessary for physical and mental vitality,* he assessed, his mind drifting again to the image of Kayna, trying to give his bizarre experience some rational accounting. A knock on the door of his cabin interrupted his thoughts.

"Seaman Derrick, one of the new recruits, has sores on his face and arms, with a high fever," Dr. Soadey began when invited into the cabin. "It could possibly be smallpox, and I canna take a chance on it spreading. We need to quarantine him until I see what develops—keep him in quarantine if it be smallpox or spotted fever."

"We can't let any of the others know what you suspect," Penberthy returned.

"I'll keep him aft until we know. If it proves to be no more than fever, we can move him to a cuddy cabin until he gets better."

"Keep me posted."

Open sores could also be the result of old scurvy wounds. Several of the crew suffered from the depression that often accompanied the disease, but it was unlikely it was what ailed either them or Derrick. They'd not been to sea that long. Still, he worried that without proper food soon, the men might become too weak to adequately handle the ship if added strength should be required.

While finishing his tea, he felt a change to the motion of the ship. Barometer readings had dropped slightly. It was not enough for immediate concern, but he knew the situation required monitoring and went up on deck. There he found a strong wind from the southwest. The weather was pleasant with sunny skies to the east, overcast to the west, certainly nothing alarming. It was the erratic motion of the ship that bothered him. He was as sensitized to the ship as he was to his own body. Something wasn't right.

Throughout the day, he kept a watchful eye on the

barometer for any drop in pressure, a sure sign a depression was tracking north. In the evening, he was on deck as the dim sun slipped toward the western horizon. The sky turned roseate, and high, dark cumulonimbus clouds began to gather.

"We canna count on a pleasant day tomarra, I'm feared. Those be weather breeder clouds t' west," Ennis offered, pointing.

Ennis' omen read like a weather forecast, confirming the captain's apprehensions. As night came on, Penberthy stared into the dark, noting the faint appearance of Orion before it disappeared in the clouds, taking with it his opportunity of sighting the pole star or *Dog's Tail*. Ennis wasn't the only one who suspected strong weather was approaching.

Once the crew had been billeted, with only the watch on deck, the captain went to his quarters. Even though the barometric pressure had dropped only slightly, trouble loomed. Lighting a lantern, he pushed Morrigan from atop his desk, pulled out the rolled up charts, and spread them out to confirm their position. It was late in the season but, while in the Gulf Stream and moving north, they were directly in the path of hurricanes. Plagued with worry, he fell asleep with his head resting on his desk.

The ponderously rolling motion of the ship roused him early morning. Looking at the barometer, he saw that it had fallen. There was no doubt that a hurricane threatened. If one should pass even a hundred miles from them they would still be in danger, depending on which edge they rode, and he began questioning what tactic to institute to get them away from it. They could steer east then south hoping to avoid it but, if it curved east as was typical, they'd head right into its path. The only way he could see to beat the violent weather about to descend on them was to get to the west edge of the Gulf Stream. It would mean crossing the shallow waters of the Georges Banks but appeared to be their best option. West of the Gulf Stream they would be at the less severe edge of the hurricane, farthest from the eye. In colder waters its impact would be minimized. On deck, he gave the order to run the ship northwest across the Gulf Stream and make a beeline for Boston.

Seas were calm with very little wind. The current pushed them easily along at about three knots. Sargasso weed could be seen floating in the water. While the men watched dolphins, jellyfish, and man-o-war swimming in the clear water, Penberthy kept his eye on a barometer that continued to drop. Though content they were doing well for the moment, he was not at all complacent. He carefully monitored the ship's motion and reaction to the gathering disturbance from his cabin, hourly consulting the barometer and weighing options.

Late morning they began crossing the Banks, battling a barrier of strong winds from the northwest. Shallow waters meant rough seas—the square waves, short and steep. They rode it out all day and, when the wind slackened and seas calmed toward evening, they appeared to have come through the worst of it. But, in his quarters, Penberthy watched the barometer continue to fall.

"Why isn't the hurricane turning east?" he questioned aloud.

By morning light, the seas had grown heavy. A smir could be seen on the surface of the water. The swells were still widespread, the slopes moderate. The surface water was smooth, but he could feel turbulence beneath. Waves started to build and the water turned oily. Dark cirrus clouds spelled danger, spreading their warning across the sky. There was no wind. An eerie silence hung in the air as though holding its breath in anticipation. There were no seabirds in sight. The thick dark clouds grew more ominous. As the wind picked up, the halyards flapped and rigging sang, and a great sense of urgency descended upon him. *The hurricane is continuing north.*

"We need to get out of here," Penberthy confided in Ennis. "Crowd on the sail."

The men went quickly to the sails. The more experienced seamen knew trouble was brewing, conveying their anxieties to the others. In anticipation of violent weather, hatches were battened down, seams caulked with oakum, cracks stuffed with canvas. Anchors, longboat and gig lashings were double-checked. In the galley the cook turned their scant food stores into meals that could be eaten cold so the fires could be dowsed.

Within hours swells were evident, as well as drastic changes to the wind. The ship heeled off the wind as the size of the waves began rapidly building. The barometric pressure rose briefly, then plummeted. The crests of the waves were longer than the ship for a time but soon became short and choppy.

"T'is a foul wind 'at blows," Ennis advised with false bravado. "I think we need more 'an a cat aboard. We need a naked lady t' keep t' storms away."

Watches kept their vigil through the night. The captain paced on deck, stem to stern then across the beam. Around midnight the wind slacked off some, giving them reason to hope. It picked up again before dawn, coming from the south and bringing pelting rain. Their only light came from random flashes of lightning. Thunder cracked so hard it shook the ship. Below deck there was little sleep. Not only was there worry over the approaching hurricane but, having made the ship as watertight as possible, there was no ventilation. The crew's quarters were soggy and hot, the bilge smell strong.

By early light, Morrigan, at Penberthy's heels for most of the night, had disappeared into the bowels of the ship. The captain kept an eye on flattening waves, unfurling clouds, and a darkening sky. Responding to the steady surge of the sea, the ship rolled and pitched. The sky hazed over and visibility was less than a mile. They were in a bad spot.

Late morning, the hurricane bore down with a vengeance. A wall of dark clouds tumbled rapidly toward them. In surrounding darkness, the wind and rain intensified. The temperature was warm and it was a wet wind that tore at them. The deck was continually awash as massive waves barraged the ship.

"Run a life line from aft t' bow," Ennis roared.

The deck crew braced themselves against the wind, struggling to obey and hanging onto anything stable that might hold them. Fierce winds and heavy spray caused confusion in their minds, taking away their power and creating a sense of helplessness. The ship leaped another wave, making it impossible for the men to keep their balance. As they slipped and slid, pandemonium ensued, and the ship's operation deteriorated into chaos. In the disorder, a man was washed overboard. There was no way to rescue him. Somehow death was always more painful at sea—a tragic reminder of inevitable dangers to those who survived. Some of the men refused to obey orders, instead seeking the shelter of the berthing deck. Several became injured sliding down the ladder as wave after wave crashed over them.

Rain pelted the ship horizontally, and they couldn't distinguish sheets of rain from massive waves. Strong winds blew the tops off the waves, sending foam flying through the air. The wind suddenly changed direction, hitting on the beam, as the ship pitched and yawed. A man was slammed into the deck house, his limp, lifeless body washed overboard. In the driving rain, it was impossible to tell who it was. The ship was handling poorly and began to fall off the wind. As it swung around, the helmsman tried with all his might to correct their motion, but it was no use.

"Chegwin, keep t' wind on t' starboard bow," Ennis barked to the helmsman from the taffrail, his words vanishing in the wind.

Realizing Chegwin couldn't hear him, Ennis began making his way along the life line to the quarterdeck. Bending forward, he faced the strong wind, inching his way across the slippery deck. As the ship wallowed into the next trough, there was an intense flash of lightning. The helmsman shouted something to him he couldn't hear. Seconds later, the main mast splintered. The top gallant blew off and all the running and standing rigging came crashing down, sprawling at Ennis' feet, blocking his passage. Stepping over the raffle, he made his way to the quarterdeck, grateful to have narrowly escaped injury.

Penberthy also had climbed to the quarterdeck. Steadying his stance, he reassured himself that *Mordonn* was a long ship with more stability than most. But the ship had lost its rhythm to the horrible storm. The bow rose up as the vicious sea crested then broke into a hollow of brief calm, reared up again then plunged into the next trough to face another wave. He'd been on rough seas before, riding waves as wild as untamed beasts, but never any as strong as these. From the way the ship was handling, he suspected the rudder had broken.

"Lash the helm," he screamed at Ennis. "Let the wind take her."

The ship started rearing. Waves curled over, relentlessly crashing against the port beam. With the next crashing wave, the ship shook and trembled, rolling dramatically over to starboard. Two men, unable to navigate the severely angled deck, slid into the sea. Ennis crawled across the slippery deck on hands and knees, as howling winds and tumultuous waves tossed the ship. Water poured over the deck nearly washing him overboard. Struggling against the hiss and tumble of the hurricane, each man did what he could to fight the elements.

Rain continued but, by midnight, the hurricane had spent its force. Then the rain slackened, the wind died, and a foggy mist floated on the water. By the gray light of dawn, the survivors could see the ship had been seriously damaged but, thankfully, was still afloat. The sails were ripped off, they'd lost a mast, rails were broken, and the deck was strewn with debris. A spar had come down and broken one longboat. The other one, as well as the gig, had been ripped from their lashings—presumably blown away with the wind. The bowsprit was broken, and shredded sails and rope hung about the ship like cobwebs. In places, they could see through the weather deck to the one below. Pieces of the ship and cargo floated on the water. The men were exhausted, most were bleeding. Their clothes were soaked with rain, and they were chilled to the bone. In addition to all the damage to the ship, their remaining food stores and supplies had been lost. Five men, including Coltrane, the cook, were missing.

Seas remained high for most of the morning, the remnant waves of the hurricane rolling rhythmically beneath the ship. Seaweed floated on the water. As the sea lay down, fog rolled in, surrounding them like a gray cocoon. It was so thick it condensed on masts and what was left of furled sails, dripping onto the deck. Captain Penberthy could smell land, knew they were off the steeply sloping North America continental shelf and at the west edge of the Gulf Stream. But, by his calculations, they were 175 miles from Cape Cod, in the Gulf of Maine. They had avoided catastrophe, but were much farther east and north than desired.

Later in the day when the fog thinned slightly, he could see islands off to larboard. Making landfall was tricky and dangerous at any time. In fog, the concern was in being driven ashore, onto shoals or rocks, at the mercy of the tides and current.

Penberthy knew where they were positioned relative to the islands, but which islands they were, he didn't know. If the fog cleared and he got a better glimpse of them he could take compass bearings. Without sightings or the usual means of celestial navigation, it would be impossible to get adequate bearings. He would have to navigate by taking soundings and dead reckoning.

"Start taking soundings," he prompted Ennis.

At the order, the bosun and first mate retrieved the lead-line, tallowed the end to take bottom samples, and threw it over the starboard rail as far ahead of the ship as possible. Taking soundings would tell the captain not only the depth of the water but also identify conditions of the bottom, whether sandy, muddy or covered with shells or rocks. He could then compare his findings with what the charts indicated and determine exactly where they were. After reading several bottom samples, he determined they were off the coast of Maine.

The next morning, the fog browned up and burned off, but it was a gray day. In the distance, over the larboard rail, could be seen the mountaintops of the Atlantic, an archipelago that rose up from dark blue-green seas. The islands lined up like moored ships with their prows pointed southeast. Some of them looked like little more than bird rocks. The island closest to them was small, the most southerly the largest, with a sheer rock cliff rising at least one hundred fifty feet from the sea. The captain had read about the islands, created millions of years before, during the age when a sea of ice tore the mainland to shreds. They were first settled over two hundred years earlier, in the 1600s, and coveted for their offerings of fish and fur.

Taking bearings on the islands, Penberthy determined they were about ten miles from the outermost island. On deck, he held up his thumb to the western horizon. *Never come closer to danger than a thumb's width,* he recalled from his navigational training. *We're way past closer,* he reluctantly conceded. Scanning the maps, he looked for a way around the islands, hoping to locate a safe harbor. He was uncertain the ship was seaworthy but, optimistic they would be able to limp into protected waters, he set the men to fixing the rudder and jury-rigging the ship. From charts, he knew the shores of the islands to be ledgy. He stared across the bow, trying to read the water color, but gray skies made it impossible. His hope was that the sun behind them would strengthen as it rose higher. When in its zenith, they could more readily see the ledges beneath the water and avoid them when they skirted the islands to find a safe harbor where they could haul in for repairs.

The men worked all day trying to get the ship back in order but there was only so much that could be done. By evening the wind picked up slightly. Through the night it pushed them west toward the outer islands. The next morning the wind died and the fog rolled in, at first on cat's paws. Looking leeward, and taking into consideration fog distortions for speed and distance, Penberthy figured they must now be about three miles from the first of the offshore islands. The sun gradually burned through the fog and it cleared. Gulls circled overhead. The men warmed themselves in the autumn sun, trying to dry their clothes and, with the help of Dr. Soadey, nursing their wounds. By noon seas were calm but the wind grew cold.

Penberthy suspected they were not yet out of trouble, and in for more foul weather. The ship was badly crippled but there arose in him an urgency to get to shore.

While the men struggled with the rigging, he gazed out over the water from the quarterdeck. Watching the dimming sun in the western sky, marking its trajectory, an eerie feeling came over him in noticing there were no fishing smacks on the water nor were there any shorebirds. These were not good signs. The stillness became palpable as a bank of fog emerged with a terrible grace from the east. At nightfall it rolled over them like a giant platen, pressing its illusions into the sea. Morrigan, who had made an appearance on deck, sitting on the samson post and wistfully staring westward toward the islands most of the day, had gone into hiding. Going to his quarters, Penberthy saw that the barometer had again dropped. Another blow was coming—their problems about to escalate.

A fierce wind picked up around midnight, coming at them from the northwest. Seas began running at odds, the waves building. At dawn, worry seized the captain as he watched dark clouds gather. The sea grew more confused, the storm quickly gained momentum, and nasty weather was soon upon them. Immense waves crashed against the ship, threatening to drive them into the graveyard shoals surrounding the islands. Because of the damaged rigging they couldn't go windward, and their options were limited.

Rain began pelting the ship, quickly becoming a torrential downpour. For hours they battled the rain, sea, and wind, tossed with the crippled ship. There seemed no end to the storm's fury—far more powerful than any line squall.

Riding angry waves that looked like the bottom of the sea had been heaved to the top, exposing sediment and seaweed, they hoped and prayed that each wave would be the sea's final outburst. The rain briefly slackened but a cold wind blew straight against them, hammering the ship. He could see immense briny waves plunging against the rocky island cliffs facing southeast then spilled, transferring their energy alongside. The ship was too close to the islands and, without much sea room, not in a good place. Windward, as night came on, a full silver moon in its perigee rose from the rim of the sea, briefly lighting the scene before disappearing into the clouds. Everything felt distorted and, for brief moments, Penberthy couldn't tell the difference between illusion and reality. His mind wandered to his childhood, and he feared he was having one of those life reviews he'd heard dying people experienced.

He couldn't keep his thoughts from summarizing his life with Kayna. They ran through the streets of Porthusek together, stole their first kiss on Bodmin Moor. In his mind's eye, he ran his hands through her raven-colored hair, stared into ebony eyes that had compelled his affections so early in life—her love for him a miracle for which he had always felt undeserving. Their first night together as a married couple came to mind and, despite great present danger, he felt his face blush in recalling her tender body, fresh minty scent, downy neck, and soft lips. Kayna held their first born in her arms, handing Tremayne to him, and he recalled how he'd feared he might drop their child. Little Gwennap had been the second joy from their union. His memory resurrected their times together as a family, his life with his beloved Kayna rather than their days apart, and he had to wonder if he was being prepared to see her once again in the afterlife. Suddenly his moribund fate no longer mattered. Tired of life without her, he welcomed the idea of seeing her, being with her. If he died it would be all right if he could again experience Kayna's eyes.

He didn't want to have to tack, but the current and wind had pulled them too close to the islands. Desperate to get ashore, he gave the order to institute tacking maneuvers. The crew understood all too well the urgency of the situation but were exhausted and weak from hunger, their arms sore and shaky, their spirits low. As they started their tack, three massive waves in rapid succession slammed against the hull, and Penberthy realized they were in deep trouble.

"Buggar," he muttered aloud, involuntarily feeling for his pocket as he did multiple times each day to assure himself Kayna's letter was secure.

Thank goodness Lamorna didn't come along with me, he thought, suddenly questioning his fate. *What if I never see her again? Who will care for her? I promised her I'd take her with me when next I sailed to America. I've never broken a promise in my life. If, somehow I get through this, I'll keep that promise and go back to England for her. And, where is Morri? What will become of her? A letter and Morri are all I have left of Kayna.* Catching his thoughts, he sighed, resigned to the cat's fate. *With men's lives at stake, I can no longer worry about a cat.*

"Let go," he ordered Ennis.

Though void of all hope, the men did all they could, giving their ultimate effort to get the anchors lowered and the ship around, but it wasn't enough. They got one anchor lowered then a massive wave rose up and the anchor rode snatched, jerked, heaved then parted, and they were captives of the wind. Duties forgotten, they clung to the lifeline, belaying pins or railing—anything they could grab hold of to manage the threatening waves and a heightening wind.

In the darkness men called on God for pity, their mumbled prayers like the drone of bees. Mutterings of confessions and promises filled the air, swirling with the ceaseless wind. Through the din, Penberthy felt the ship hit rock. He could hear *Mordonn's* timbers creaking as she started to settle and knew the hold was filling with water.

They missed the tack. Just as they were about to make the turn, a rogue wave rose high above them then descended. Their forward momentum was halted, and the ship started moving backwards. Tossed by a mass of black water, the ship was driven hard onto the rocks, and the keel broke. A wave lifted the ship and slammed it down onto the ledges like an angry child throwing down a toy. The impact crushed the hull and pushed the keel up into the ship, leaving it open to the sea. No longer afloat, the ship settled like a brick on the ledges. As if predestined, the next wave rose up above the horrified men and swept the deck of her hulk. Bodies flew through the air and into the churning sea.

— CHAPTER THREE —

She struck where the white and fleecy waves
Looked soft as carded wool,
But the cruel rocks, they gored her side
Like the horns of an angry bull.

Her rattling shrouds, all sheathed in ice,
With the masts went by the board;
Like a vessel of glass, she stove and sank,
Ho! Ho! The breakers roared.

From *The Wreck of the Hesperus* by Longfellow

When the rote of the sea splashing against the sheet of gneiss ledge awakened him, he was lying with his head in a niche in the rocks. The shallow end of a wave lapped at his battered cheek. His head throbbed and burned—the rest of his body an indefinable mass of tangled and tortuous pain. Ceaseless wind swept over him, singing its mysterious notes. *It must be the voice of one of the Oceanids,* he concluded, swooning, assuming himself dead. The caw of a crow caught his attention for a moment. Then a woman's voice, soft and low, spoke to him, but he couldn't distinguish her words enough to lay hold of their meaning. His mind strayed, drifting as he focused on bits and pieces of unfamiliar words and muffled sounds, as from a great distance.

"Ici, depechez-vous—il est en vie!"

Feeling himself turned over, he lay submissively on his back, staring up into mahogany eyes framed by hair as black as a starless night. The porcelain, pure skin of her oval face and regal neck were in dramatic contrast to the coarse holland of her simple indigo dress. She knelt beside him, lifting his head to lay it on her lap. Her head was shrouded in a mist, an amorphous pale mauve nimbus surrounding it. Beyond her, blue sky and sun blinked in turns through patches of fog. Again and again he refocused his eyes, trying to stop the swirling scene, trying to see her more clearly. Eventually, too weak to separate vision from reality, he quit trying to sort it out, concentrating instead on the steady rhythm of the surf, the fishy, salty smell of the sea, and cries of gulls overhead. *Cries of gulls are said to be the spirits of dead sailors bemoaning their fate*, he thought, wondering if they were speaking for him, wondering how he knew they might. None of the sensations he was experiencing matched the watery grave envisioned when first awakening.

A tall man, somewhat dreadful in appearance, naked to the waist and with brown skin, lifted him to a standing position then hoisted him onto his back. Not one part of Lanyon's body was free from aching. It was a composite pain that filled him. He weakly groaned an objection but it went unheeded, dismissed. The brown man, steadying his legs, adjusted his burden, and moved forward. Laying his head against the man's strong back, Lanyon felt some of the tension ease from his body with the knowledge he might be alive. At the direction of the woman, he was carried from the beach up a well-worn pathway. Remnants of gray fog rolled past them in wisps, and the wind slackened to a trembling breeze. Lifting his head slightly, he looked toward a whitewashed cottage smothered in red rose bushes. The gable end faced the sea, a path curving toward the front to the left. A clump of dark forest rose behind it. Gray-blue light mixed with amber surrounded him. He could only assume the ethereal quality of all he saw before him to be a product of his weakened state of mind and body. The cottage looked familiar, but he couldn't explain why, couldn't wrap his mind around anything he saw, heard or felt. Only the salty taste and smell of the sea registered. A bone hanging on the vertically planked door caught his eye as they entered, something about it stirring mysterious and foreboding feelings within.

"Mettez-le ici!" the woman instructed, motioning to the far corner of the room.

The man lowered him onto a crude cot on the outer wall. The pine straw of the mattress crunched as his weight pressed into it, his bones thankful for something soft to lie on. Glancing about the room, he found it modestly furnished. A large central stone fireplace, where a small fire brightly burned, rose from rough hewn floorboards on the opposite wall. The scent of yew hung in the air, and he saw a sprig hanging next to the fireplace. Sunlight streamed through the open doorway, casting a dust mote haze across the room. He could smell meat, maybe pork, browning in the spider on the hearth. Trying to sort out the ache of hunger in his belly from one more generalized, he involuntarily drifted away from lucidity.

When he awakened, he was covered with blankets and animal skins. The woman squatted at the side of the cot and the tall man, very off-putting, stood behind her. She began dabbing at the wound on his forehead, the white cotton cloth quickly soaked with blood. Her gentle touch felt like a hot poker thrust into his head, and he screamed out. Soothing his forehead with the back of her hand, she continued ministrations. The pain was intense but, without the strength to resist, he could only grimace and moan.

"Wounds must be cleaned and tended," she reassured, moving her hand from the gash in his forehead to one on his cheek.

With salt water, she washed the wounds, patiently pushing his hands back each time he raised them in painful protest. The stinging was nearly unbearable. Producing a clean cloth, she dipped it in fresh water and again dabbed. He was surprised at the lovely fragrance, even more so to recognize it as witch-hazel. Images of her, then another woman, floated in space, merging then separating, merging then disappearing entirely as he again lost consciousness.

"Calf's foot jelly," she said in answer to his quizzical look when he again awakened. She daubed some smelly salve onto his forehead and cheek. "For healing."

Staring at her shifting image, he tried to grasp what was happening, who she was. Three different images were superimposed on her face, appearing then fading, all with black hair and dark eyes. The effect was apocryphal, confusing his mind, and he questioned his sanity.

She forcefully tore some white cloth into wide strips, then wrapped his head, leaving only his eyes, nose, and mouth exposed. His mind wandered in and out. At times, he could feel her touch, see her face, smell her scent. At other times he felt drawn toward a veil of fog, somehow knowing that through its mists lay something more familiar. The woman seemed important to him, but his mind wouldn't produce the reason why. Someone beyond the mist called to him. Before he could answer, the present again summoned. Looking into her dark, glistening eyes as she tended him, he tried to ask the woman her name but the words only formed in his throbbing head. His cracked and bleeding lips could not speak them. She indicated he shouldn't try, putting her warm fingers on his cold lips then patiently applying salve to them.

With the brown man's assistance, she removed his wet vest and shirt, then tucked blankets around his chest and neck. The warmth was welcome. When he turned to look at her, hoping his eyes would speak the gratitude his lips couldn't, pain shot up his leg into his groin and he groaned. She went immediately to the foot of the cot, a look of great concern on her face. Tugging off his rough sea boots, she examined his legs then firmly shook her head.

"This one is broke and must be set," she stated matter-of-factly.

After saying something to the man, in a voice too soft for him to hear, she wrapped her shoulders in a cape and went out the door. While she was gone, the man took off Lanyon's nankin breeches and stockings, setting them near the fire to dry. He then retreated again to the shadows, invisible and strikingly silent. When the woman returned, she carried two pieces of relatively flat driftwood. At the fireplace, she scraped the pieces smooth with a penknife then scrubbed them clean. Motioning for the stoic, silent man in the corner to assist her, she went to the foot of the cot. He came forward as requested and stood at the side of the bed.

"Redressez la jambe—Enveloppez-la et serrez fort," she advised.

Before Lanyon could object or even react, she took his right leg in her hands at the calf, just below the knee, and gave it a frightful jerk. A wrenching pain made him scream out in agony. Placing the two wood planks on either side of Lanyon's leg, and directing the man to hold them in place, she slipped leather thongs beneath and wrapped them tightly around. Unable to bear the pain, he slipped into that misty world of unconsciousness.

It was night when he surfaced from his delirium to find her singing, working at her loom. She had covered him with wool coverlids and skins, tucking them around his body. Though he was comfortable, his moan expressed the general pain he was experiencing. Turning toward him at the sound, she saw that he was awake. Standing, she lit a beeswax taper ln a pewter holder on the broad, hand-hewed mantle. *Where are the other candlesticks?* he found himself wondering. Glancing around the room, he could see no sign of the brown man.

"I'll prepare tea," the woman called from the hearth.

She placed a kettle on the crane, swinging it over the flames. Then, carrying a copper warming pan, she came to him, raised the blankets and slid it under near his feet. For a time he drifted with the warmth, then his heavy eyelids slid shut into dreamful sleep.

— CHAPTER FOUR —

In that building, long and low,
With its windows all a-row,
Like the port-holes of a hulk,
Human spiders spin and spin,
Backward down their threads so thin
Draping, each a hempen bulk.

At the end, an open door;
Squares of sunshine on the floor
Light the long and dusky lane;
And the whirring of a wheel,
Dull and drowsy, makes me feel
All its spokes are in my brain.

As the spinners to the end
Downward go and reascend,
Gleam the long threads in the sun;
While within this brain of mine
Cobwebs brighter and more fine
By the busy wheel are spun.

Ships rejoicing in the breeze,
Wrecks that float o'er unknown seas,
Anchors dragged through faithless sand;
Sea-fog drifting overhead,
And, with lessening line and lead,
Sailors feeling for the land.

The Ropewalk by Longfellow

"Tim-berrr," Magnus wailed.

The men scattered as the giant tree creaked, tot-
tered, then crashed with a force that made the earth trem-

ble and drove the wooden peg far into the frozen ground. Limbs and debris flew in every direction as the tree kicked back. After the tree had been scarfed, the choppers had gone to work with powerful axe blows at opposite sides of its base—the deeper cut insuring the butt would face the direction in which it was to be hauled out when it fell. Seeing how well they'd done, the men proudly experienced the satisfaction of their labors.

"It fell wheer we knew it wood hae," Magnus offered in his strange Scottish patois, as he put down his axe and stood akimbo, brushing the perspiration from his forehead. "Paey up, men."

"That was a big one—nearly thirty-two inches," Alistair assessed. "Glad we bed it well."

Pinus strobes, because it retained resin the longest, was coveted for its suppleness. The woodsmen had worked for weeks to clear smaller trees and pucker brush from the area in which the tree was intended to fall. Their expertise enabled them to gauge where so accurately that they'd put a wooden peg in its path, wagering whether or not they could hit the mark. If it had fallen otherwise, someone might have been injured or killed. The tree also could have gotten hung up in adjacent trees or landed on an area not properly bedded and become damaged, rendering it useless as a mast.

The larger branches, widow-makers they called them, had earlier been chopped off the tree as well as those surrounding it, to minimize damage and injury. Smaller branches and slashings were kept to cushion its fall. Now that the tree had been felled, its length for use as a spar would be determined. Then the head and remaining branches would be chopped off while they waited for the heavy snowfall that would make it easier to transport the huge tree to the river.

"At least this un tain't rotted," Jules Gorman, the head of the team commented, as he fingered the broad arrow mark on the trunk. "No moahr dry ki this season."

The last tree they'd felled had been rotten. It was illegal to dispose of any trees with the broad arrow blaze reserved for the Crown, even to possess boards measuring twenty-four inches or wider. Though trees of modest measure, or those damaged or rotten, were useless as masts, stiff fines were levied if caught with them. The rotten tree had been divided into smaller sections to erase the mark then hauled by sledges and scoots to Burrows' Creek mill where it was sawed into planks and shingles. The men had been fortunate enough to get it completely sawed up before any possible visit from the surveyor-general of the woods. It was told that he was suspicious of any supply of timber awaiting shipment. Even if his critical eye couldn't prove the tree had worn the broad arrow or was of illegal size, he was known to overstep his authority and seize the lumber.

"Retahn to the kip," Gorman ordered, once the tree was resting on the ground. "Tomorrah we work on t'road agin so git some sleep."

Mast teams from past winters had cleared a road, but there was always more that needed to be done, including an ongoing search for stumps or rocks that could damage the tree when hauled out. The submissive oxen, belled then turned loose in the forest to manage on their own over the late spring and summer, had been rounded up and recalked. Their primary labor would be to haul the mast tree to the river, but they would also be used to pull out more chocks and boulders. Once the mast road was completely cleared, the men would pile smaller branches and leaves in the path to add a cushion.

The lumber camp associated with the stand of pine at Koasek had only recently been established. Several seasons ago the mast agent had gone interior to find the stand, calculating its location relative to navigable streams and rivers that would facilitate transportation of the timber. Topographical maps had been drawn up noting hazards like hills, bogs, and other potential obstacles. The mast road needed to allow the most safe, straight, and unobstructed path possible for the removal of trees. Notations had also been made regarding the location of springs where a lumber camp could be sited, and meadows as provender for the oxen. Wells for watering the oxen had been dug along the route or arrangements made with land-owners for the use of their water source, and suitable sites for overnight quarters had been established.

The result was a functioning and efficient lumber camp, with a redoubt built to protect the men against Indians. The kip the first mast team had built was a crude, square log cabin with no windows, but served its purpose. Berths lined the perimeter of a large room. Mattresses were spruce boughs. It was nearly as cold inside as out— the moss used to chink between logs only a partial defense against freezing winter winds. A table made of split logs sat in the middle of the room in front of a central fireplace. On the other side was the cook's realm. A dingle, separate from the kip, housed their gear and food stores. It was sturdy and tightly built with logs set close enough together to discourage bears and hedgehogs. Gorman was determined their camp be as complete as others he'd worked at so, while they waited for snow, the men had been told that in addition to preparing the mast road they would be put to work building hovels for the oxen.

Leighton was assigned to check on the oxen. Gorman advised him to take a coil of rope in case one of the beasts had wandered into a fen and needed to be led out. It had turned quite cold. Trudging toward the forest at even-tide, the coil of rope in his hand, he looked up at the moon's silvery light glistening through the high, fleecy mare's tail clouds. *It won't be snowing tonight*, he mumbled within. The huge bright stars, shining in the cold night sky, looked close enough to reach out and touch as, shivering from the cold, he searched for the oxen. He was anxious for snowfall and eager to get the tree to water so he could be done with lumbering.

The forest was so dense that dead trees couldn't fall to their eternal rest, instead remaining propped up in the branches of those surrounding them. Channels of pine extended to infinity. Hearing a crow in the treetops, he lifted his face to the silver splintered light of the November full moon streaming through the trees. The horizontal maze of pine branches extended in all directions like dark interlocking arms. His thoughts were of the December full moon, wondering if they'd be hauling out the mast tree by then. He'd been away from his Genevieve nearly two months—an eternity. Recalling her words, he stared heavenward at the lunar light, assured she was watching it as well.

"Watch the silvery full moon each month, knowing I'll be watching it with you and counting the days until we're together again," she had advised.

They'd met when he'd worked in the rope walk, indentured to Nathan Easton. He had taken Easton's bylander along the coast then up the Mgeso River, delivering rope for the pulleys and wheels at Van Hoek's mill just south of the French fort on Pountegw or Rapids River. Riviere, as the settlement became known, was where she lived with Van Hoek and his family. She had been bound-out at a young age to the miller for room and board by her father, Pierre Batiste. Though French, she didn't hold Leighton's place of birth against him and said she admired him for coming to America on his own, even though in servitude.

The French had a less possessive attitude regarding settlement and land ownership than the British. It created friction between the two countries. Their relationship with the Indians was also entirely different—the French, more amicable. They used the Abenakis as scouts or shock troops to intimidate the English, even paying them bounties for their scalps. Fearing the Abenakis might turn face, the French did all they could not to annoy them, but their dealings had been frustrating. The Indians, remarkably resistant to commands, came and went as they pleased.

Both the British and French built forts to protect their interests. When the British captured Fort Riviere, most French in the region fled north into Canada or went back to France. Once the French were gone, the Abenakis began raiding settlements in the region. After a series of devilments, Batiste, a fur-trader who had chosen rustication deep in the north woods, moved his family, sans Genevieve, closer to the fort. The Indians had regarded him as a friend but became suspicious of anyone getting along with the English. A marauding band raided the fort and small huddle of houses surrounding it, killing all, including her entire family. Living with the Van Hoeks down the Mgeso River several miles, with no one left to tell, Genevieve didn't hear of the massacre until weeks later.

At the mill she milked cows and goats, fed pigs and chickens, washed clothes, spun fibers into cloth, sewed, and gardened. Sometimes she helped in the mill alongside Van Hoek's two burly sons who did most of the work. She regarded them as brothers and was taught to read and write along with them and their sisters. Compelled to stay until she was eighteen, she eagerly awaited her emancipation, hoping to teach school in Riviere, but had not anticipated meeting tall, lanky, blonde, and blue-eyed, Leighton Parnell.

Following the faint sound of the oxen bells, he found the wooly beasts where they should be, lowing and chewing, their warm nostrils exhaling frosted breath. Putting aside his thoughts, he tallied the oxen. Finding all accounted for, he laid out marsh hay from the shed then returned to the kip. Most of the men were talking or playing cards, waiting for their supper. The rope he'd taken with him had become partially uncoiled, and he took the time to neatly fake it in the storeroom. Then, crossing the room, he went to warm his hands by the fire.

"Com'n git it," Murdock yelled in his hoarse, gravelly voice.

The men dropped whatever they were doing and clattered to the table. The cook had prepared a rabbit stew with sour-milk biscuits for the evening meal, and the ravenous men enthusiastically plunged into their food. Leighton sat next to Hodgkins. The stew was good, the meat resilient, but tasty.

"This rabbit's tougher 'an boiled owl," Hodgkins objected.

"Quit your complainin'," Murdock defended. "I doubt you know the difference 'tween owl and rabbit all told."

"I dassent know why we can't get something sides rabbit fah our suppah." Hodgkins shot back, accompanied by a chorus of assenting grumbles.

"Oh, you be? Fix it yahself or shut you up an' eat." His words brought the men up short, and they returned apt attention to their food. Most meals were the same—beans, salted beef or pork, potatoes, and game when it was available. The days had turned into weeks, the weeks into months, since they'd had anything green or fresh. Any departure from endless and tedious routines was welcome, even tough rabbit.

Evenings in the kip at the mast camp were not unlike those in the forecastle of a ship. The men sat at the table or huddled around the fire, telling stories or singing. Most songs were bawdy, others tested their memories. Only a few of the men were able to sing all thirty verses of the Old World version of *The Flying Cloud* from start to finish. Stories, grown larger than fiction, were about the days when the woods had been full of bears and wolves, the worst blizzards they'd survived, the women they'd conquered. There were also hunting anecdotes, and yarns about giants and the supernatural.

"It used t' be thahr's wolves in these woods but now thars tew meny men," Connick, a Welsh old timer lilted. "I still remembah some wintahs ago when it 'as so cold the smoke froze in t' chimney an' t' wind were so strong it blowed t' teeth off t' sar, changed d'rection and blowed 'em back on. That be t' wintah we sar wolf tracks headin nahth. The wolf haint been seen hereabowts since."

"Ayeh, and I seen a white blackbird," Remy ridiculed.

Remy Arsenault was an old fur trapper and trader, gaunt of form, stout in mind and spirit—a real *coureur de bois* in the early days of settlement. He had tall tales of his own, mostly about the Indians, but today it was a fisherman yarn he blandished.

"I got a tale true," he began, his lips barely visible through his thick, white, shaggy beard. "This heah fishahman met up wit a snake in t' woods. This snake had a toad in 'is mouth and t' fishahman wants it fah bait. 'What'll you give me fah t' toad?' the snake asks. 'I'll give you a sip a ma whiskey,' t' fishahman answers. He give t' snake a sip of 'is whiskey. 'I be back fah moah bait next week,' he tell t' snake. He go fishin' then com back t' woods an' meets up wit t' snake agin. This time t' snake 'as tew frogs in 'is mouth."

"You be tight as strings ona fiddle, Remy," Alistair put in, passing the keg of Dutchman's courage. "I knowed this woman in our village people sed be a witch. She could come and go as she pleased, appeahring then disappeahring. She'd be standin' thahr, t' next she'd be a gray cat a sittin' on t' windah sill. Once a man seen worms crawlin' owta hah hahir, hah eyes big as trenchahs. All sed she smell of mint. When hah husband die, murdahd they say, she be gon, but he hed cat claw mahks found on his neck an' all his blood hed run otta him."

Timbering was hard work and there was the ever present fear of a blow down or fire. Either one would not only destroy the trees but their livelihoods. Though it was a concern that hung in the languid air of the kip each night, it was unspoken aloud, therefore not the subject of conversations. Grumbling was aplenty. The men were not typically defiant, happy for the work, but when out of earshot of their foreman, were quite vocal regarding the mast trade. Leighton focused on his supper, listening but unwilling to throw in his opinion, knowing it would go against the majority.

The controversy had begun with the Navigation Act of 1651 which limited importation to England, and her colonies, to English vessels only. The great London fire of 1666, as well as the need for ship masts destroyed in sea battles in a series of wars with Spain and the Dutch, greatly increased the demand for suitable wood. England turned to its colonies. North American white pine was sought for use as masts and spars due to its light weight and resiliency. If cut while the resin was still in them, and if not destroyed in battle, they lasted six years or more. Trunnels, and the wood by-products of tar, pitch, and turpentine, were equally desirable. The Naval Stores Act, of which the Broad Arrow Policy was a part, tightened regulation of the lumbering and mast trade in the American colonies. The widespread policy the French called *martelage*, sanctioned the right of the navy to mark and cut any trees in their kingdom for use as naval stores. For France, this included Canada. England had imposed such a policy in its homeland until the mid-17th Century when it was overthrown but had resurrected it for application in the American colonies.

Controversy regarding the attempt at regulating the timber trade was most pronounced in the Province of Maine. Resentment centered on legislation, but also overbearing officials, to wit Harpswood, the Surveyor-General of the Woods. A very notional and cavalier man, he accused the woodsmen and millmen of violating the Charter and not doing their work well. By the time the Molasses Act, as part of the Navigation Act, was passed in 1733, imposing a tax on molasses, sugar, and rum imported to North America from non-British colonies, indignation had grown to a fever pitch.

"Can we help it if t' British fahrests be gone—have been fah a hundred yeahs," Dodson, one of the drovers, began. "An' they be takin' ah masts fah a hundred yeahs, tew. Those Jackboots an' Frenchies, that's all they do is fight at sea fah who's in chahge wit' battles breakin' up masts, spahs and bowsprits then comin' heah fah moah. I heahd they used t' git naval stahs in t' Baltic 'til privateahs messed that up. T' whole idea ah t' naval stahs policy in t' fahst place was t' protect sea lanes an' get us away from t' wool trade. They think we don know 'at? Them English cain't stand t' competition, I'm guessin'. An' all weah supposed t' do heah is help 'em git rich on ah backs?"

"They want ah old growth white pine heah because they's lahjah than any othahs they kin find," Alistair offered. "But they be needed fah ships bilt heah and what ah we supposed t' have fah lumbah?"

"The idea of reservin' ah trees of t' finest kind fah t' Crown makes my blood chill—and that surveyah-genahral, appointed by t' king, " McGee put in, "hell, he thinks he's king, goin' 'round mahkin' all t' trees fah t' Admahalty wit' that broad arrah then getting' us t' hahvest 'em fah cheap. I dint lot on such a trade."

"We'd make bettah money on Indian scalp bounties," Alistair added.

"The surveyah-genahral is supposed t' show us how t' grow hemp an' distill pine pitch and tah, like we don't know nothin'. Then he protects the fahrest so we cain't cleah trees fah ahselves," Hodgkins complained.

"How's a body t' make a livin' if he cain't even cleah t' land fah crops, buildin' a howse or sell t' wood he's got t' buy t' tings needed?" McGee griped.

When an agreement was reached between a mast contractor in England and the Naval Board to provide masts for their ships, a mast agent in New England was alerted and charged with forming a mast team. It was his responsibility to find the trees then insure that their cutting and transportation to the mast ponds, mast houses, and waiting ships went smoothly. West bound cargo had to be arranged by the contractor in England then a license obtained to bring masts back. The ships left England late spring, arriving in New England with their cargo of English goods mid-summer. The stands of trees had been located the previous summer, and those to be cut marked with three slashes of a hatchet, called the Broad Arrow, Crow's Foot or King's Mark. The mast teams started preparing the area around the mast trees for felling in the fall, as well as mast roads for transporting them from forest to port, timing their delivery and hewing with that of the arrival of a mast ship from England.

"They got it good in t' southahn colonies, them mahchants do," Morrison put in. "They got slaves t' do t' wahk fah free, linin' theah own pockits wit' huge profits. Heah, wheah t' fields ah covud wit' snow and t' ships moahed at whahves in t' wintah, t' growin' season an' fishin' ain't much. B'sides a short mastin' season, we got t' fight off t' damn French and t' Indians evah time we tahns ahround."

"It git hardah evah yeah t' eke out a livin' in t' Province. We ought t' do tahpentine. Don't run as long as in t' south but a lot easier t' make than distilling pine tah. I think it'd be a lot moah profitable than lumbahin'," Dodson added. "Or we could jest grow hemp an' go inta t' linseed oil bizness."

"Why doon you just do 'at now, Dodson," Morrison inserted. "Get you a cockleshell an' take it on up t' Boston, even t' southahn colonies if ya dahr. You kin take wool an' dried fish, even pottahry. When you git to Vahginia, bring me back some of 'at tobackah."

A favorable shift in the economy had occurred when Puritan politics transitioned into the merchant class. Industries associated with ship building opened up new opportunities for carpenters, engineers, smiths, and for rope making, as well as the production of turpentine, tar, pitch, and masts. However, these activities came into direct competition with English markets. Prohibited from trade with France, Holland, and Spain, the lumbermen and other colonists turned to smuggling. Yankee ships, built lighter and faster, also began posing a threat to the English ship building trades. English merchants pressed the Crown for tighter controls and taxes on goods sent to or coming from the Colonies, the beginning of the oppressive acts that would eventually lead to revolution.

Sedition was in the air. Desirous of more independence, the colonists grew resistant, hardened to British rule whose proven ignorance of life in New England thwarted legislation. More than a vast ocean separated the American Colonies from Britain. Disputes surfaced over land ownership and especially the naval stores policy, threatening the imperial relationship between the colonies and motherland. Large tracts held by absentee land owners left ample opportunity for squatters, jealous of them, who wanted to profit directly from their woodland labors. Continually harassed by British officials of one kind or another, they were hauled into court for cutting trees supposedly reserved for the Crown.

Unless the granted land or plantation was owned

before the 1691 Charter, title was not recognized by the court. The first White Pine Act of 1711, while an attempt at more control, provided quite a bit of latitude in its interpretation, and the colonists were quick to take note. It had claimed all trees over twenty-four inches in girth not on private land. To circumvent the Act, paper townships, argued to be bodies politic, were established. This extended private land ownership where trees could be freely lumbered, limiting the number of trees that could be reserved.

"The British don't like us shippin' ah lumbah t' Europe so they decided t' make t'ings tuffah, but that White Pine Act shah was stupid, if ya asks me," Cornell offered. "Trees undah twenty-foh inches can only be used as top masts and theys welcome t' 'em sticks. By saying we can cut all the rest of 'em meant no trees around heah would evah grow lahg enough t' be used as masts."

"Ayeh," Hiram assented. "How come no one stopped t' think abowt what would happen t' thehr white pine nahsahry then?"

The acknowledgement that eventually they'd have no trees for masts caused the Board of Trade to toughen the act, replacing it with another in 1722 that put the burden of proving trees were legally felled on the woodsmen, claimed all white pine on public land for the Crown, gave the Admiralty Court jurisdiction in enforcing the act, and extended the duties and responsibilities of the surveyor general. Because it was impossible for him to oversee the extensive land area he was charged with managing, his actions became sporadic, often, in frustration, punitive. Oppressive activities of seizure and harassment became commonplace. The result was that making a living by the timber trade, much less meeting market demand, grew very difficult for colonists and English merchants alike.

Loyalty to the Crown, George II, eroded, as millmen, sawyers, and woodsmen successfully sought new and more inventive ways to circumvent British legislative authority. English merchants bore great expense in the initial outlay of money for harvesting masts. Complications in getting repaid by the Royal Navy meant payments for the masts were greatly delayed, often spread over several years. As a result, many merchants grew tired of the difficulties of compliance in legally removing timber from New England forests and lost interest in the trade.

Meanwhile, local millmen, whose livelihoods came from the forests, thrived in the selling of lumber. Tons of trees, not hewed to Royal Navy specifications, were smuggled as ton-timber or balks to European and West Indies markets where profits were immediate. In protest to legislative demands, masts were often left in the sawmill ponds to rot instead of being processed and sold to English mast contractors. The demurrage for delays in shipments cut into eventual profits, further crippling incentive.

"Seems like with all t' effaht we put t' gettin' t' mast trees t' salt watah a little moh undahstandin' could be felt fah that it wahn't no easy task t' avoid damage," Elwood complained. "I didn't lot on this much wahk fah nothin'."

"All they cahr abowt is t' profit. They cahr nawt fah us or how hahd we wahk," Dodson threw in.

"If 'at jack-booted Guineaman, Harpswood, comes snoopin' 'round t' sawmill, I've a mind to give him a piece of ma fist," Elwood threatened. "We kin make a lot moh money selling this heah tree t' Millman Burrows fah ton-timber than t' cozy it along t' the masting pond at Pezegawan."

The complaints of the men only made Leighton more determined not to get involved in the trouble he saw brewing. He silently ate his supper with intent, steering his thoughts another direction—to Genevieve. Following a dream in which she'd seen him walk across roiled waters to her, she had begged him not to leave the island that fall. It didn't bode well, she had told him, but he was determined to complete his last woodsman season. After his third year of working in the dark winter woods, he would finally be able to save enough money to allow them to become island-sufficient.

Lumbering was honest labor, but the winters were

long and hard, the wages not what they could be. The worst part was being away from her. He worried about leaving her alone on the island for months at a time with only their distant island neighbors to look after her and occasional visits from the Indians. His commitment to be back early spring, long before their first child was to be born, allowed him to put aside his anxiety. To bolster him she had, in the end, assured him she'd be fine, though with less zeal than the previous falls when he'd left. Minimizing her unease, he had climbed over the gunwale of his sloop, swung off the island, and let go, as she bravely waved from the shore. Looking back through a cloud of gulls, he had seen her turn and walk up the path to the cottage, a definite slump to her thin shoulders.

He would remember his entire life and beyond the day, late winter, when he'd first seen his Genevieve as she ran through the barren, frosty meadow toward the mill. Her linsey-woolsey skirt billowed out from under a cloak, exposing her cotton underbody and knit stockings. A gray wool hood sat loosely on her head, the strings wagging in the breeze as she ran. Her eyes were of smoky quartz, her cheeks round and rose-red, her hair, raven-colored. Unknown to him at the time, she'd also noticed him as he and Van Hoek carried the heavy rope to the mill in an oxen-pulled dray. After unloading rope from the wherry at the icy water's edge, Van Hoek had offered to finish the task, but Leighton insisted on seeing his work to conclusion with the rope resting, coiled neatly, on the storage room floor. Had he not accompanied Van Hoek, he would never have seen Genevieve.

"Who's that?" he had questioned.

"Genevieve, our milkmaid and serving girl, wandering from her tasks as usual," he gruffly offered through a twitching, black mustache. "She shows more interest in the bounty of the woods than anything else around here. I don't know what she does with all the culch she gathers."

With the rope stowed, Leighton's thoughts returned to the girl that so captured his attention, in his mind devising a means of meeting her. Seeing her come from the house and head for the river bank, he followed, under Van Hoek's watchful eyes. There, beneath the bare, swaying willow branches, they stood in the snow, talking, sharing their terms of servitude and vowing to meet again. She was seventeen, he twenty. Getting to know each other would be difficult and it would be several months later, in the spring, until he saw her again.

At the rope walk, Easton had been a fair man to a degree, but a task master with a pestilent nature and little regard for his indentures. With a hunched back, more like a carapace, his coarse appearance matched his nature, belying a softer side he kept well-hidden. Bushy black eyebrows partially concealing steel gray eyes, narrowly set, nearly covered his low brow. He was a bilious man— short, stocky, and of measurable girth, ambling more than walking as he strode from one end of the rope walk to the other, keeping an inscrutable eye on his workers. Some were free men, laborers who tolerated the stink and filth of the rope house for low but steady wages. Most, like Leighton, were indentured servants, working to pay off their passage to freedom.

Seeing ships at anchor in the harbor, held with heavy cable, Leighton recognized that sea-going vessels needed thousands of feet of line, rode, halyards, and sheets—rope that had been hatchelled then smoothed and made water-resistant by tar. Rope had for years come from the Caribbean in exchange for linseed oil, lumber, and cord-wood. Since sea-going vessels were now being constructed in greater numbers at New England harbors, and rope was in even more demand, some farmers had started growing hemp. In response, rope walks sprang up throughout the region.

However important he knew rope-making to be, he had long grown tired of the sweaty tasks, yearning for fresh air and the freedom of the outdoors. The long wooden rope house was confining, hot, and smelly. Men unloaded bales of hemp from a wherry on Moonlight Estuary—a place the French had once called Riviere Le Claire de Lune. There, water was diverted to run through the building, powering the wheels for winding and twisting the rope. He'd unloaded hundreds, perhaps thousands of bales of hemp to be retted and scutched, his hands tingling in remembrance of their rawness in handling the coarse fiber. Hemp was used because it was supposedly easy to work—a conclusion with which he could not agree.

When the fibers had been soaked, they were beaten to remove dirt, then laid out on the rough-hewed wooden floor and dampened. In the summer they were dew-retted on the grass. The bales were then carried to the hackle, a spiked apparatus, to separate them into straight threads. As the fibers were combed, hemp dust hung in the air like sea smoke, creating a surreal atmosphere and masking the always present danger of it igniting. His greatest concern was that a fire, destroying the ropewalk, would forestall his path to freedom.

Always watchful for fire or the punitive eye of Easton, spinners wrapped the straightened threads around their waists, and walked backward the seven hundred-foot length of the rope house. They then moved the thread from the traveler to a jack or spinner, like a capstan on a ship, where it was threaded onto hooks and slowly wound and twisted. A top, with notches in a handle, regulated the amount of twist in the rope as it was moved from the jack, gathered into junks to prevent tangling, then soaked in vats of pine tar for seasoning. Once the excess tar was squeezed out, the junks were wound onto bobbins then skewered onto creels to dry.

Rope was produced through a series of opposing twists—the fiber twisted one way into yarn, the yarn the opposite way into strands, the strands into rope. Single threads of hemp yarn were twisted to form strands for rope, rode or line. In turn, strands were twisted together, three at a time, to form hawsers or three hawsers together to form cables, to be wrapped around capstans for towing or mooring a ship or to drive the pulleys of grooved mill-wheels.

The Sisyphean work of the rope walk was pure drudgery and he, a mere cipher. But at least he had escaped the British press gangs that sometimes descended upon the rope house or docks, commandeering free men. It would have been more preferable to him to have been collecting cobblestones from riverbeds to take by coaster up to Boston or out to the islands like his friend Duncan, also indentured with Nathan Easton. But his lot, to endure the smell permeating the air and filling his nostrils as he stirred the molten tar in the rope house, had been sealed for one last year.

Smelling the residue of the distasteful tar on his hands from handling rope for the oxen, Leighton retrieved his thoughts, got up from the table and went to his berth. Lying down, he turned to face the wall, attempting to shut out the loud voices of the men. The air was close. Tired from a hard day of work, he soon drifted into the deep shadowy side of sleep.

— CHAPTER FIVE —

How often, oh how often,
    In the days that the ebbing tide
Would bear me away on its bosom
    O'er the ocean wild and wide!

For my heart was hot and restless,
    And my life was full of care,
And the burden laid upon me
    Seemed greater than I could bear.

But now it has fallen from me,
    It is buried in the sea;
And only the sorrow of others
    Throws its shadow over me.

From *The Bridge* by Longfellow

A foul smell awakened him from parcels of the past. The woman sat on the edge of the cot holding a crude earthenware mug to his lips. The contents smelled of tar and he refused it, drifting, as the hueless gray light of dawn cast rosy shadows across her persistent eyes. Attempting to focus, he couldn't sort out the present from the past—both equally foreign to him, and yet, at some level, strangely familiar. *What of dreams and fantasies*, he found himself asking, as he swooned.

He was more alert for a time, but became confused as his eyes darted past her, drawn by bright spring sunshine bathing the doorstep of the cottage. Folded rose petals spread their thorny stems across the dust-moted light, stretching around the door-jamb as though searching for shelter within. Without realizing he'd drifted again, he awakened to faint footsteps pattering about the room. Looking to the right, he found the woman at the hearth. A gray cat was curled up on a chair near her.

A gentle shower fell outside the open doorway and a quiet fire sparkled in the fireplace. The smell of rain was refreshing and, as he inhaled its cleansing fragrance, his mind was carried away as though caught in the current of a stream. He floated over the scene for a time, slipping the bonds of reality and sliding first into a familiar past, then one that seemed to be happening to someone else. Like strange and mysterious codes, it was impossible to decipher or separate one experience from the other enough to grasp it or thoroughly examine what was real, a dream or fantasy. The phrase *cataract seas that might break a ship's back* came to him, and he frowned, then groaned, as a memory struggled to surface. Hearing him, the woman got up from her weaving. After pouring a cup of steaming water into a mug, she walked toward him.

"You must drink this tea," she offered, her eyes examining his.

Trying to raise his arm in protest, he briefly pondered the idea that she might be poisoning him. Looking into the depths of her soft eyes, he quickly concluded there was no logical reason to bolster his suspicions, and relaxed into receptivity.

"You have nothing to fear from me," she explained without reproach, reading his thoughts. "Herbs and roots—for healing—for the fever."

With the help of the brown man, appearing from the shadows, she raised him up on pillows so he was more upright. As the man looked on, she gently lifted Lanyon's head, urging him to take short sips of the hot tea. The smell was revolting. It was not black tea but tasted like she'd boiled sticks and tar together.

Amber light danced through the window panes beyond her. It was twilight, and the door was open. He could hear the faint slosh of the sea against the shore, crickets chirring, the murmur of bees, and smelled meat cooking. The warmth of the cozy fire lulled him, and he drifted through dreams. Soon after the hot tarry liquid slid down his throat like a dulling narcotic, lethargy overtook him and he felt himself subside, falling down and away from her into a familiar past of which he had no waking recollection.

— CHAPTER SIX —

The tide rises, the tide falls,
The twilight darkens, the curlew calls;
Along the sea sands damp and brown
The traveler hastens toward the town,
And the tide rises, the tide falls.

Darkness settles on roofs and walls,
But the sea, the sea in the darkness calls;
The little waves, with their soft white bands,
Efface the footprints in the sands,
And the tide rises, the tide falls.

The morning breaks, the steeds in their stalls
Stamp and neigh, as the hostler calls;
The day returns, but nevermore
Returns the traveler to the shore,
And the tide rises, the tide falls.

The Tide Rises, The Tide Falls by Longfellow

The smell of meat cooking at the hearth in the kip awakened Leighton. Seeing that the other men were up, he rose, sitting on the edge of his berth to pull on his boots and face another day.

For weeks, some of the men had gathered the smaller growth pines and, under Gorman's direction, started to build hovels. Smaller slashings, as well as bark and moss, would be used as roofing material and to chink the logs. Other men built or repaired scoots, used to haul out the mast tree. Leighton worked with the men and oxen on the mast road, removing boulders, stumps, and laying slashings. Lesser trees for bowsprits and spars had already been hauled out. While they'd had snow, the cover was still not adequate to cushion the huge mast tree and so they worked and waited.

Weeks passed. The days were short, the nights long, the cold more severe. Like every other day, Leighton was exhausted by evening. A crow cawed from deep in the woods as he turned the oxen loose. Looking to the night sky, he noticed Betelgeuse at Orion's shoulder, the brightest of the winter stars, hanging low above the horizon. Genevieve's words came back to him as he watched a full moon rise in the east, casting its silver light through the rows of pine.

"Watch the Long Night Moon of Winter Solstice, knowing I'll be watching it as well," she had told him before he left in the fall. "'Tis when the days are shortest, the sun at its nadir, a time of death and rebirth—the death of our time apart and the rebirth of a time when we will watch all moons together, whether they be waxing, full or waning."

After returning from his oxen chores, Leighton ate a boring supper and retired to his bunk. The men's voices came into and out of his awareness as he dozed. He could sense great anger and anxiety in their voices. Life was not easy for any of them. Just trying to make a decent living was hard enough in an untamed land, especially for those without property. The continuum of threats, coercion, and subjugation by British officials wore thin with the colonists. Oppressive English dominance, strict navigation laws, and unfair taxation caused open defiance of authority. Some turned to treachery. Many loyalists returned to England or conducted their business in America from London. Others, who had been loyalists, became aligned with the colonists when seeing the advantages of freedom from English rule.

Adjusting his position on his cot, praying for snow, Leighton's thoughts again turned to his days in the rope walk. Though he hated the work, it had compelled him to seek a better life. There was something about the islands that had called to him from when he'd first set foot on American soil. He had dreamed of living on one of them, to gain his livelihood by fishing or trading, and never again smell tar or wet hemp. He pictured a reefy islet with a secluded cove where the waters were as transparent as blue crystal and full of fish—a place where he could hunt, with a meadow in which to build a strong and sturdy cottage able to withstand the strong winds and high seas of winter. All his dreams suddenly seemed possible the day he'd met Genevieve, but could not be brought into reality until she became his wife.

In the spring, when he had again taken the wherry loaded with rope and other goods to the mill at Riviere, Genevieve was waiting for him at the dock—her cotton bonnet pushed back to reveal a bewitching smile. Shyly, she took his hand and squeezed it once he'd secured the boat. She watched from the mill door as he unloaded the tarry rope and carried it to the storeroom as instructed. When he cut himself faking the rope, she was immediately at his side with a cloth to wipe the blood and a soothing salve, drawn from the pocket of her shift, somehow knowing they would be needed.

They aimlessly walked together through blue flags and yellow bastard daffodils in the meadow. In the woods, she showed him woodbine, snow drops, and other early bloomers, as well as wild mint. Together they strolled along the river in the cool spring breezes, inhaling the earthy smells. He wove a wreath of wildflowers for her hair. In their stolen moments together, they vowed their affection for one another. Under a full moon, its golden light flowing down on them like honey, they kissed for the first time.

"The moon is Ostara," she told him, presenting him with a twig of sage, "the vernal equinox marking the balance between light and darkness. The days are brightening as is our love for one another. The new moon that draws lovers together will next occur while you are away from me. Twelve days after that, by the time the moon is again full, you will think of me and know my love for you."

The morning he left, he braided some early spring green blades of grass into a ring and placed it on her finger as a promise. Leaving her that day had been one of the more difficult things he'd had to do. She told him they'd be together again soon, and he found encouragement in her comforting words. During the darkness of the next new moon he felt sullen and distant from her but, gazing at the full moon that followed, strongly feeling her love, he realized he never wanted to live without her.

When he had returned to the mill early summer, she wasn't waiting at the landing and his heart nearly stopped beating until he spied her in the meadow above the millpond picking violets. Upon seeing him, she ran lightly to him with a delicate air. Violets and yellow and white daisies spilled from her splint basket, and the skirt of her blue broadcloth dress flapped in the breeze, revealing bare ankles and feet. The hem of her dress was rent, her delicate feet dirty, a patch of berry stained her cheek red, all as endearing to him as her angelic face and sweet voice.

"Only the white or blue violets have the lovely scent," she commented, leaning into him and placing a bunch of them under his nose. "The red violets are very private and so they give off no fragrance."

In the evening, when his work was finished and she had put her spinning aside, they met as agreed under the rock maple at the back of the mill near the elder copse. There they made their plans, then went to Van Hoek for his blessing. In a twelve-month, when Leighton was free, they would be married. Deliriously happy, he couldn't imagine what saints of heaven he had fooled to win her heart.

Hand in hand they walked near the tidal estuary early the morning he was to leave, hardly noticing the dew thick on the tangled marsh grasses as they sat proclaiming their love. He promised to return in the fall then left her standing on the river bank, waving to him. Carrying with him the image of her bonnet-framed face, he was stricken with doubt, swallowing a powerful fear he might never see her again as he rowed out into the strong current of Mgeso River.

That summer in the rope walk had been lonesome as he listened to the pulsations of his captive heart. Working conditions were brutal, hot enough in the searing midday sun that several of the men fell victim to calenture. Stealing whatever time he could for himself, he began answering some urgent inner need, exploring the offshore islands in a borrowed sloop. Scudding the craft eastward, in the dim light of a rising sun, he set sail from the harbor, using the oar as a rudder.

An ethereal mist shrouded the islands. He had heard others call the fog sea smoke and could see why. Though he wasn't one for the myths and legends Genevieve often talked about, knew by heart, the islands and haziness surrounding them created in him an indescribable other-worldly feeling, bringing to mind the mysterious island of Avalon she had described. It was like the islands floated not on water but dangled in the fog, coming and going, appearing and disappearing in the mists. Genevieve had said that the mists held secrets, suspending the barriers of time between the worlds or dimensions. "At the time of Samhain, the night the year turns to winter," she said, "the barriers are thinnest and one can shift with ease from past to present to future then back again, if they so desire it."

With a soft backing wind, he steered fearlessly east, driven by inner cravings and a strong sense of longing. By the time he'd crossed Kokokhas Channel, separating the first islands from the shore, most of the fog had burned off. Blinding sunlight glittered off the waves as he wove his way around the first two islands. He wasn't sure exactly what he was looking for but heard one of the islands calling to him.

Over the summer he visited both the inner and offshore islands, hoping one would welcome him. He went ashore on each, exploring from one end to the other, meeting the people that lived there, inquiring about possibilities. But, after each excursion, he returned to the mainland disappointed. The islands were all beautiful, with coves, cliffs, ledges, shoals for fishing, woods for hunting, but none seemed just exactly right. He had begun to think it was Avalon he was looking for—a perfect place that existed only in legends.

On the last trip of the season, he had come upon the most remote island, the last stop from the mainland before the open sea. Leaving Stone Island, he crossed Bitawba Reach to get a closer look. Drawing close to the island, he found it such a beautiful sight he nearly lost his balance when he stood up to ascertain a proper anchorage. The western shore looked like a good place for a landing site but, wanting to explore it all, he rowed around the southern tip. High cliffs rose up from rough waters, making landing impossible. There were inlets between the cliff faces but, with the waves breaking violently into them, it was not a place to steer a boat.

As he moved to the eastern shore, a ship showed in the offing. Having seen one like it in port, he recognized it as a whaling vessel. On shore was a sunken reef where cold salt water combers crashed. Landing looked difficult, if not hazardous, so he moved on, but not before noting nearby shoals that promised a fisherman's harvest. On the north shore there were more ledges but also a cove where rippling waves gently lapped the shore. Strategizing his landing, he feathered the oars and chased the boat into the cove. Swallows swooped overhead, diving at him, as he grated the sloop over multi-colored beach rocks, snugged it into the bight, and secured it, wrapping the painter around a large stone.

It was a sightly place, smaller than some of the other islands he'd passed, but idyll. In evidence were tidal flats for digging clams and mussels. The surrounding sea was very accessible and sure to provide an endless source for fish.

His youth and innocence kept him from taking into account all that living in the weather extremes of a remote island might entail. Convinced the island would provide all they required, and it was where they should live, he mentally positioned their cottage above the grassy knoll near the beach. He pictured it gable end toward the sea, patterned after those of the village in England he'd left in his youth. It would be a simple cottage, but adequate to their needs, warm, and comfortable.

The tide was in, the ocean covering all the flaws of a rocky shoreline. Stepping over carrion fish, he walked up the gradual slope to a flat meadowland, where he determined there was plenty of space for pasturing and raising crops. Off to the side he found a midden as evidence of the past. Wondering about the revenants and spirits Genevieve often talked about, he picked up a talisman for her. At the far end of the meadow was a series of stones that seemed to be the outline of a circle. An oak tree clearly marked the center, with smaller stones extending outward in four directions.

A piney scent was strong and refreshing as he walked through the ranks of trees. It made him think of Christmas. The woods teamed with chickadees and several other bird species. As a blue jay scolded in the distance, he stood staring through feathery branches overhead. At the periphery of the pine forest he discovered yew, juniper, birch, oak, maple, poplar, and nut trees as well as plum, mulberry, and apple. Dewberry and gooseberry bushes, as well as the red checkerberries of the wintergreen, were in abundance. Blueberry barrens and wild strawberries spread like a colorful blanket across the fragrant meadow.

His wanderings brought him to the south end of the island, where the rocky cliffs he'd seen from below plunged a hundred feet to rias running in from the sea. Light clouds hung on the distant hills to the west as he stood gazing, entranced by incessant waves rambling toward shore. The day seemed boundless.

Hours later, he walked back along the beach on the eastern shore. The tide was going out, leaving seaweed draped over rocks, abandoned to dry in the sun. Seaweed patterns left in the muddy sand looked like pieces of art— jellyfish with long hanging tentacles, or stylized botanicals with their roots showing. In places, it looked like a whole group of trees clumped together, resembling a primeval forest. He stared at the beautiful patterns, sad in knowing the on-coming tide would wash the beach clean, erasing them.

It was a fragrant summer's eve with a silvery waxing crescent moon rising over the horizon as he made his way back to the cove where his boat was secured. Salty water lapped over gneiss ledges. The first ledge, farthest out, broke the sea before spilling more gently over the second. The closest ledge, soaking in shallow water, was lichen-covered. Gulls soared high into the air, hovering, dropping mussel shells onto the rocky shore to break them apart before diving down to claim the meat inside.

Watching a thin fog move toward him over the expanse of sea, he wished his Genevieve was with him. The next day he would be back to work but, as he untied the line of the boat and climbed over the gunwale, he took a moment to savor his island discovery. When next he saw Genevieve, he would tell her all about their new island home surrounded by endless sky, light, space—and sea smoke.

Working in the rope walk, he had for years mechanically moved through his tasks, automatically, unthinking, often reprimanded by Easton who had threatened to extend his servitude if he didn't work harder. He remained unsure that was possible but couldn't risk it, finding periodic enthusiasm for the work. After meeting Genevieve, he'd taken his work more seriously, vowing not to let anything get in the way of their being together. And so he had toiled, dreaming of his beloved.

When they were married, they'd move to the cottage he'd build on the island. There they'd raise their children and live off the land. He had it all planned—a modest cottage, an orchard, a garden. They'd fish and hunt for their food, only going ashore to sell or trade dried cod or other raised and gathered goods to buy their staples. It would be an extraordinary life.

Returned from his discovery of the island, he'd inquired about its ownership and found out the Indians called it Sobagw Pekeda Menahan, translated to Sea Smoke Island. As was often true with Indian names, shortened by white men, it had become Sobagpeka. It wasn't known who laid claim to it, but he was told the island could be had by *squattin'* on it.

Whether dreaming or day dreaming, he thought of little else than Genevieve and their life on the island, vowing they would move there as soon as possible. When he again visited the island that fall, there was no sign of the swallows seen in the summer. Migrating geese lay over in the fresh water pond near a spring at the center of the island where they could be easily hunted. An adjacent bog held an abundance of catkins and cranberries. Beaver lodges were also in evidence. The woods seemed filled with game that could provide an endless supply of deer, rabbit, mink, squirrel, and turkey.

Strong winds blew without ceasing over the island. Standing at the south end on towering cliffs was like being at the quiet edge of the world. As the sea crashed and roared below, a salty spray rose up, dowsing him. He stared at the sea marching silently toward him from a distance, wondering at the source of its waves and what shoals, ledges, and reefs they would pass over before reaching the island, pushing thick weather before them. A sense of foreboding came over him as the mists rolled in, but he shook himself free of it and walked to the north end of the island. At low tide, a series of small islands no more than bumps in the sea, breached the water. Someone had told him they couldn't be called islands unless he could stand on them at high tide. There was a cormorant rookery on the one farthest from shore. Gulls, facing east like moored boats, perched on several others.

He constantly talked about the island to all who would listen. Through extensive inquires he learned more about its history and mystique. Some of the news was good, some not. Most people he talked to felt prompted to dissuade him from interest in it, saying it was too remote.

"Winters be hahsh, brutal. You'll find only t' sough of wind on t'isle," his friend Duncan warned.

"At least with the wind blowin' all t' time yew won't have no mosquitoes. At Foggy Hahbah they be so thick you kin reach out and grab a handful," Harris commented.

"Pahrates haunt t' outah islands, all tell," Lewis cautioned, "and not jest fahthah south in Massachusetts Bay."

That fall when he again saw Genevieve, he gave her the talisman he'd found near the midden as evidence of Indians and told her all about the island, including concerns voiced regarding its remoteness.

"We'll have neighbors on nearby islands and soon, a family to keep us company," she encouraged. "The Indians must always feel welcome as friends," she added, fingering the smooth talisman.

The stories he related of ghosts that walked the island, heard about in port from a sensitive with second sight, did not dissuade her. Nor did stories of shipwrecked sailors caught in a nor'easter, eating rockweed, mussels, and gulls to stay alive. Other stories revolved around bitter winters and squalls that capsized ships, sending sailors to their sea graves or onto ledges, eventually starving but not before eating one of their own. Tales were also of pirates, dead pirates, roaming the island looking for lost treasure, a will-o-the-wisp seen over the catkins at the salt marsh late evenings. It was said that hundreds of cats, once inhabiting the island, had eaten a man alive who had been lost at sea and strayed onto its shore. Yet another rumor was of a woman from England who sailed to America to be wed. Upon arrival, she learned that her betrothed had been killed by Indians, his inland home burned. Renegade Indians, fearing reprisals, fled to the island, taking her with them as their slave. Genevieve listened but remained strong in her conviction they should be together and live on the island. How could he possibly think otherwise?

"I'm not afraid of phantoms and shades. And how can we get lonely when we'll be so happy," she innocently offered. "We'll have wild berries to eat and can grow corn for cornmeal, grinding it into cakes to eat with our fish. We can trade with the nearby islanders and maybe even the Indians. I'll prepare the food and tend the garden—and the children," she added, blushing. "I'll live with you anywhere anytime, but you must do one thing for me, Leighton Parnell. I want roses in the dooryard—lots and lots of cinnamon roses."

"Then roses you shall have," he promised.

"Cinnamon roses?"

"Yes, cinnamon roses."

He'd do anything for her, loved her with an intensity he couldn't have thought possible before their meeting. Sometimes he missed his parents, both dying during a cholera epidemic in England, and wished his own dear mother could know and love Genevieve as he did. If he hadn't been farmed out as a laborer at the age of ten to a man in Yorkshire who pastured a dairy herd, he would have suffered the same fate as they. At fourteen, he'd arranged passage on a ship bound for America as the servant of Nathan Easton, brother to the farmer for whom he'd worked for four years. It would take seven years to gain his freedom, but he had been eager to go, eager for the adventure of it.

The passage west had been more difficult than he could ever have imagined. At the start he was unafraid and enjoyed the mellow sea, but too soon the weather grew threatening, quickly altering his level of comfort. Never before had he experienced a sea's fury. Gushing waves indiscriminately tossed the ship, showing no mercy for captain, crew, passenger or lowly deckhand. When he wasn't overcome by seasickness turning his stomach inside out, he worked as part of the crew. Sometimes, he helped the cook with errands, hauling supplies from the storage room, cleaning, and scrubbing. Most of those on board, galeres all, had gained passage in the same way he had. Indentured servants, they were treated with the disdain their lowly status dictated, a clue to their reception in the new country and, in particular, Nathan Easton. The passage took three months, the longest of his life until that winter, the last of his servitude, waiting for the day when he could go to Genevieve, a free man, and wed her.

"We be free men," Elwood yelled, startling him

and jarring his thoughts. "Shud be free enuf t' act like it, not be under t' rule of no English.

"Ayeh, Ayeh," several voices resounded.

Most of the men by now had gone to their bunks, knowing a good night's sleep would be needed for the work to be done the next day. In some ways felling the tree had been the easiest part of the work.

"Shut you up," Dodson roared from his bunk to the men still at the table. "We need ah sleep."

The men, not usually compliant, rose from the table and shuffled to their berths. Leighton shifted in his bunk and was soon asleep amidst his misty dreams and illusions.

— CHAPTER SEVEN —

A slumberous sound, a sound that brings
The feelings of a dream,
As of innumerable wings,
As, when a bell no longer swings,
Faint the hollow murmur rings
O'er meadow, lake, and stream.

And dreams of that which cannot die,
Bright visions, came to me,
As lapped in thought I used to lie,
And gaze into the summer sky,
Where the sailing clouds went by,
Like ships upon the sea.

From *Prelude* by Longfellow

"I'm wrapping the thongs tighter around the splint," she sheepishly explained, as his eyes snapped open in response to the pain. "Awake at last?"

He tried to speak, tried to move, but couldn't. Fearing he'd again lose consciousness, he bit his lip and bore the pain. A strong, fishy smell hung in the air. Raising his head enough to see what she was doing, he saw that she'd removed the splint, wrapped his leg in brown kelp, and was again securing it.

"Too tight?"

Even though it hurt like hell, he shook his head in denial. The salty smell of seaweed, mingled with smoke from the fire, gagged him as he fought the pain. Pulling a chair from the table, she sat beside him, gently removed the bandages from his head then washed his wounds with witch-hazel water. The fresh scent stopped his stomach from churning. Something about the smell stirred emotions of sadness and grief.

"This one be very bad," she commented, motioning to the gash on his forehead.

He had no response, being in no position to assess his wounds. All he knew was a body wracked with pain and a mind astray, plodding through visions of the past—or was it the present or future? He couldn't tell. Thoughts and questions barraged his mind, coming and going, circling. Some were coherent, others not at all. He hadn't the strength to sort them out nor could he get his mouth to speak the words swirling within.

After wrapping fresh linen around his head, she eased him back onto the pillows. Standing, she smoothed the coverlids and propped his splinted leg up onto some bundled furs. Sitting next to him again, she took first one arm in her hand then the other, rubbing tallow into his bruises. He gazed past her to the sun-washed open doorway—against his will, drifting away.

When he next awakened, the room was candle-lit, the feeble light reaching out into the far corners. He could hear the snapping of the fire and see her sitting at the table with the cat at her side. A stray thought that the table should be bigger creased his mind. The door was closed, the windows black. The opaque darkness of the panes reflected candle and firelight back into the room as drizzling rain beat against them. He stared at the window panes, mentally measuring the muntins and wondering why. Fighting the feeling of sinking again into the darkness of unconsciousness, he tried to sit up. She heard him stir and turned. Her eyes looked through him, like she read his Soul and he blinked, unable to bear the intensity of her gaze while trying to force some remembrance.

The cat didn't stir as the woman tranced to the fireplace—her shapely figure silhouetted against the amber light. Feeling he shouldn't steal a look, he shut his eyes.

"I've made some broth," she offered, lifting a pot from the hob and placing it on the table. Turning again to the fireplace, she hung a kettle on the crane over the fire. After ladling broth into a crockery mug, she set it down and came to his bedside. Her simple indigo dress, gathered at a slim waist, waved gracefully about her as she glided toward him, surrounded by a rose mallow light. Leaning over him, she lifted his shoulders slightly and slid another pillow under his head. Her strangely familiar fragrance was sweet and fresh.

After retrieving the mug from the table, she sat beside him. Staring into her bewitching eyes, he was shy as a young lad. *How do I know this stranger?* he silently questioned.

Certain his blushing face revealed the embarrassing heat rising from his groin, he was glad for the mask of bandages. Passion seemed a stranger to him, and he found his involuntary response to this unknown woman alarming. *Perhaps it is nothing more than gratitude for her aid that I feel*, his mind defended.

"This will give you strength," she advised, spooning the savory broth to his lips.

The gamey taste was good and he took the broth without resistance. Sipping, he wondered how many days it had been since he'd eaten anything—how long he'd been in her care. Her hair flowed like black silk, her glimmering eyes, warm pools of ebony. As she sat close to him, he could see patches of wear on the sleeves of her dress with threadbare cuffs. Her hands were small and feminine, gentle in touching, their softness a comfort. He wanted to know her name, but decided to wait until he'd finished the broth to ask, hoping this time his lips wouldn't fail him.

When he'd had all he could manage of the broth, he pushed the spoon away and tried to speak. He grew dizzy as his mind wandered, words he intended to speak became fractured. Unsure he'd actually uttered them, he tried again.

"What—is," he started in feverish gibberish, immediately forgetting what he wanted to ask.

The door opened and the tall, brown man entered the room, rain drenched, with a musket in his hand. Two rabbits, fresh killed and strung on a thong, were slung over his shoulder. His jaw was square and serious.

"Mateguasak," he said, holding the rabbits out for her to receive.

"Merci," she answered, rising to meet him and taking the rabbits. They spoke in low tones. He couldn't understand what was being said, but it sounded like a mixture of French and some other tongue which, in a lucid moment, he concluded must be Indian.

"Du petit bois, s'il-vous-plait," she requested.

He left as silently as when he'd arrived. She laid the rabbits on the table then went again to the fire, removed the kettle, and poured hot water into a mug, stirring herbs into it. The man soon returned with an armload of firewood, dumped it on the floor next to the fireplace then squatted to stack it. When finished with his task, he rose, briefly warmed himself by the fire, then nodded to her and walked silently to the door.

"Pull the door to when you leave," he heard her say to the man, as she approached the cot carrying the mug of steaming brew.

Sitting beside him, she saw that he was trying to speak and laid her fingers gently on his lips to silence him.

"Don't speak. There will be time enough for that when you feel better. You must drink this now and rest," she directed, raising his head and encouraging him to drink the hot, dark, smelly liquid.

Lying back against the pillows again, he turned his head to the right, watching her as she floated to the fireplace with the cat following at her heels. Her image and the cat's kept merging then separating as she stirred the fire and added wood. Taking up her knitting, she sat at the table humming. A taper sat in front of her, a mug of tea at her elbow. The cat sat on an adjacent chair. The woman's silhouette shifted as he gazed toward the diffused mauvy light surrounding her. The edges of her body first became more solid then liquid then solid again. Looking about the smoke-filled room, he drifted, unable to get his bearings, unable to place himself in a single dimension. An inchoate fear nothing was real haunted him as he stared at the stacked cordwood, wondering if the brown man was her husband. In a haze, he tried to focus on a distant memory just out of reach, falling into a deep sleep toward a dream that would not let him be—a dream that, more and more, he wished to manifest into the present.

— CHAPTER EIGHT —

In the first watch of the night,
Without a signal's sound,
Out of the sea, mysteriously,
The fleet of Death rose all around.

The moon and the evening star
Were hanging in the shrouds;
Every mast, as it passed,
Seemed to rake the passing clouds.

From *Sir Humphrey Gilbert* by Longfellow

It had been yet another hard day of work at the lumber camp. Gorman saw to that. With time on their hands in the evening, the men grew progressively more restless and bored. Snoring was always the most prevalent sound in the kip but a couple of the men, lying head to head in their berths, whispered far into the night. What few words Leighton caught rang of treachery against the surveyor-general and the Crown. He wanted no part in it—only to complete the work for which he'd contracted, and return to the joy and calm Genevieve and their island provided. While remaining loyal to the Crown, he could also see the unfairness of England claiming trees the squatters needed for their livelihood.

Everyone in the Province farmed. It was hard-scrabble farming, but they were able to eke out staples of food and drink, so there wasn't a market for vegetables, flour, meat or ale. Other English goods like tools and cotton cloth could only be obtained if money was earned. Many colonists fished, going out in shallops each day for their catches and returning with a load to cure and sell. Some made use of the woodlands to produce lumber, shingles or barrel staves, worked in sawpits or cut and carried cordwood to the lime kilns. Others, like him, worked on coasters or by-landers, sloop-sailing goods to the off-shore islands, down east, and to southern ports. Still others smuggled illicit cargo to the South Islands, returning with rum, molasses, cane sugar, and coffee.

Though the mast trade was often a topic of contention, as evidenced by the men talking far into the night, new opportunities had come as a result of it. Sawmills were built wherever a stream could be blocked to create a mill pond. Those who didn't work at sawmills, hewed masts at the mast house, worked on mast teams harvesting the giant trees or were shipwrights, sail or block makers. Merchants sold spars, masts or ton-timber for shipment to foreign markets. Many worked in the rope houses—the thought of it always making Leighton shudder in remembering the foul smell of tar. He was grateful for the income masting provided each winter, and it was much more palatable than work at the rope walk had been, but he was eager to be independent and making a wage by his own initiative. Most days it felt like he was just marking time—each one away from his beloved, harder than the last.

Genevieve had proclaimed seven to be a magical number. They had been married Whitsunday, the seventh of May, just a week after Leighton became a free man. It was a proper day with a mild breeze but without much sunshine. Patches of snow still lay in low places. The river roared past as they stood beside their favorite boulder in a grove of pine. Leighton wore a waistcoat, frock coat, and breeches. Genevieve looked radiant in her wedding dress of yellow sprigged calico with a furbelow at the neck. Her black hair was gathered in a chignon and a chain of wild flowers crowned her head. Mrs. Van Hoek had kept her busy all winter sewing the delicate stitches of the bodice and skirt she wore over a linen shift. Katrina, one of the Van Hoek girls, had gone to the forest and picked apple blossoms for Genevieve to hold in her hands as she and Leighton pledged to stand by each other in fair and foul. Lying in his cold, rank bunk, he could smell the gentle fragrance of those blossoms as he thought of it.

Feasting with friends and neighbors followed the ceremony, the likes of which had not been experienced in many months. Though food supplies were low after a long and hard winter, somehow enough was found to go around, prepared in a great variety of savory dishes in celebration of their marriage as well as spring. A fiddler took up his bow and began playing a reel. Without further prompting, the men lined up on one side of the clearing, the women the other. Leighton and Genevieve met in the middle, linking their opposite elbows. While everyone clapped in rhythm to the fiddle music, Leighton swung Genevieve around and around. Soon other partners joined in one at a time, dancing down the center and following them. Leighton had eyes only for Genevieve, unable to believe how beautiful she was—unable to believe the boon from heaven that finally belonged to him. That night, in the complete darkness of the new moon, their conjugal relationship began when at last he knew her body for the first time. In their moments of passion, her loosened hair fell onto his face, smelling of mint.

Easton, at the last, had tried to talk him into continuing at the rope walk, but Leighton refused. Though uncertain as to what he would do next, he only knew it wouldn't be working in the rope house. He and Genevieve couldn't move to the island until he'd built their cottage and earned enough money to buy furnishings, supplies, and staples to get them started in self-reliance. When Van Hoek offered him a job at the mill with the idea of coasting flour and meal to the islands in season, he accepted.

He worked in the mill until early summer then began slooping. Despite his harrowing experience on the passage from England to America, he liked being on the water and felt confident in his ability to handle a sloop. With Van Hoek's permission, he expanded his trips to include stone slooping up to Boston to make extra money, always cautious of pirates and wreckers that preyed on coasters, rumored to live on the off-shore islands of Massachusetts. On trips to Boston with the thirty-foot sloop, Duncan usually went with him. Coasters were fore and aft-rigged like schooners and it was possible, though somewhat difficult, for one man to reef the sails—easier with two. Sloops, beamy vessels that could carry heavy loads, were built to ground out at wharfs to facilitate loading and unloading. Since they were relatively slow, cargo had to be stores that wouldn't spoil, like stone, cord-wood or coal, if he was going any distance.

Van Hoek helped Leighton build a smaller, twenty -foot sloop with a high narrow stern that was less beamy. The single sail, also smaller in size, was easier to raise on the mast, allowing him to take it, solo, to the islands. Since he could make it out to most of the outer islands, deliver his goods and be back in one day, cargoes weren't limited to nonperishable items. Each coasting trip to the islands included a foray to Sobagpeka. He would like to have started felling trees right away but knew, with the sap running, the logs would shrink. He hauled shells from the midden on a wooden sled. Later they would be crushed, added to lime, sand, and water and used to chink the logs. Gathering stones from the shore, he built the central chimney, making sure the hob in the fireplace was spacious and level. The crane had been brought from Boston, and he installed it at a height he knew would be convenient for Genevieve. Upon completion of the chimney and fireplace, he experienced the satisfaction of a job well done. It also provided assurance their plans were progressing, and soon he and Genevieve would be able to move to the island.

He worked hard but always took time to enjoy their island home—wandering its edges, wading in the coves, breathing in the fresh air and, for hours, watching the surrounding sea as it crashed against the shore. Most of all, as a recent free man, he cherished the feeling that endless space elicited in him. Though Genevieve had never been to the island with him, he knew the same sense of space and freedom appealed to her and made her want to live there. Trips included gathering some of the island's bounty—berries, wild apples, cranberries, and fish or game to take back to Genevieve and the Van Hoeks. It was sad to see summer drawing to a close. Shorter days limited the amount of time he'd be able to spend on the island when coasting.

Late summer a few of his friends made trips to the

island with him to help build the cottage. Leighton had made a plan but, after sharing it with Duncan who was a more experienced builder, he made some modifications, though not the one his friend stressed the most. Duncan advised him to site the house farther up from the shore, in the center of the meadow. Leighton insisted the meadow was for planting, and the cottage needed to be situated close to the water. He kept the details of their new home from Genevieve, how it would look or the progress made, as a surprise.

"Sobagpeka, is it?" Duncan said when first seeing the island. "Oughten you change t' name, like t' Parnell Island?"

"Does it mean somethin'?" Lewis inquired.

"The original name was Sobagw Pekeda Menahan but islanders shortened it to Sobagpeka. It means Sea Smoke Island," Leighton answered, smiling with the knowledge that he knew the island better than most.

"They got 'at right," Duncan put in, glancing at the foggy dark haze on the eastern horizon. "This island is thick o'fog I heerd."

"Why do you want a Injun name?" Harris asked.

"It's bad luck to change the name of a ship, and I expect it's bad luck to change the name of an island," Leighton countered. "The name stays."

Seeing the bounty and beauty of the island, his friends agreed it might be a good place to settle but were inwardly concerned about the remoteness. They, too, had heard the stories, discussing them among themselves. Not wanting to lessen Leighton's zeal however, they said nothing to him.

For two months the men cut trees into logs with fast and furious axe blows, hewing them with hatchets and broadaxes then notching them at the ends. Duncan threw a rope over a tree limb that hung out over the building site to be used like a parbuckle, and they hoisted up the logs, guided them into place, and crossed the notched ends flush at the corners to form a two-room cottage around the chimney. Next, openings for windows and doors were cut, then lintels, jambs, headers, and sills were framed in. Leighton was determined that Genevieve have as much light as possible in the cottage, with windows on the outer walls of each room.

Often, while they worked, the Abenaki Indians would come, securing their sea canoes in the cove, then sitting on boulders to observe the construction. Their faces, bare chests, and arms were painted in horrific designs of black, red, and white. At their waists they wore brightly colored sashes, with a knife or hatchet tucked in and often a tobacco pouch. Their heads were shaved except for a strip of hair at the crown. Some wore braided scalp locks with beads and feathers woven into them. Silver pendants hung from holes in their noses and ears.

"Ni-do-ba," they'd say, each time they came.

The men weren't sure what it meant but assumed it to be a friendly greeting. Few Abenakis spoke English, communicating mostly in sign language or broken French. After watching for some time, they'd go to the woods to hunt or to the cove to dig for mussels. Each time they left the island, their canoes were loaded with berries, shellfish, and game. Never once had Leighton considered it stealing from his island. There was enough bounty for them all. Sometimes the Indians helped carry marl and shells to the building site, dumping them in the tall grass surrounding the cottage. Leighton always thanked them for their help, presenting them with tobacco or sugar, gained on his trips to Boston.

After raising the tie beams, king post, and joists, the ridgepole, and finally the rafters were placed. Because he wanted to eventually daub the exterior of the cottage, he decided to wattle the roof, using sticks and marsh hay to thatch it. On his most recent trip from Boston, he'd brought wrought iron hinges, a latch for the door, and oiled paper for the windows. While he placed the oiled paper in the window openings and sawed the boards to vertically fasten together for the door, his friends began to chink the logs, packing moss, crushed shells, and marl into the cracks between them to keep the rain and wind out.

There was no way he could ever adequately repay his friends for all their help.

"I appreciate all you men are doing for us," Leighton offered, on one of the last days they worked together. "If you ever need my help, I'll always be willing."

"None of us has a wife, so we won't be needin' no house," Lewis put in.

"How bowt yew name yer first born after me," Duncan suggested.

"Now why would anyone name a child Duncan?" Harris teased.

"Well sure it wouldn't be Harris or Lewis 'less, 'course, it's a girl like yew," Duncan returned, as they all laughed.

When the trees grew hoary with frost, Leighton made his last trip of the season to the island. A southerly smeach came up as he loaded his coaster in preparation for leaving after a long day of working. With the tide coming in, he thought it best to spend the night in the cottage and leave early morning, rather than risk the long trip to the mainland in a storm. It gave him pause as he experienced first hand the unceasing winds and salt water sprays battering the island but he put it aside, with no thought for changing plans.

As he went inside the cottage, a cold wind waved through the trees to the west, the dimming sun cast ghostly shadows across the door, and a crow that seemed always at hand, cawed from the branches of a nearby tree. Retrieving his knife from his pack, he whittled some shavings of wood, struck flint, and lit a fire in the newly finished fireplace. The smoke immediately drafted up the chimney as he knew it would. Several squirrels had been trapped to take back to Genevieve. He roasted one on a spit over the fire for his evening meal, along with the last of the cornbread she had sent with him. Watching the fire burn, listening to the sea moan, and the bitter wind blow, he slept.

By morning the cove had iced over. Though the ice was thin, it was difficult to get his boat launched. Undaunted, at slack tide, just as it was about to turn to flow, he wrenched up the killick anchoring the sloop in the lees and put out. The air was refreshingly chilly as he cut through rough waters. A thick brume was receding as he rode moderate waves. South, southeast winds were variable. A giant bull seal, thinking his harem threatened, roared his disapproval, startling Leighton as he drew close to a bird rock. Scudding with the icy cold wind, the sail chowdering, he slipped through the reaches between islands and crossed Kokokhas Channel, relieved when back on the mainland. The bottom in the harbor was foul and he anchored his boat securely.

Tired from fighting the elements to get to port and sore from all the work he'd done on the island, he decided to spend the night before heading home. Sneaking past the men he knew in the tavern, he retreated to his room for a good night's sleep. The next morning he was up early and soon on his way, rowing his small craft along the jagged moraine coastline to Mgeso River then upstream to Riviere. He was eager to tell Genevieve all about his latest trip, day dreaming of the day they would live on the island instead of enclosed by land.

Genevieve always greeted him with enthusiasm, ready to share all that had happened in his absence. It was nothing of great importance to anyone else, but he patiently listened, happy to again hear the sound of her lilting voice. The Van Hoek's had been very kind to them both, offering assistance when they could and befriending them in every way.

Leighton and Genevieve lived in a small cabin near the mill. Though Leighton spent a great deal of time away, and Genevieve missed him, she never complained, knowing his absence was necessary if they were to eventually move to the island. She spent her days gathering nuts, herbs, roots, and other culch from the woods or harvesting water cress from the spring. Her arms seemed always filled with seasonal blooms. She helped at the mill, and assisted Mrs. Van Hoek in teaching her two youngest children to read, seeing it as practice for her own eventual offspring.

In Leighton's absence, nights were the most difficult for her. She would gaze up into the sky at the evening
star, wondering where he was spending the night. Other
than the Van Hoek's who knew her well, people saw her
as strange. She was one to be more concerned with those
aspects of life that most people neglected or ignored—the
phases of the moon, the croaking of a frog at the pond, the
song of the sparrow, the cawing of a crow, the hoot of an
owl at midnight, how the wind blew, where stars were
placed, the bulging cheeks of a chipmunk, the sadness in a
deer's eyes, where bees hid when it was cold. Seeing her
whimsical nature, Mrs. Van Hoek had taken great pains to
teach Genevieve the more practical side of things—
anything she thought might be useful for a woman to
know in establishing a new home and raising a family.
The challenge was holding Genevieve's attention for long
on things basic.

When Leighton was home, he worked with Van
Hoek and his sons in the mill. Evenings, he and Genevieve rambled through the vibrant meadow of white yar-
row blooms, holding hands and speaking of when they'd
met, or sitting on the river bank making plans for the future.

"Once we're on the island, we'll never ever leave,"
Genevieve offered.

"I'll have to leave you at times, until I no longer
go coasting, but we'll be together the rest of the time."

"When will we be able to move to the island?" she
questioned.

"As soon as I earn enough money so we can," he
answered.

"I hope it's soon," she responded.

Birds tucked their heads under their wings to sleep
in the branches overhead, the night sounds surrounded
them, and the rose-orange sky faded as the sun slipped
over the horizon. They gazed at the starry sky for a time
then Leighton took Genevieve's hand and led her to their
cabin. Carrying her inside, he laid her gently on their bed
and unbound her hair. Nights were filled with passion as

they pledged their eternal love, vowing always to be together.

Leighton had made good money coasting but, eager for them to move to the island, became overanxious about the progress in establishing their home. In winter there were few weather opportunities for taking a bylander down the coast, and he had to work in the mill. It was not entirely to his liking, although he was thankful for the work. Hearing from a friend of mast teams going into the dark interior forests to cut mast timber marked for the Crown, he decided to join up. He had worked for two winters cutting mast trees, in the midst of a third.

The rest of the year he had coasted—between trips going to the island to clear and burn trees to create fields and a garden space for Genevieve. He also worked at finishing the cottage. Though it neared completion, there was something about it that didn't feel right to him. Even with a fire blazing, it felt inhospitable. On his last several trips from Boston, he'd carried pewter spoons, apple shoots to graft onto thorn trees, and cinnamon rose bushes to plant in the dooryard. All these things he hoped would help turn the cottage into a home, but something felt missing, and he grew concerned that Genevieve wouldn't be happy there. Unable to decide what it was, he saw nothing else to do but continue to make it ready for them to occupy, hoping she would be satisfied, if not amazed and ecstatic.

On frequent trips to Boston, he offered to bring needles, pins, and cloth for her, but she wanted to use the resources of the island, like fish bones for needles, herbs for flavoring, fragrance, and healing. "We will have sheep," she proclaimed, "for producing cloth that I'll spin and weave. I'll not have *boughten* cloth." They would grow their own corn for meal to make biscuits and pone. A large garden would augment fish and game, completing their provisions and food supply. Their hopes and dreams were completely aligned, and all they talked about when they were together was the day they would move to the island and make it their home.

Hearing murmured voices and the snorts and

wheezing of the men of the kip, Leighton realized dawn was at hand. Another hard day of work would face them in the morning. Lying awake for a time in his bunk, he again drifted with days past, thinking of Genevieve. It had been especially difficult leaving the island and sea that first fall when he'd joined the mast team—even harder to leave her with the Van Hoeks who alone would have the advantage of her company. His departure hadn't gotten any easier in subsequent years. He missed Genevieve most of all, but it was also with reluctance that he left the sunshine, refreshing air, and open space of the island for the deep and dark inland forest.

— CHAPTER NINE —

The sea awoke at midnight from its sleep,
And round the pebbly beaches far and wide
I heard the first wave of the rising tide
Rush onward with uninterrupted sweep;
A voice out of the silence of the deep,
A sound mysteriously multiplied.

As of a cataract from the mountain's side
Or roar of winds upon a wooded steep.
So comes to us at times, from the unknown
And inaccessible solitudes of being,
The rushing of the sea-tides of the soul;
And inspirations, that we deem our own,
Are some divine foreshadowing and foreseeing
Of things beyond our reason or control.

The Sound of the Sea by Longfellow

Hearing the dash of a shuttle, he floated up from that fuzzy realm between sleep and wakefulness. It felt like he was surfacing from a remote region or a deep, dark well. His senses followed a fragrance sweet and pure as he opened his eyes slightly. He could hear her at the loom. The door was open. It was night time. A mild breeze swept through the room, and the light of a dimming fire stretched across the darkness, casting its eerie light. Soon the sound of the shuttle ceased, and he could hear her faint footsteps. Seeing a long gray shadow appear across his chest, he opened his eyes wide. She was standing over him. The severe-looking brown man was gone. Lanyon had heard about the dark-skinned Indians of the American Colonies but was ignorant of miscegenation, surprised in realizing it did not please him to think of her with the man.

"Dassent you feel better?"

"Yes," he answered, amazed to feel his lips move and hear his voice.

"You look better? Your head—does it hurt you?"

"Not—as much. How—long—have I slept?" he asked.

"Time is an illusion."

"Time is—," he began, trying to repeat what his mind couldn't grasp.

"Your strange words while asleep tell me you be here and not here. Mostly you have slept. You keep drifting into the past when asleep, I'm afraid."

"Whaa—?" he tried to ask.

"We can talk later, when you feel better and are more present. Your mind is wandering. Rest is the best thing for you. You must rest."

One more question formed in his head, distinguishable from all others, and he felt compelled to ask it.

"Wh—who you be?"

"My name be Emma. And yours be?"

He thought for a moment before answering. "Leigh—Lan—I don't know," he finally answered, surprised to find the simplest memory lost.

"That's all right. You'll perhaps know in time."

Gazing into her lustrous eyes, his mind straightened slightly, and he realized he had been drifting through illusions for days—scouring his past for remnants of a happiness lost in time. The dreams depicting those days were such that he didn't mind. He actually hoped to again return to that time and space when he was so in love, where he felt a sense of belonging, and seemed more aware of who he was, what he wanted—no longer grieving, but for what or whom he didn't know.

"Where is your husband?" he asked with temerity.

"He's not my husband, only a friend. His name is Askwedaid."

"Ask—?"

"He Who Is Fire," she added, when his look became quizzical. "He is the sachem of the Cowasuck Indians. He and his people have been driven farther north so do not come here often anymore. Do you feel well enough to sit to the edge of the bed?"

"I'll try," he answered, attempting to rise.

Helping him, she swung his feet over the edge of the bed and pulled him into a sitting position. His head pounded, leg throbbed, and he nearly passed out. When he swooned, she caught him under both arms, drawing very close to his face. Her fragrance was like a balm, erasing a brief remembrance of salty seas and the musty smell of a ship. He found the smell of her soothing but, it was more than that. There was something about her fragrance that drew on his memories, played with his mind—something familiar yet foreign, pleasant but painful.

"Do not try to get up," she instructed. "The blood is rushing to your leg."

"I should lie back down?"

"No, we can make it better."

Going to the table, she got a chair and carried it to him. Seeing the chair confused him, and he found himself absently searching the room for a bench. She folded a blanket and placed it on the chair then propped his wounded leg up onto it, positioning and adjusting it to make him as comfortable as possible.

"Is 'at better?"

"Yes—thank you," he weakly replied.

"You must eat something, for strength, then sleep again. I made stew."

For the first time he noticed the smell of cooking in the room. It smelled good, and he would like to have found it appetizing, but became repulsed at the very thought of food. Knowing he needed nourishment in order to heal, however, he nodded his head in acquiescence. The fire had drawn low. Emma busied herself at the hearth, removing the pot from the hob, setting it on the table, then feeding the fire. The cat followed her every move with its eyes as the woman brought a bowl of stew and some cornbread to him.

He tried to lift the spoon but could not. Emma sat down next to him on the cot, holding the spoon, directing it to his mouth, as the cat curled in and out between her ankles, mewling. The stew was very good—rabbit, he guessed, recalling the game the Indian had brought her. She intently watched him during intervals between spoonfuls as he chewed and swallowed. Her look was visceral, like she knew his thoughts, knew everything about him without his having told her anything. *Intuition is the merging of the Soul with the Universe* flowed through his mind, and he wondered if the words had come from her. He found it difficult to hold her look. The intensity caused him to glance away then feel compelled to gaze again into her profound eyes.

When he'd had a few mouthfuls, he pushed her hand away. She didn't press him to eat more, instead carrying the half-eaten bowl of stew to the hearth. Watching her remove the kettle from the crane, pour water into a mug, and add herbs, the barriers of illusion thinned for a time, and he felt certain he knew her. It was only a fleeting thought, gone before he could fully grasp it. As his mind attempted to focus on the present, he had a vague remembrance of others or something missing.

"Where's—?"

"Have more tea then rest," she advised, returning to him with the steaming mug.

He tried to tell her he didn't like the tea, but could only obey as she lifted the mug to his mouth and encouraged him to drink. After a few sips, she helped him lie down and moved his legs back onto the cot.

The next thing he knew it was morning and a silvery-mauve haze drifted in through the open doorway. It had apparently rained because he could smell the fresh scent of wet earth mixed with the salty smell of the sea. Gulls argued in the distance and he thought he heard the faint ringing of a bell. A fire burned low and wispy curls of smoke floated out into the room.

"We will change your bandages," she asserted, interrupting his thoughts.

Carrying a supply of cloth strips and an assortment of salves, she came to sit on the edge of the bed. She unbound his head, washed his wounds with witch-hazel water, gently applied salve then wrapped his head again. Rising, she went to the foot of the cot and tightened the thongs of his splint.

"Where am I?" he questioned, bearing the pain.

"Quiet yourself. You must sleep more. When you again awaken perhaps you will be able to have more stew. I'll keep it warm for you. We'll talk then, but now you must let the tea work its wonders and sleep."

More questions formed in his head—where was he, who was she, why was he there, were there others, who were the others he only vaguely remembered? His questions dissolved as easily as they'd formed, his mind unable to focus. She helped him turn onto his left side to face away from her, positioning his splinted leg comfortably on a pile of furs to take the pressure off. Staring at her shadow on the wall, he drifted away.

— CHAPTER TEN —

The sea was rough and stormy,
The tempest howled and wailed,
And the sea-fog, like a ghost,
Haunted that dreary coast,
But onward still I sailed.

From *The Discoveries of the North Cape,*
A Leaf from King Alfred's Orosius by Longfellow

Gorman was barking orders, and the men scurried to obey. It was still dark as they finished breakfast and were prodded to get to their work. The days had been colder than usual and, as he trudged outside, Leighton wrapped his muffler tightly around his neck in anticipation of a raw wind. He could smell Genevieve's fresh scent on the gray scarf she'd knit for him.

Though there had been several snowfalls, Gorman wasn't satisfied it was enough to adequately protect the mast tree. After each storm, the men had packed down the snow on the mast road to make it icier but still more cover was needed. A wolf with yellow eyes stared at Leighton as he entered the dark woods to tend the oxen. Watching the wolf lope back into the woods, his attention was drawn to a full moon sinking over the trees to the south-west. It was the Hunger Moon of February. Standing amid the wooly beasts, he calculated that Genevieve would have already observed Candlemas. To her, it was one of the most sacred rituals of the year when winter was half way through. He had watched her as she honored St. Bridget, blessing candles and the light they provided, chanting. *If Candlemas Day be bright and fair, Winter will have another flight. If Candlemas Day be shower and rain, Winter is gone and will not come again.* The thought of her celebrating alone made him more homesick.

It was another long and hard day of work—one in a seemingly endless chain of lumbering routines and chores. Morale was low. The men were tired of the cold, worn out, and their main challenge yet awaited them. The oxen bellowed and snorted as Leighton turned them loose in the woods that evening. Wearily, he coiled his rope in the shed. As he tromped back to the kip it started to snow.

"It's t' be a snowin' hahd t'night makin' a good surface fah baulking t' tree," Gorman informed the men, as he joined them in the kip. "In t' mahnin' we hitch t' oxen."

Over supper the kip was abuzz with enthusiasm. Though hauling out the mast could be the most risky and dangerous part of the process, all were eager to get started with the task. The talk of the men continued as Leighton retired but it was of home for once, rather than complaints about their livelihood, Gorman or the surveyor-general.

While they slept in the crude shelter, snow continued to fall. By morning a fresh blanket of nearly two feet covered the packed ice laid for the mast road. Leighton awakened early morning. The sound of men heavily breathing and snoring filled the room. Since the cabin was inky dark, it meant the fire had gone out during the night. Cold damp hung in the air like icicles, and he briefly considered getting up to add logs to the fire. He poked Remy to stop his snoring—a useless gesture. Pulling the blanket up to his chin for more warmth, he thought of Genevieve.

Soon after Leighton returned from the woods their third spring together, he had finished the cottage on Sobagpeka. With great care, he rough hewed planks for the floorboards and laid a stone hearth for the fireplace. A log had been positioned above the fireplace opening when he built the chimney, but he spent a day hewing it into a mantle with a drawknife, knowing Genevieve would want to set things on it.

Their long made plans were finally coming to fruition. He'd earned enough to provide their basic needs and allow them to move to the island. Times would be thrifty, their stores and furnishings meager, but they were ready to begin life on their own. It was with heavy hearts they bid farewell to the Van Hoek family who had been so much a part of their lives. Before they departed, Mrs. Van Hoek had a warning for Genevieve.

"Life on the island will be lonely, Genevieve. You'll not have women folk for company as you do here in Riviere."

"I have not buck teeth," Genevieve put in, "with no time or interest in women's gossip. I'm eager for the open space of the island. It is said that islanders are both hardy and hearty people, unaffected by the wiles of the sea that surrounds them. I want to learn such guile and become sturdy like them—a true islander."

The air was cool as Leighton stowed their personal belongings in the cockpit of the boat and helped Genevieve aboard. She drew her cape closely around her delicate shoulders as he pushed the boat out from the river bank. They caught the strong current of Mgeso River and rode it as it wound its way to the sea at Pezegawan, also known as Foggy Harbor. Both were silent, drinking in the beauty of the river for the last time, focused on their future. From Pezegawan they rowed out to where the sloop was anchored. The tide turned from flow to ebb as he loaded their stores into the boat.

After lifting Genevieve over the gunwale into the sloop, he weighed anchor, steered them into the waves, and raised the sail. The previous day he'd ferried the last of their goods and supplies, so their gear was light this trip. Genevieve had with her the books she'd acquired for teaching, now to be used for educating their children. She also brought a spinning wheel, tools for shearing the sheep and carding their wool. Leighton promised to make her a loom once they got settled. Her personal belongings included a brooch of red and gold that had belonged to her mother, a dress of wool, another of calico, new boots, a bonnet from Mrs. Van Hoek to keep the sun off her face, and some safely guarded calico bags of seeds, roots, herbs, and potions. His personal effects, an extra shirt and pair of breeches, fit into a small satchel, and he wore the new seaman's boots Van Hoek had given him. Van Hoek also gave him several tools.

The dungeon of fog in the early morning had sealed up, browned off, and it was a beautiful day. Genevieve was a picture in her simple collarless indigo dress and gray wool cape. She sat primly on the middle board, her dark hair streaming with the wind, happy as a clam at high tide.

The Van Hoeks had warned them about the Indians, but Leighton and Genevieve chose to believe the best about them. When the Abenakis came to the island to watch Leighton and his friends build the cottage, they had been very friendly. Duncan had told him that hostile Indians lived to the north and inland, and that the islands were actually safer than the mainland—often places of shelter for settlers fleeing Indian attacks. When Leighton had passed this piece of reassurance on to Genevieve, she was nonplused.

"Why would they ever harm us?"

"I thought you might be concerned because of what happened to your family," Leighton responded.

"I want to be friends, learn from them. They have much to teach me."

Genevieve said it was bad luck to move into a cottage on a Saturday and also to set off on a Friday, so they had left for the island on Monday. The trip out was choppy, but the sloop rode the waves well, dipping through the hollows.

"The waves remind me of ruts in the road," she commented, as they sailed to eastward.

It was then Leighton realized she'd never been to the ocean, and he considered her brave for not only being on the sea but wanting to live on an island. His assessment of her as an extraordinary woman had increased greatly in their years together and, although he never thought he could care for her more than before they were married, with each passing day his love grew ever stronger.

"This be Kokokhas Channel," he informed her, as they proceeded. "Kokokhas means *owl*. I don't know why it's called Owl Channel because I've never seen any owls out here. I heard an owl one night, however."

"Owls are only out at night, to hunt," Genevieve put in. "During the day they won't let you see them, but they watch everything. That's how they gain such wisdom and know so much. They're thought to be the wisest of all animals and birds, representative of Athena, the goddess of wisdom."

The channel was wide but, with the aid of a westerly wind, they crossed with ease, making their way past several of the outer islands, and he named them for her as they skirted by each one.

"This be Mosbas or Mink Island and the next is Akigw, Seal Island, then Kaakw or Gull Island in the distance. That one over to the right is Nolka, Deer Island."

She was interested but could not conceal her eagerness to finally see her island home, stretching her long neck to try to get a glimpse of it. Eagles soared overhead, their wings far spread, as Leighton and Genevieve rounded the north shore of Stone Island and tucked into the reach.

"This be Stone Island," he told her. "The Indians called it Sen Menahan. And the Reach is called Bitawbagok or Bitawba. It means *the waters in between*."

Crossing the reach, he pointed out Sobagpeka in the distance. The cottage was on the north end of the island at the base of the meadow but, with a grassy knoll and trees behind it, barely visible from the reach. Genevieve strained her eyes to see it but could make out little more than a partial outline.

"Crossing the Reach is taking forever," she impatiently complained."

"It's only a few miles now. We'll be there soon."

"Not soon enough for me," she teased.

With that pronouncement, the breeze freshened as if by magic, filling the sail and speeding their journey. Genevieve donned her bonnet, tying the ribbons under her chin as she gazed eastward. She trailed her fingers in the water over the side of the boat, eyes fixed on the cottage as though willing it to manifest before her. Finally, Leighton reefed the sail and they rode the waves into the cove.

After securing the boat, he lifted his wife over the gunwale, carried her through the ebbing tide to the beach, and set her firmly down. He grew nervous, wondering if she'd like her new home, watching as she walked slowly up the slope toward the cottage. Stopping, as if in a daze, she stared.

"Oh, Leighton, it's wonderful," she burst, running to hug him.

She then took his hand and pulled him along toward the cottage, stopping at the first rose bush.

"Thank you for all the lovely rose bushes—cinnamon roses, just as I'd asked. I love them. I love you," she exclaimed, hugging him again. Cupping the thorny stem of a rose bush in her hand, she laughed. "They're beautiful. See how the fresh morning dew still sits on the shiny green leaves—how velvety soft the red flower petals be."

The cottage had been carefully built, fashioned with love as well as skill but, despite his best efforts, it still felt cold and uninviting to him. His concerns grew larger as they stood in the dooryard. *What if she doesn't like our new home, finds it too rustic, too crude? What if she wants to return to the mainland to live?* He tried to stall, to take a minute to explain what he felt, but she rushed ahead, tugging him toward the door.

Opening it, she stepped inside and screamed with delight. It was a modest cottage, but to her a castle could not have been finer. There were two bays with a keeping room on one end and, beyond the fireplace, their bedroom. Light streamed into the room through oil-soaked paper windows. She admired his work, running her hand over the smoothed mantle of the fireplace and stones of the chimney.

"I hope to eventually add glass paned windows with muntins, and I'll stucco and lime wash the exterior of the cottage then whitewash it," Leighton offered.

"That would be lovely, but I love it even now," she responded.

"The loft will be for our children," he reassured

her, gesturing upward.

They had thought that, after three years of marriage, they would have been blessed with a baby. Seeing Genevieve's eyes turn slightly teary at the thought, Leighton distracted her by showing her around. The meager furnishings suited their needs. In the bedroom there was a rope bed, blanket chest, and chiffonier, as well as a dry sink, pitcher and bowl near the door. A sideboard stood ready to hold their dishes in the keeping room and, near the fireplace, was a small Pembroke table with two benches. Three pewter candlesticks sat on the mantle along with a clock the Van Hoeks had given them as a wedding present. It was their most prized possession.

Genevieve put down her belongings, untied her bonnet and laid it on the table then wandered through the cottage while Leighton brought the rest of their dunnage from the boat. By the time he returned, she had put the trenchers carefully in the sideboard where they wouldn't go adrift, started a fire in the fireplace, placed their two tankards for special occasions on the mantle, stowed the blankets, and put their indigo and white Love Apple quilt Mrs. Van Hoek had helped her make, on the bed. He watched from the doorway as she placed three candles in their holders on the mantle then lit a match stick in the fire and reached her delicate white arm up to light them.

A surreal sense settled on him as he felt the cottage heave then gasp, taking a deep breath as one would their first in life. He could feel the walls of the cottage expand outward then contract into a comforting warmth, surrounding Genevieve then extending out to him—the cold, stark space transformed into an inviting home by her mere presence. He couldn't get over the sense that she belonged in the cottage, had perhaps always lived there, would always live there. Wondering where that notion might have come from, he put down their gear and walked toward her.

"Three candles in a row is bad luck," she explained, moving two to the left side and leaving the other on the right.

"We want none of that then," he replied, holding

her close.

They stood before the fire, staring at it, enveloped in each others arms, savoring for a time the moment they'd worked and waited for so long. Then she reached up to snuff out two of the candles. Carrying the third, she led him to their new bedroom. The same ethereal light surrounding them in the keeping room followed them to the bedroom, warming the room and heightening their senses. Their love making was more intense than it had ever been before.

Their first evening together on the island, Leighton suggested a walk, and they stepped out into the dooryard where the roses bloomed. Genevieve stopped at each bush, admiring it, and praising Leighton for making her the happiest woman on earth. Picking a rose, he placed it in her hair then took her hand, and they walked the perimeter of the island. He showed her his discoveries, happily sharing all he'd learned of the island. Genevieve surprised him in knowing more about it, at least geologically and as to flora and fauna, than he did. At the salt marsh, she pointed out dog stone growing near the edge and, in the woods, mushrooms. Some of them were small and long like fingers pointing up, others squatty, flat and round.

"This is the circle of stones I told you about," he told her, pointing.

"The stones be crystals—the outline of a ceremonial site. The Indians gather to celebrate all different kinds of occasions like marriages and burials. The four lines extending out from the center represent the quaternary symbols in our world—the cardinal directions, the elementals, fire, earth, water and air, the phases of the moon, the tidal changes, and the seasons. The sacred oak tree stands in the middle for balance, to anchor the energies of the circle. I hope the Indians will always feel welcome to continue using the sacred circle and will come to visit soon."

It was like she'd lived there her entire life, almost like she was an organic, inseparable part of the island or its human embodiment. They stood at the south end on cliffs overlooking turgid waters. Sea smoke swirled around them as they watched a silver gibbous waxing moon rise to the east. Strolling back to their cottage, their hearts were filled with love and heightened passion. Lost in her dewy warmth and deep tenderness, Leighton felt complete peace, like a long journey had ended and he'd at last come home. Time stood still as they made love, drifting in a state of ecstasy he wished would last forever—his body, mind, and soul willing captives of his Genevieve.

Leighton continued to coast that season while they established their stock. From the mainland he brought crates of chickens. Mrs. Van Hoek, as well as others in the settlement, had told them that chickens could not thrive in the damp weather, subject to roup, but Genevieve was determined to have fresh eggs. He also brought along two sheep, two cows, and two horses.

"Just like Noah's Ark," Genevieve teased, as she watched him snug the boat into the cove, unhobble each of the animals, and lead them ashore.

She immediately set them free from their tethers, patting them on their behinds and urging them toward the meadow.

"I'll call the horses Prince and Molly. I'll have to think about proper names for the cows and sheep."

She stayed on the island, with no interest in going to the mainland, educating herself as to the island's resources—*treasures*, she called them. She and Leighton worked hard that spring and summer. He felled trees to clear a space to grow a forage crop of ladino clover the next spring. The topsoil was thin. He'd heard it called mink dirt. It wouldn't be easy to grow things above ground, and they'd have to depend on tubers and succotash as their staples until the garden produced what it could.

They often walked to their favorite place on the island, amazed at its beauty, as they watched the sun linger over the pine forests silhouetted against the horizon toward Stone Island to the west and the distant peaks beyond. They watched sea smoke drift in and felt the earth tremble beneath their feet as they stood on cliffs wracked by pounding surf. If the wind was just right, indistinguishable sounds were carried to them over Bitabagok Reach. Genevieve read signs and portends in the solemn wind but kept them secret, even from her heart. Gazing at the star-scattered night, she talked about the constellations of Pegasus or the Milky Way sweeping across the western sky. Noting Ursa Major, hanging low in the sky, she held Leighton's hand, extending his index finger to trace its outline. Above it was Ursa Minor, with Polaris at the end of the handle. Returning to their cottage one night, passing the pond, they heard the mournful cry of a loon. Genevieve's playful mood suddenly turned deeply earnest. Looking heavenward, she pointed out Lyra, the Lyre, explaining that it was home to the star Vega.

"Lyra has a very special meaning to me," she offered, as they walked. "It is my home."

He didn't know what she meant, but nothing she said that might be odd or stray mattered when she was at his side. It was like she'd cast a spell on him from which there was no escape—from which he had no desire to escape. He found the smell of her intoxicating and everything she did precious and dear, no matter how unusual or different. Unfamiliar with the ways of women, he assigned it to his inexperience, willingly addicted to her enchanting nature.

Many of her ways were mysterious, especially during the space between dark and day when often he'd see her walking in the meadow or coming from the forest.

"What are you doing," he'd asked, the first time he found her kneeling in the meadow.

"Herbs for healing must be picked in the light of the full moon with this special knife so they are the most potent they can be," she had briefly explained.

After that he never questioned what she was doing, her interest in the Indians or the healing herbs and potions she used. Sometimes, though, he found her talk of fetches, wraiths, and spirits unsettling, and things that happened, odd—plants that grew when and where, by all reasonable expectations, they shouldn't, the cow's bloody milk suddenly turned pure white under her hand, hens that had quit laying began to lay again after the subtle and brief incantations she softly uttered.

She seemed to know things one shouldn't, talked to animals and birds, read the sky, landscape, and sea like a book, and heard things in the wind no one else did. Fishermen had shared with him the weather portends—how smoke coming to the ground, flies in the cottage, clouds at sunset, morning mists, and the cry of loons all meant rain, how gulls flying inland, birds sitting quietly or seeing a storm petrel meant a blow. She knew without seeing any of these signs—*knew it in her bones*, she would say.

The island was a long-established resource and fishing grounds for the Indians. When they came in sea canoes to fish, hunt, and dig for mussels, they were welcomed as friends. Communication was awkward to Leighton, but Genevieve understood them—overjoyed at their visit, making a fuss, and eager to please. In the late afternoon she fixed a nice dinner of steamed mussels, with vegetables from her bountiful garden.

Against all odds, she had coaxed an impressive garden full of vegetables and herbs, but felt she could do better. In their exchanges, a blend of French and the Indian language, she eagerly absorbed the information the Indians gave her about planting according to the phases of the moon—seeds for above ground plants during a waxing moon, those for underground during a waning moon. She couldn't wait until the next season to put this new knowledge to work. During the waning period of the full Harvest Moon in September, she would harvest her garden and prune her precious roses as they had advised.

She knew all about growing herbs, but her association with the Indians expanded her knowledge of the art of healing by making further use of things found in nature. In addition to the usual balms, salves, and teas, she gathered witch-hazel and lady slipper from the forest, and swamp water for treating burns. She made sumac liquor for skin rashes, used swamp lily root to keep the kidneys healthy, blood root and mullein leaves for breathing difficulties, and alder bark, when chewed, for application to cuts and bruises. Her knowledge of the natural resources of the island was not restricted to healing. In the woods she probed the laurel bush, extracting cinnamon from the inner bark, and found bay leaves to use as yellow, sassafras for red, to dye her wool. At the salt marsh she gathered glasswort and burned it to create barilla for soap making, adding herbs for fragrance. From the Indians she also learned to make splint baskets, sometimes dying the strips she wove. On his trips to the mainland, Leighton sold her handiwork or traded them for staples. Soon, she became known for her craftsmanship, but remained the mysterious woman on Sobagpeka.

At Litha, the summer solstice, they enjoyed the long hours of daylight. Walking the island with him, Genevieve spoke to him of fairies and elves, saying they lived in the woods and meadows, and were helpers all.

"The Indians call them Bokwjimen or Little People. They are the keepers of summer."

He held tight to her hand, listening and trying not to judge her words with his rational mind. Staring into her venerable eyes, he focused instead on what his heart was telling him—that it was enough to be with her and nothing else mattered.

Late summer Genevieve boiled down brine for their supply of salt. Islanders considered the surrounding sea theirs, harvesting all they could as one would a garden. Fish were their cattle of the sea. Leighton's garden was full of fish, and he worked his lines. He caught cod, haddock, and pollock, then helped Genevieve salt and dry them. He made a storage space under the keeping room floor, fastening a trap door with leather thongs so she could easily open it. It would store tubers from the garden which would be a substantial part of her winter diet. When the corn was ready to harvest, he hollowed out a log to make a trough for crushing it with stones. Genevieve could shell the corn then grind it into meal as needed. Two more logs were hollowed out—one to catch rain water and another to hold water carried in piggins from the spring by the pond. In anticipation of a tough winter, they built a crude three-sided shed of wide gray clapboards, with the opening turned west, to shelter the livestock from harsh winter east winds, then stocked it with bundles of hay cut from the salt-water marshes. It wouldn't keep the weather out entirely but, with their thick coats of fur, would be enough protection for the animals.

Leighton worried about fierce winter weather and leaving Genevieve alone on the island. He encouraged her to stay with the Van Hoek's for a few months while he was away, but she would have none of it. Not wanting to leave the island, she'd convinced him she would be fine with only occasional visits from the Indians. "As to winter weather, I can tolerate whatever Mother Nature sends my way," she assured him.

In the fall, just before he was to leave, the Indians came again, this time with their shaman, Mdawlinno, medicine man. They promised to take care of Genevieve, visiting often during the winter months when they came to gun game birds, jack deer or hunt and trap. Leighton offered for them to sleep on the floor of their cottage when they came, and they gladly accepted. To honor their shaman, he built a cot for him in the far corner of the keeping room, and Genevieve sewed a cover for a mattress, stuffing it with pine straw.

The rose bushes had been trimmed and, when the gold and red leaves fell from sullen trees, and the mountain ash hung heavy with orange berries, they knew it was soon time for Leighton to leave again. Those days were difficult, anticipating their separation, but they had not yet been able to manage without the woodsman's income. Late September, Genevieve prepared a fine dinner of fish chowder and cornbread. For dessert she made blackberry cobbler.

"T'is the last of the blackberries we can eat," she commented, setting the wooden bowls of steaming cobbler on the table. "Tomorrow t'is Michaelmas and we must never eat blackberries after that day."

"Why is that," he innocently inquired.

"T'is the day Satan lost his heavenly war with Saint Michael and fell from heaven to land on a blackberry bush. The autumnal equinox has passed and the days grow shorter. I will light candles and ask Saint Michael, the angelic warrior, to protect you as you go to the forest."

"Ask him to protect you here as well," Leighton put in.

Though a nonbeliever, in Genevieve's presence anything seemed possible, and he simply accepted whatever she told him of her pagan beliefs as truth, aligning his thoughts with hers.

"To honor Saint Michael, we will have goose tomorrow if you will go to the pond and get one for us."

"That I will do, if you so wish."

"Please do not shoot it from the sky as it flies. Instead, wait near the pond and wring its neck after it has eaten its fill of tender shoots. I'll make a bannock to go with our goose, and we can have the last of the greens from the garden."

The next evening, Michaelmas, they dined on the goose that Leighton had gotten for her. As with every meal she prepared, she thanked for the bounty. If the meal included game, she thanked the spirit of the animal for its sacrifice, requesting that its nourishment and strength be transferred to them. She considered this a special meal in honor of the protection they were seeking.

Over the next couple of days sadness descended, as the fact that he would soon be leaving settled heavily upon them. After dinner their last evening together, they walked one more time to the cliffs above the sea. Apples turned silver in the light of the moon, hung pendulously from trees at the forest's edge.

"The moon is a maiden who rules the night sky and guides the tides," Genevieve offered, as they stood together watching the moon's light stream toward them across the sea. "If clouds race across the moon it means a storm is coming, and you must ask the moon goddess to guide you safely home to me."

When they returned to their cottage, she lit the

three candles on the mantle. They sat for hours, savoring each other's company then shared their passion once more before months of separation.

Exhausted from his mental wanderings, and earnestly missing Genevieve, Leighton turned over in his pine bough bunk in the kip and was soon asleep.

— CHAPTER ELEVEN —

Ah! What pleasant visions haunt me
As I gaze upon the sea!
All the old romantic legends,
All my dreams, come back to me.

Sails of silk and ropes of sandal,
Such as gleam in ancient lore;
And the singing of the sailors,
And the answer from the shore!

Like the long waves on a sea beach,
Where the sand as silver shines,
With a soft, monotonous cadence,
Flow its unrhymed lyric lines.

From *The Secret of the Sea* by Longfellow

The mattress of pine straw scrunched as he shifted. Wondering where he was and who would be there, he opened his eyes. The room was familiar but it took another moment to orient, to realize Emma should be there, and he was in the cottage, not billeted in the kip. Finding himself in a different place each time he opened or closed his eyes was playing with his mind—fading the margins of consciousness. Yet half-asleep, he couldn't reconcile past and present or sort out his dream phantoms from reality.

There was no one in the cottage. The door was open. Sunshine streamed through it and the scent of pine hung in the air. The gray cat sat on the windowsill in a rosy glow, licking its paw and cleaning its face. Lanyon felt measurably better. Thinking how good it might feel to go outside into the sunshine, he sat up then tried to stand. The cat jumped down and ran out the door. Emma suddenly appeared through the doorway, running to him in time to catch him as he tipped and fell back onto the cot.

The basket of eggs she carried was nearly upset in her haste to assist him. A frayed gray wool shawl on her shoulders covered a faded and drab, blue, threadbare dress. Her worn attire did not suit her fresh, cheery composure and strong, captivating fragrance.

"How about some fresh quail's eggs this morning—and some pork?"

"That sounds good. I'm hungry as a horse."

"How can a horse be hungry? They eat all day long," she laughed, as she set the basket of eggs on the table.

Her laughter sounded to him like the lilt of a chipping sparrow at dawn.

"I'd like to sit—if you'll help me to that chair?" he requested.

She came to him, put her hands under his arms, and pulled him again to his feet. Dragging his splinted leg and heavily leaning on her, he limped to the chair at the table in halting steps. What little strength he had drained from him as he plopped down onto the chair.

He watched her closely as she busied herself at the hearth, the phrase *true love cannot be eclipsed by time or distance* wafting through his mind. Looking about the room, he saw hanks of wool dyed indigo hanging on racks alongside the loom. A spinning wheel sat to the right of the fireplace. The sideboard, in addition to holding pewter mugs and trenchers, contained a series of books.

Emma interrupted his survey, placing a meal of in eggs and pork from the spider, sour-milk biscuits from the stone oven in front of him. The smell of food no longer gagged him and, though it took all his effort, he heartily ate. She joined him in eating, but no words were spoken. He was afraid to talk to her for fear his emotions would betray him—afraid that talking to her might make her less real, and she would disappear into that misty realm from which he kept reappearing. He and Emma both seemed unwilling to venture into the growing bond that had been involuntarily established between them. He was unable to decipher his feelings, liked to think it was only the gratitude of a man saved, but couldn't deny they were much stronger. In her presence he felt complete, as in his dreams, and the grieving, lonesome, sad or lost feelings no longer haunted him. When in Emma's company, he couldn't reconcile fond memories from the past with those forming in his heart. After he'd eaten his fill, she helped him stand, and they trudged toward the bed.

"You feel better?"

"Some," he lied.

His head was pounding and his leg ached, but he said nothing as he sat down on the edge of the cot. After pouring steaming water from the fireplace kettle into a mug, she coaxed him to again drink the horrible tea. His mind in conflict, wanting to stay with Emma yet hoping that in drinking the tea he would again drift into that other world where Genevieve waited, he sloshed it down. Feeling the drowsiness envelope him, fears crept into his mind. *It's good the tea is healing me but will this all go away when I'm healed? If I no longer need Emma, will she disappear from my life? What if Genevieve is no longer where I left her?* Emma drew close and he inhaled her fresh, familiar fragrance. She helped him swing his legs onto the cot and lie down. Gazing into her eyes, he felt himself drift into their deep chasms of warmth and lost his grasp on reality.

— CHAPTER TWELVE —

I saw the long line of the vacant shore,
The sea-weed and the shells upon the sand,
And the brown rocks left bare on every hand,
As if the ebbing tide would flow no more.
Then heard it, more distinctly than before,
The ocean breathe and its great breast expand,
And hurrying came on the defenseless land
The insurgent waters with tumultuous roar,
All thought and feeling and desire, I said,
Love, laughter, and the exultant joy of song
Have ebbed from me forever! Suddenly o'er me
They swept again from their deep ocean bed,
And in a tumult of delight, and strong
As youth, and beautiful as youth, upbore me.

The Tides by Longfellow

The smell of pancakes awakened Leighton and he found himself again in the kip. He sat on the edge of the bunk, still somewhat groggy, rubbing his leg and trying to reorient. Pulling on his boots, his thoughts turned to Genevieve and her wonderful blueberry pancakes, jarring him into the moment. In recent days, nearly every waking thought was of little else but their being together soon. Eager to hold her, eager for the birth of their child, he wondered how she was faring in his absence.

"Look lively," Murdock, the cook bellowed from across the room. "Food's gettin' cold yew lazy scala-wags."

The men scrambled from their bunks. Those up late, talking far into the night, struggled to their feet, receiving no sympathy from the men they'd kept from a sound sleep. It was early morning, before dawn. Despite their shortage of sleep, the men hustled, bolstered by the strong smell of coffee. The cook had long been up and the fire was brightly burning. Flapjacks smothered with maple syrup, biscuits, and pork piled onto platters awaited them. Their incentive was more than food—more than an eagerness to get to work. They were ready to haul out, get the mast tree to the river, and get back to civilization as they knew it.

"We've fresh snow. Hitch up t' oxen," Gorman yelled from the door before they'd finished eating.

Snow had left a good cover, continuing to fall as the men tramped out into the dim predawn light. The tree branches overhead were stacked with white fluff, creating a fairyland of quiet, disturbed only by the muffled footsteps of the men trudging to their duties. Before the sun could rise in the eastern sky, they were all hard at work. Leighton and Remy were assigned the task of retrieving the oxen and set off to find them. Carrying a lantern, they entered the quiet whiteness of the dark woods.

They found the oxen in the adjacent meadow munching marsh hay and led the ponderous beasts to their tasks. Their tangled and matted shaggy winter coats were snow-covered. While some of the men took charge of the beady-eyed oxen, Leighton, Remy, and Dodson retrieved the gear from the shed, carrying it to the clearing where the animals were held. Hawsers had been wrapped around the mast tree, the lines waiting to be attached to oxen yokes.

While a team of oxen pulled one direction, the men on the opposite side of the tree, using sturdy sticks or poles as levers, twitched it up an incline of boards onto the waiting scoots. It required a Herculean effort. The tree was so long that four strategically placed scoots were needed to support it. Once the tree was secured on the sleds, bridle chains were run beneath the scoots and attached to the yokes of the oxen. The lead oxen, four abreast, were first to be hitched into their yokes—the off ox, Bright, on the far left and the nigh ox, Star, on the right. Four more teams were hitched behind them in front of the tree. Two teams were hitched on both sides of each scoot to help haul and to keep the tree from rolling or shifting. When all bridle chains were secured to the yokes, the oxen were ready to be driven.

"Nae doubt, all this effaart, we be riskin owr lives with the Abenaki for 'em nabobs oe'r in England or the money-hungry millmen," Magnus, complained in his Scottish burr. He was a large, morose man with hair like rope yarn. "I hate the thocht of it. When a's said and doon it taakes twal of us tew month to git one tree wi' the crow's fooot maark oot 'n doon to the maast pond. Anither wund to git it ship fit. This one'll bring a faancy profit but dew we get paaid for the size of it? Nawt! Always the saame paey no matter."

"Better not let Gorman hear you talkin' like that. He'll have you strung up," Leighton put in.

Nodding toward Gorman, Magnus cocked a snook. "Let 'im try."

From the time they'd first entered the old growth pine stands at Koasek, the woodsmen had toiled for over four months. A mast road, already established, ran from the camp to Burrows' Creek but, since they'd gone farther interior to get the tree, the road had been extended. Sometimes as many as two or three mast trees could be felled and taken to the waterway in any one winter season, but when more clearing was required, or the tree exceptionally large, usually only one fine specimen could be harvested per team.

The tree was to be taken to the saw mill at the confluence of Burrows' Creek and Mkeswontegw or the Elbow River. The store of mast trees, the result of several teams' work, would await a spring thaw. When there was open water, they'd be twitched in to begin the trip down the Elbow River to the masting pond near Waban. There, the Elbow River converged with Moonlight Estuary, the overflow of the Moonlight River, and an arm of Baie la Claire de Lune. The pond was too shallow to accommodate the large ships they would eventually be loaded onto but a good place to protect and store the trees.

Masts needed to be three feet high for each inch in diameter. Following inspection by the mast agent at the pond, they would be twitched into the estuary at high tide. When tied together they'd be floated to a mast house and depot abutting Moonlight Bay at Pezegawan and hewed to sixteen sides, as required for all Royal Navy masts. While the woodsmen felled the trees and transported them to the landing then yard, the mast agent arranged with the captain of a masting ship for transport to England. Once the deal was set, the hewed masts, harvested from various lumbering camps, were hoisted aboard the ship with capstans, hauled through a port in the hold, and nestled among the sternposts. When fully loaded, the port, nearly awash, was caulked to seal it shut. The mast ships often weighed between four and six hundred tons and carried up to one thousand tons burthen. There were usually thirty to fifty masts in the hull, with smaller spars fitted in between or up on deck. A Royal Navy ship, guarding the shipping lanes, would insure its safe passage to England where the sticks would be tapered and finished by mastwrights.

While the cutting teams and hewers earned a decent wage, the big profits were to be made in England. It took two months to unload the cargo and reload the stern with masts to be exported, but more often of late there were no masts to ship. Problems with delayed shipments and additional demurrage occurred. Sometimes Indians attacked, destroying the trees or threatening the settlement, making it impossible to get the masts to the waiting ships. If the trees sat in the water too long, they were ruined and all profits lost. Land owners who received a bounty for the trees felled on their property saw it as meager compensation relative to the expense of cutting and removing the trees, and grew increasingly reluctant to harvest them.

"Let's go," Gorman bellowed, his frosted breath shattering the silence.

"Gee, Star," the driver shouted, standing at the butt end of the tree.

Birds, harbingers of dawn, chirped their winter songs, and the first rays of sun streaked through the branches. The lead oxen moved laboriously to the right,

then forward through the files of pine, dragging the twenty
-ton tree. They were hitched two to a yoke to allow them
to pull more than twice what one alone could. Even so, it
took all forty-four to move the tree. The story had been
told of a tree several seasons ago that had required eight
sleds and one hundred oxen to haul it out. It was a giant of
a tree, more than fourteen feet around and two hundred
fifty feet tall.

Drovers herded the spare oxen alongside the
baulking team as the men grabbed their accoutrements and
followed along. The cold wintry wind shifted, scooping up
fallen snow and blowing it in their faces as they went. It
was difficult for the oxen to gain momentum, and their
progress was slow in the beginning. Once they got going
it would be an easier pull, but then stopping could be difficult. The topography inland was somewhat varied and so,
no matter where they hauled out a tree, there were likely
to be a few hills to conquer. The length of the mast tree
was always a factor. The longer it was, the more difficult
to maneuver over hills and around even modest curves in
the road.

All went well until they got to the first hill. The
oxen got up the gradually sloping hill all right, but beyond
it was a particularly deep hollow. Snub lines were
wrapped around adjacent trees to slow the tree's progress.
By the time the lead oxen had made it into the hollow, the
last two teams were dangling from their yokes in mid-air
at the top of the hill. The men feared the beasts would
choke before they could get the forward oxen moved into
the hollow enough to set them back on the ground. His
first year of masting, Leighton had seen two of the oxen
choke to death in such a manner. Two more had to be destroyed when their legs were broken by the chains as the
scoot came back down hard onto the frozen ground. As
quickly as possible, they had been replaced by a spare
team and the tree again moved forward, but the incident
had been disturbing. The men had been consoled by the
hope they'd have fresh beef to eat for most of the trip but
never tasted a morsel. Word had it the mast agent had con-
fiscated the meat for his own use. Trudging along with the

men and beasts, Leighton hoped there wouldn't be any unnecessary delays this trip. His eagerness to return to the island and his wife grew more avid with each halting step.

The second winter of masting, he had followed the mast tree all the way from the stand at Koasek to Burrow's Creek Mill then to the masting pond and finally, the mast house at Moonlight Bay. That season there had also been problems along the way, though of a somewhat different nature. One of the oxen had been killed by wolves. Worse yet, once at Burrows' Creek, some of the men that had contracted to take the tree all the way to the waiting ships at Pezegawan got sick and, without replacements, it had made more work for those who were left. Two of the men died from the sickness and there had been concern regarding contagion for a time. Unable to be taken home or their wives notified until spring, they had been buried in the deep woods. The widows, living in Waban, first learned of their husbands' deaths when Elwood delivered their boots. There was a late thaw that year so the masts weren't twitched into the river until April. Then problems with boulders in the river, uprooted and displaced by giant ice floes, caused further delays. The oxen used to pull them out had long since become as worn and tired as the men. Leighton was a patient man, but it felt like that trip had taken forever.

When finally they had reached Moonlight Bay late spring, delivering the trees to the mast house, he had been the first one to leave. As soon as he could, he lashed his gear, including the two goats Genevieve had requested when he'd left. He also had a keg of maple syrup, another of molasses, to sweeten her hasty pudding. The goats bleated pitifully from the bottom of the boat where they lay hobbled. It was a neap tide, a low tide, higher than usual as he pulled up the killick, scudded into the harbor and set the sail, tacking through a strong, cold nor'east wind. The channel was open water but drift ice coated the shores of the islands. To be safe, he skirted them, out far enough to avoid ice gullies along each shore. The eerie sound of creaking ice as the tides pushed against it carried over the water to him, creating some concern about Genevieve and conditions he'd find once at Sobagpeka.

It was late afternoon by the time he rounded Stone Island and headed for home. Genevieve, sitting on the grassy knoll above the beach, saw him coming in the distance. He struggled into the protected cove, his boat laden deep. The chipping sparrows, hatched in the winter, sang out as he snugged his boat in, let it settle on a tidal flat and dropped the killick, relieved to be home at last. She stood near the shore and ran to embrace him the moment he was on dry land. A gray cat rubbed against her legs as they held each other.

"Where did you get the cat?" he asked, loosening his arms from around her.

"The Indians found her in the woods and brought her to me, saying she would be good company," she explained. "Her Indian name is Chibai, for ghost, but I call her Macha. Look, she has mismatched eyes."

Knowing how much she loved cats, he wished he'd thought of it—something to keep her company in the house on cold winter nights. She'd faired well enough in his absence but had grown somewhat limsy, even pindling. Ardently embracing her thin frame, he could tell that hunger and solitude had taken their toll.

The cat, Macha, took to him immediately, twisting through his legs and meowing loudly as they walked up the slope. He picked her up, roughed up her fur and set her back down on the ground where she inserted herself between them. There was something about the cat that felt almost haunting, resurrecting conflicting feelings difficult to separate. He remembered a cat from his childhood, a stray his mother had taken in, assigning his emotions to that, even though it had not been a gray cat.

"Why do you call her Macha?" he asked.

"She is gray after all. A gray cat is a primary lunar animal," she explained, holding him.

He looked at the cat blinking back at him and, without understanding, accepted the explanation.

"You brought the goats I asked for," she suddenly exclaimed, hearing them bleat. "Let me help you carry them ashore. They cannah like being hobbled so," she called back to him, running toward the water.

He followed her back down the sloping embankment. While she stood waiting on the shore, he waded out to the boat then, one at a time, carried the goats to her. She quickly unbound them, setting them free and urging them toward the meadow. They leaped and kicked as they ran, soon disappearing over the rim. Watching Genevieve, her black tresses blowing with the wind, he wondered if his worries had been for naught. She was so full of life. Despite looking a somewhat spent force, she was as beautiful as ever and had managed well in his absence. There were still patches of snow on the ground and a chill wind blew but apparently it had been a mild winter. Even though mornings continued to be rimed, she had started the garden. Already coriander, mint, fennel, dill, and anise were in evidence. Birds called from the woods as he unloaded the rest of the dunnage and, together, they carried the stores to the cottage.

"What's this?" he asked when they were at the door.

"That be the wishbone of a goose," she responded. "The goose we had just before you left in the fall. For good luck!"

He found the idea of any talisman for luck somewhat disturbing, but trusted her instincts. The kettle was on the crane, the water for tea heated. Somehow she always knew when he was to arrive, even though the day had never been set nor was never the same. Sitting at opposite sides of the table, they had their tea while she told him about her winter on the island and he, his life in the woods, both thinking wistfully of the day when they could share their winter rather than an accounting of their time apart.

Genevieve told him about the visits from the Indians. She had learned more about them. Their name, Abenaki, meant *people from the dawnland*. Arriving in their winter garb, they wore leggings of buckskin, had colorful wool blankets wrapped about their bodies, and leather moccasins fitted to their feet with leather thongs to hold them on as protection from the cold and snow. She had admired the smooth, soft leather and decorative details.

"Their muskets were slung over their backs, held with a leather strap, and knives hung from their necks in leather sheaths adorned with porcupine quills."

"The guns didn't make you afraid?"

"No, never. They also had bows and arrows for hunting. I learned that they like the feathers of gripe best for their arrows because they don't sing when shot, alerting the prey. Michabo is the Great White Hare, the creator of the sun, moon, earth, and stars. Kchi Niwaskw is the Great Mystery, the First Creator. Watsowsen or Wind Eagle sits on top of Mount Ktaden to the north and makes the wind by flapping his wings. They stayed for several days, teaching me about, among other things, conjures. Mdawlinno has magic powers and is training me in dreams and trances."

He had some concerns about how much time she was spending with the Indians and all they were teaching her, but her enthusiasm made him reluctant to say anything that would depress her spirit.

"He showed me how to make a drum," she announced, retrieving it from the mantle and handing it to him.

Thoughtfully, he turned it over in his hands, admiring the artwork on it—a red horse, three cranes, some stars, and the moon in three different phases.

"It's lovely," he praised, handing it back to her.

Watching her return the drum to the mantle, he decided that what the Indians were teaching her was surely harmless enough, seemed to make her happy, and he forgot his unease. As she continued to chatter on and on about the Indian's visits, he realized anew how alone she'd been without him—glad they had been a comfort and good company to her.

"One of these days we'll go to the neighboring island for dancing and singing," he offered. "Would you like to do that, to meet our neighbors?"

"That would be fine. I'll show you the garden," she began, as the cat sat at her elbow listening. "The Indians taught me how to companion farm, planting in mounds. Corn is at the center then beans are planted around them so they can climb the corn stalk. Squash and pumpkin, planted around the stalk, have plenty of room to spread out into the sunshine. The leaves of the gourds help hold the moisture in the soil for the corn and beans. Isn't that clever? They also gave me yellow, red, and blue wheat to plant. The blue will ripen first to quickly restore that used up over the winter months.

"One of their warriors died in the fall and they buried him up near the bluff, not far from the woods. Apparently there are several buried there. As I've suspected, it is a sacred site."

"Is that the small mounds we've seen up there near the circle of stones?"

"Yes. They let me watch the burial, but only from a distance. First the elders came to bless the site with tobacco then, with drum and song, they called in the ancestors, asking for their approval and blessing. When they brought the body, wrapped with sinew in white birch bark, it was the first time I'd seen their women. They're quite beautiful, with hair darker than mine, so black it looks blue. The men dug the hole, placed the warrior in it, and turned him on his right side, facing west, with his knees drawn up to his chest. They blessed the site with tobacco before, during and after burial, then chanted songs and again drummed. Leaves and branches were put over the site to hide it until grass can grow again. It was a very moving experience to witness."

"I'm glad you were allowed to be a part of that."

"I felt honored. They've said they will use the ceremonial circle again, and I've made sure they feel welcome to do so."

"Does that mean they'll be here more?"

"Yes, especially in the months of warmth. All their ceremonies, which begin at sunrise, include honoring the Creator, Mother Earth, Father Sky, and all their relations, with tobacco and gifts. I'd like to help them place stones for the circle, if they'll allow it. Now, tell me about your winter."

"The same thing I do every winter. Remy was there again. He and I were, for the most part, in charge of taking care of the oxen. We didn't mind and actually enjoyed the task. Gorman gets more demanding by the year. At night in the kip I heard a lot of talk. The men are very upset with the Crown and feel the laws regarding the masting trade are unfair. They say the officials are overbearing, especially Surveyor-General Harpswood. It sounded like they've had enough of him. The trees we take out are legal so I don't know what the concern is— only that they don't like being told what to do by the English, I think."

"Did you have any difficulties along the way this time?"

Deciding not to worry her about the sick men, their deaths or the oxen killed, he began another direction.

"Not too many. The river was really high and so we had to haul out a lot of boulders that were in the way. With the water moving so rapidly, it was difficult to control the flow of the trees down river, but we managed."

"What do the men do when they're not cutting or hauling the tree?" she innocently asked.

"There's not a lot of time between work and sleep, but they play cards or wrestle. Sometimes they have axe or hatchet throwing contests. Me, all I do is dream about you."

"Leighton, you don't."

"Late winter I went sapping with the cook and some other men," he said, in conclusion of the accounting of his winter activities. "We were eager to have sweet maple syrup smothering our pancakes so we pitched in."

"Can we do that here? We have maple trees."

"Yes, when I'm here early spring we can do that. It has to be done before the sap rises in the trees."

"How do you do it?"

"After locating a sugar maple, the cook chopped a space in the bark with his axe then drove in a wooden spout and hung a piggin on it. I helped the men construct a tripod from which to hang the iron pot of yellowy liquid over an open fire. We took turns stirring. It has to be boiled and stirred a long time. I watched carefully to see how the process was done so we can do it."

"That will be fun. Every morning I'll fix you a stack of pancakes with maple syrup poured over them. It will be a stack so high it will touch the moon."

"And I will eat them all if they be made by your hand," he cooed. "I brought some wine from Waban. If you will get the tankards from the mantle, we'll celebrate my return and our being together again."

He watched her as she reached up to get the tankards. She had a straight and lean neck, fit for diamonds, and he wished he had more than wine to offer her. She never complained. He knew that only tubers and baked beans had been her fare for several weeks, but she said nothing of it, happy for the goods he'd brought her. She was always singing, never seemed unhappy or saw anything she did as drudgery. If her bone knitting needles weren't clicking or she wasn't at the spinning wheel, she was carrying firewood, nurturing the animals, gathering fruit and nuts or working with her herbs and roots to make lotions, potions, salves, and ointments.

As they sipped wine together, he gazed into her obsidian eyes, assuming her to be entirely happy, but she was hiding a secret unhappiness from him. There was one thing missing from her life that he had not been as sensitive to as he might have—baby bunting. She could heal the sick, make ewes lamb, hens lay, plants grow, cows content, wild animals tamed, but what she desired most, a baby, eluded her.

"The swallows have returned and made their nest in the chimney to rear their young," she explained, leading him outside to where she'd built a fire pit. "I don't want them disturbed so I cook here, like you did to make maple syrup."

Their first meal together consisted of clam boil and goose tongue, the first greens of the season cut from between the rocks. To follow, she had plum duff. Before it grew too dark, they walked together to the shore and stood, staring eastward across the ocean. A family of grebes floated on the water near shore, bobbing up and down as waves moved beneath them.

"Are those loons?" Leighton asked, pointing to several birds that scooted along in front of them as they walked toward the meadow.

"The Indians called them wobbles. They're like loons but can't fly because they don't have long feathers in their pinions."

Near the pond she stopped to pick wild mint, holding it in one hand while her other held his tight.

"See the yellow flowers on the pond? They be water lily. The Indians eat the roots and also the deer that feed on them. They kill the deer as they browse with their heads underwater so they don't know their death is coming, like how you killed the goose you got for our last dinner in the fall."

Strolling to the south end of the island to their favorite place, they stood above the cliffs. The cat had followed but soon disappeared into the woods in pursuit of a huge black turkey. A first quarter moon hung in the sky like a tipped silver bowl as they returned to the cottage to enjoy each other's connubial embrace.

By first light he was up. Genevieve was gone. Standing at the open door, the cat at his feet, he watched the sun throw sparks of light into the sky then rise into brightness as it broke the rim of the ocean to the east. The grass was stiff with frost. Wind whistled through the spruce trees beyond the flowering meadow, animals grazed in the pasture he'd cleared, and he could hear the song of the warbler. It was good to be home. He had brought several more rose bushes to Genevieve the previous summer and could see she'd planted them next to the cottage. The apple shoot grafts had taken. The trees were blossoming and looked healthy but it would be a couple of years before they could expect apples. Some trees grew wild near the woods and, for the time being, Genevieve was satisfied with windfall apples. As he sat on the doorstep, she came from the brambles by the woods, beaming with delight. A basket of eggs swung from her arm. She held herbs in one hand, a bundle of catkins in the other.

"I have picked herbs and mushrooms for our breakfast to go with our hen eggs," she offered by way of explanation as she approached, handing him the catkins.

After a hearty breakfast, Leighton got busy grubbing out the stumps left over the winter to rot, clearing a space for the clover. In the days that followed they settled back into a routine. As yellow buttercups and wild flowers bloomed in the dooryard, blue flags in the meadow, Genevieve's vibrancy and vigor gradually returned, and they renewed their life together as though they'd never been apart. While Leighton toiled, Genevieve kept busy with a variety of tasks, often disappearing into the woods for hours at a time. He thought nothing of it—her strange nature as dear to him as ever. She had planted the pink seeds he'd brought her the summer before, and they attracted a multitude of bees that murmured as they hovered over the flowers. One afternoon a swarm of them flew into the cottage, and he feared she'd get stung, but she only laughed.

"Leave them be," she insisted. "They must be welcomed."

Plowing and planting had taken up a great deal of his time that summer. He made use of island resources, stuck close to home, and made few trips to coast goods to the islands for mainland merchants. A crude fishing shallop he'd constructed allowed him to fish for menhaden and porgy to feed their hens and as fertilizer. The oil extracted from them would be used for lamps or to sell. Haddock and mackerel flocked to his hand lines to be salted or smoked on flakes. He'd been told that herring preferred the colder, deeper Atlantic waters but, seeing a green, phosphorous slick near the shore one afternoon, he knew they'd come in close. He stopped off the cove to form a weir then stamped and made noise on shore to drive them into the nets, soon overhauling his wealth of silver. When he proudly showed his catch to Genevieve, she waxed philosophical.

"Some fishermen believe that the herring are led by a king who shouldn't in any way be harmed because he leads the other fish to their nets. Others think he should be caught with the others as punishment for leading them to their peril."

"Which do you believe?"

"The governance of fish is beyond my understanding. I only know you shouldn't count the fish you've caught, lest the others decide not to bite, so just empty your nets and thank the sea for its bounty."

Though her ways were odd, he loved her true. It didn't matter to him that she escaped from him into her mind from time to time, a sadness streaming through her expressive eyes, that she knew things before they happened, that she took extra precautions in anticipation of problems, performed rituals to ward off potential difficulties, that she disappeared or reappeared in surprising ways—that she seemed inseparable from Macha. Often, when he awakened at night, he'd find them gone, presumably to the woods. Once, in search of her in the early morning hours before dawn, he found her under the full moon in the Indian ceremonial ring of stones, chanting, as the cat sat on a rock intently watching and listening. He never asked her to account for her ways, and she never offered explanations.

Sometimes he watched her as she went about her chores and activities. She boiled water in the black iron pot suspended from a tripod over the fire pit to wash clothes. Always mindful of cleanliness, she kept an immaculate house—sweeping, scrubbing, always filling the air with her fragrant herbs and incense essences. She made beeswax, bayberry scented candles and soap, made healing potions and salves from herbs, sheared the sheep, carded their wool, spun yarn, and always prepared lovely meals—all as if produced by magic, and with a grace that belied effort.

Besides the ease with which Genevieve produced everything, did everything, the island mysteries and contrasts intrigued him. The tides, governed by the moon, patiently and relentlessly washed against the island as though attempting to push back its shores. The water was clear and still on the west, dull and raging on the east. There were high cliffs on the south end, a flat, sloping shore on the north.

Early summer on the western shore, where the water was clear, he placed offal in a hole in the rocks to capture the lobster that would come at high tide—netting them at ebb tide. Genevieve fixed lobster for their dinner along with mushrooms gathered in the woods. She tended an immense garden, carefully nurturing the herbs, vegetables, and flowers she'd planted according to the phases of the moon. The goats were immediately put to use producing milk for cheese and, when Leighton got a cold, nanny plum tea to clear his breathing. The grape seedlings he'd brought for her the year before had sprouted tiny leaves and would soon be stretching their long vines over the lattice work she had constructed of wood slats between stakes.

The Indians came, trading their goods for herring and working on the ceremonial circle. He was too busy to help them but did observe for a time. Genevieve spent several hours with them before returning to the cottage to prepare a feast. In the evening, after a meal of cornbread and roasted turkey, she plied them with checkerberry tea and hasty pudding covered with molasses. It was the night of the first full moon of Leo, Lughnasadh—the turning point in Mother Earth's year. She had gathered the last of the herbs and wanted to celebrate, burning sandalwood at the hearth. Just as the Indians always shared their bounty, so did she. When they left, she sent many of her herbs with them in gratitude for their friendship. The Indian ways were as mysterious to Leighton as were Genevieve's, but he accepted it all. His love for her expanded outward to include everything she touched or was of importance to her.

He did some coasting but most of the time worked

in the field or cut wood. Together they harvested marsh hay and the bounty from the garden. Often he went with Genevieve to the woods or the blueberry barrens beyond the meadow to help her gather the harvest. Always the cat came with them, sometimes winding between their legs, more often standing at a distance and observing them.

"That cat knows more than she should," Leighton said one day, "staring at us like she knows everything."

"Macha does know everything," Genevieve corrected. "One day you will know that with certainty."

Duncan and Lewis had surprised them with a visit toward the end of summer. They made the trip out to the island in a sloop, bringing sugar, coffee and flour, hoping to trade for some dried cod and cord wood. The men spent the afternoon chopping wood and loading it into the sloop. While they were busy with that, Genevieve fixed supper for them. They'd not met her before, but it didn't take long for her to win their hearts as well. They left late in the evening, with only enough light to get safely back to port. It was nice to have the company, and Leighton vowed again to take Genevieve visiting. But, as the summer drew to an end, they hadn't left the island together. Their relationship was so self-contained, they were content. It was easy to remain isolated when they had each other and needed no one else.

Early fall, he trapped mink and otter with dead falls, leaving the cleaning of hides and drying of meat to Genevieve. They carried piggins of water from the spring and carefully stored food. The storage area was filled with herbs hanging on pegs to dry, as well as honey and honeycomb she'd collected from a hive near the woods. Fennel was dug up from the garden to store over the winter. He often caught silver-bellied eels, turning them over to Genevieve to fix for their dinner, out of doors, along with pumpkin mashed with ginger, vinegar, and butter.

By the time all preparations had been made and he was ready to leave, he felt confident in her ability to thrive in his absence another winter. She had grown so self-sufficient that he never feared she couldn't manage on her own but was happy the Indians would be visiting. The day before his departure, however, she wasn't as supportive of his trip inland as in years past. Her eyes were less cheerful, her smile wan, and he grew fearful something might be wrong.

"Are you feeling well?" he prodded, as they carried the last of the stores inside.

"Yes, dear, well enough."

"What then is the matter?"

"All is fine," she sullenly responded.

They watched from the doorstep as piscine clouds shifted and changed. Soon they were beset by a sudden storm. A fierce wind whistled across the island and a spate of rain drove them indoors. Sitting before the fire, holding hands, Genevieve remained withdrawn. Leighton coaxed her to tell him her troubles, but she would not. The storm had spent its rage by early evening and, as the sky cleared, they walked together. At the edge of the woods a small gray, short-eared owl flew past, and a stag peered out at them before turning to disappear into the darkness of trees. It was just past the full moon and the tide was high—spring tide. Bats swooped around them as they stood in their special place, gazing at the night sky alive with a smoke of silver stars. Genevieve held tight to him and finally confided her concern—the only one she was willing to share.

"I thought I'd have a baby growing in my womb by this time. We've been together nearly five years."

"Don't be disheartened, my Genevieve, it will happen in time. Don't you always say that things happen as they should, at the time they should?"

"Yes, but this is different."

"I don't see that it is. Think about it and you'll know I'm right."

They talked the rest of the evening, making their plans for when he'd be back in the spring, and her spirits seemed to lift. In the morning, pancakes with maple syrup awaited him when he awakened. Though he put on a brave face, it had been with a heavy heart that he left that morning to return to the forest.

— CHAPTER THIRTEEN —

Water descends on the Atlantic
The gigantic
Storm-wind of the equinox,
Landward in his wrath he scourges
The toiling surges,
Laden with seaweed from the rocks.

From *Seaweed* by Longfellow

"Parnell, quit yer dam day dreamin' and git those oxen unhitched," Gorman yelled.

The lead oxen were moved to the back, tailing the others to act as a drogue and allow more control. In years past, more than once the hawsers and chains, strained to their limit, had broken, sending the mast tree careening downhill too fast to stop, crushing the driver and oxen in its path. This year care was taken to prevent such a mishap. While the beasts stamped and snorted, the men slashed branches from nearby trees, strewing them on the downward slope of the road to provide friction. Snub lines were then wound around adjacent trees and held tight, to slow the movement of the immense tree and ease it down the hill.

Injuries were unavoidable in the masting process. Deep in the interior woodlands there was little disease to worry about, but axe wounds were frequent, sometimes severe. Sugar or flour were used to stop the bleeding. If stitches were needed, the pain was dulled with whiskey. Other maladies included dislocation of arms or shoulders and the inevitable frost bite. Murdock, the cook and doctor, was half Abenaki. He used knowledge gained from his people to combat infections with mud packs or treated the injured with compresses of alder or balsam tea.

In the hollow, the dutiful lead oxen were taken from the rear and again hitched at the front. All the yokes and bridle chains were refastened then the snub lines were unwrapped, and they were again ready to continue.

"Haw, Bright," the driver ordered.

The oxen snorted as they turned to the left and pulled hard. Their mangy coats were covered with frost, their heaving breath visible. The men tramped along beside the oxen, urging them on. It was so extremely cold that occasionally the sound of exploding trees could be heard in the distant interior of the forest. Blown by a strong wind, the limbs of the close-knit trees rubbed together, making an eerie sound. Crows screamed from the tops of trees as the teams of oxen, mast tree, and men clattered beneath them. Deer watched from thickets, and an occasional squirrel or rabbit darted across their path. A female moose appeared in a clearing, staring at them in defense from a distance through near-sighted eyes. When she moved slightly, they could see a calf at her side. The men rarely talked as they went. The grumbling of nights in the kip had turned to silent forbearance in favor of the effort required, and in the company of Gorman, their team leader.

By late afternoon the snow finally quit, and a dim sun shown through the clouds. Its light, filtered by the pine branches, provided little warmth. In the calm after the storm, the men with frosted beards slowly made their way toward Burrows' Creek, stopping at wells along the way to unhitch the oxen and allow them to drink.

They only went a couple of miles the first day. There were some turns in the road difficult to manage, but it was the modest hills that posed more of a problem. At night they camped in crude tents huddled together in the woods. Campfires blazed, fed by a rotation of men assigned to keep them going. Exhausted from their labors, they soundly slept despite the bellowing of the beasts of burden kept close to camp.

Hauling out had many challenges. Foremost of concern, was making sure the tree was not damaged in transport, rendering it useless and all their work, in vain. Most of their haul out was through wild, untamed land and woods, but sometimes they would go through settlements that had sprung up along the masting roads. Villages, with clusters of white houses, log cabins, and a requisite church, had broad, straight streets to accommodate the hauling of trees, and town squares with the corners rounded off by teams of turning oxen. The people of the settlement came to watch, amazed to see the massive trees horizontally, and impressed with the ability to move anything so large.

The men had to find water for the oxen and marsh grass or hay to feed them. Their own meals were prepared out in the open, regardless of winter's ravages. Campsites along the way had to be set up when the progress of their haul wasn't aligned with a farm or settlement. Once the hauling out began, whether religious or not, the men prayed to be spared a winter storm or gusty winds that would make their job more difficult. Oxen often became mired in mud along the route. If they came to a bog, the mast team had to cut more trees, laying them down so the oxen could get across without getting stuck. Winter thaws caused flowage which then refroze, leaving ruts in the mast road that made a rough go of it. In past seasons, storms had been so severe it had caused blow downs. Trees had to be removed from the mast road and cut up before they could proceed.

Once they had struggled more eastward and south, farther from the stand of pine, the mast road was straighter and more level, and the going got easier. For days they hauled. A few nights were spent in a settlement where they could stay in an inn or private home but most were spent in camps. Finally, when the day arrived they assumed to be their last, it started snowing again. The men were discouraged but, confident they were finally near Burrows' Creek, plodded on through the day.

"We'll hold up heah," Gorman suddenly boomed. "Make camp. Parnell and Remy, get those beasts unhitched and settled in for the night. Dodson, give them a hand."

Some of the men went about setting up a crude campsite while the cook began preparing their supper.

From previous trips, Leighton knew they were close to Burrows' Creek, and wondered why Gorman had chosen to hold up so near their destination. It was dark by the time the oxen were unhitched from their yokes. Leighton and Remy set them loose in the woods while Dodson roped off an area to keep them contained.

"What is it that's a fortnight in growing and a fortnight in dying?" Remy asked, once they'd secured the oxen and were walking back to camp.

"I sure don know," Dodson put in, "but I'm shur yer gonna tell me."

"Why the moon, course."

"Forgit t' moon. What I want t' know is why weah holding up so close t' Barhows' Creek?" Dodson asked, stopping for a moment.

"I wondered that myself," Leighton returned.

"I heerd there might be trouble at Bahrows' Creek," Remy offered.

"What kind a trouble?"

"Donno, just trouble. Don say nothin ta'other men. They don needs t' knows."

"I saw Gorman talkin' t' two men who soon left t' camp dressed for bitter cold weathah," Dodson offered. "Do yew think they were bein' sent ahead t' scout out Bahrows' Creek?"

"Could be," Remy responded.

It was so cold that Leighton was only too glad he wasn't one of those sent. He, Remy, and Dodson listened to the men talking that night in the camp, concerned for what kind of trouble might be waiting for them. They hoped to hear some clues, but the men only talked about once again being in the sawmill settlement and, ultimately, at the coast and home. It had been a hard several months. They worked well together but were tired of the smell of themselves and the mangy beasts—weary of looking at each other and ready to again see the ocean and sunshine instead of the sparse offering of winter light between the dense branches of the trees surrounding them in the dark forest. Talk ended early that evening, not only because all were tired but because Gorman was bunking with them.

Leighton, tired of the harsh cold and taking orders, was glad to soon be finished for the season, hopefully for life. Once the huge tree was moved to Burrows' Creek, his job would be done, so he would like to have kept going that day, but the decision wasn't his to make. The men teased him about his evident eagerness to return to the island, assigning a ribald reason that was only partially true. Most of them were just as eager to be done. Some of them cut mast trees in the summer, hauling them out with galamanders, a much more difficult task. Like many of them, Leighton was a man of parts and would spend the summer coasting and farming. Unlike them, he would be with his Genevieve.

"We cum t' Bahrow's Creek tomarrah men," Gorman advised, drawing Leighton's attention. "Quit yer talking and git some sleep."

— CHAPTER FOURTEEN —

And drifted onward through the golden
gleams
And shadows of the misty sea of dream,
As mariners becalmed through vapors
drift,
And feel the sea beneath them sink and
lift,
And hear far off the mournful breakers roar,
And voices calling faintly from the shore.

From *The Falcon of Sir Federigo* by Longfellow

He awakened as the clock on the mantle struck the hour. It was morning and rosy sunlight shone through the rows of clear panes at the windows. The gray cat sat in the doorway gazing out to sea, but he couldn't see the woman. With great effort, he raised himself up to sit on the edge of the cot. On the hearth, leaned against the fireplace, was a copper warming pan, and he recalled how Emma had placed it under his feet when he shook with chills. In his delirium, it had been as comforting as a mother's arms.

Lanyon pulled himself to a standing position and, noting the bench under the window, unsteadily limped across the room to a chair. Freshly picked mint lay on the wooden table—its fragrance playing with his mind. Using the chair as a crutch, he went to the sideboard to look more closely at the books he'd noticed before. There were some hornbooks, an almanac, geography and arithmetic books, and he concluded that Emma was either educating herself or others. *Perhaps the Indian*, he thought. On the mantle sat two tankards turned partially to the side. He turned them to face him. Seeing the insignia on their fronts, two swords crossed at the hilt, a sense of deja vu came over him.

Opening a trap door hinged with leather thongs in the keeping room floor, he found two small wooden barrels and several piggins, a butter firkin, candles, an assortment of teas, ointments, cornmeal, sugar, spices, and coils of rope. The tarry smell gave him pause. From the rafters, drying herbs hung on wooden pegs. His head throbbed from leaning over to look inside. Closing the trap door, he crossed in front of the fireplace and hobbled to the bedroom door. There, he hesitated before proceeding, not wanting to disturb Emma in case she might still be asleep. Cautiously, he peered inside. There was no one there. A rope bed sat against the far wall. A downy and comfortable looking mattress spilled over its edges, and an indigo and white patterned quilt was neatly pulled up over the pillows at the head. Though he hadn't seen the room before, it felt familiar. On the near wall was a chest of drawers and, next to the door, a nightstand with a bowl and pitcher. Feeling compelled to do so, he touched the pitcher's handle, traced the flower and leaf pattern on the bowl. Struggling with an eerie sense surfacing within, he turned, slowly moved from the bedroom, and walked toward the door open to the outside. On the way he noticed the loft to the left above his cot, absently wondering what might be up there. The cat scurried off toward the woods when he stooped to pet it.

Emma had told him the cat's name was Nemain and that it was a very unusual and special cat. He had thought she was referring to its mismatched eyes, but she explained that Nemain was like a phantom cat that shadowed her every move and came and went as she pleased. Acceptance of the cat had not been a problem for him. She often curled up next to him in bed or warmed his feet. Her gray coat was as shiny as Emma's lustrous hair. When he was awake and Emma absent, he found the presence of the cat a comfort.

A strong wind blew as he gingerly moved off the stone stoop and out into intense sunlight. The splint made movement cumbersome, the pain lingered, but it was good to once again be out of doors in the reviving fresh air. He hoped his muddled mind would one day clear, and he would be able to sort out events without getting lost in his jumbled thoughts. As his eyes accustomed to the light, he saw the green and placid sea through a tangle of rose bushes. A high tide filled the cove to its brink and came nearly to his toes. *I've built the cottage too close to the shore*, he found himself saying, alarmed at the nature of his thoughts.

Gulls bobbed in the water, facing into the wind with their feathers flattened against their backs. Pinks, sunflowers, and morning glories blazed in the sun. A row of lilacs stood along the right side of the dooryard. Silver-winged dragonflies flit among the blue flags. A faint quarter moon hung in the western sky and, in the bountiful garden, bees hovered over the blossoms, dipping their feet in pollen. In the distance, across the water, a fishing vessel passed over the rim of the ocean. *Most likely a whale boat or fishermen after whiting, tuna or horse mackerel*, he mused, wondering how he knew that—or how he knew the fish livers would be soaked in barrels of salt water until the oil could be skimmed off.

If dimmest of memories served him, it had been fall last he remembered but, given his injuries, he knew not to trust his mind for details. Either the passage of time had been distorted by his injured condition, or he had slipped into another dimension, because the days were always the same and ever pleasant—sunny and spring-like, with an occasional freshening shower.

He stared south, inhaling the scent of pine. Amber sunlight streamed through purple cosmos in the meadow, creating a mallow-colored aura that petulantly hung over tall grasses. Soon Emma emerged from the alder thicket at the edge of the woods on a white horse. A skullcap covered her beautiful hair. She took it off as she slid from the horse's back onto the ground in front of him, and her raven locks fell across her shoulders.

"You must feel better. I'm glad," she said, approaching him.

Her basket was filled with white star-shaped bunchberry blossoms. The fragrance was intoxicating.

"Did you see the cunners I got off the rocks this morning," she offered, gestering to the piggin by the doorstep where tails flashed in the drawn salt water. "We'll have them fresh, with pea soup and corn bread this day, instead of dried fish or stew."

When he turned to look at the fish, he saw blood on the doorstep and asked her about it. She suddenly turned and went into the cottage, ignoring his question. When he inquired again later, her answer was curt, letting him know it was not to be discussed.

"T'was a bad omen."

Deducing that it was somehow a painful subject for her, and not wishing to offend, he didn't say more about it, but his curiosity had been peaked. She had a sense of mystery about her that was difficult to compass. Knowing he had for days been in and out of lucidity, he assigned his confusion to that instead of to anything specific about her.

"Where did Nemain come from?" he questioned, seeing the cat twirl in and out under the long skirt of her dress.

"Nemain has always been," she responded, picking up the cat and cuddling it to her breast. "It is a cat of mystery, even to me, but so are many things mysterious."

When they'd had lunch, she suggested the removal of his head bandages. He sat quietly as she drew close and unwound the cloth strips from his head. Feeling suddenly exposed, he blushed as he stared directly into her beautiful eyes without the defense of bandages.

"I think a nap might be in order for you now," she suggested.

Exhausted from the little effort he'd exerted, he did not argue. She helped him to bed and tucked the coverlids securely around him. For a time he watched her move about the hearth. She was an enigma—present, yet sometimes distant and aloof, outgoing and friendly yet fiercely guarding her solitude, someone whose enchanting bright eyes lit up a room but in their depth revealed a great sadness. In some ways they were very similar and he wondered if, perhaps, in her he was being shown his feminine aspect. For reasons he couldn't explain, she made him feel whole and complete. Sorting through his baffling thoughts, he fell asleep, and drifted into the mists.

— CHAPTER FIFTEEN —

Becalmed upon the sea of Thought,
Still unattained the land it sought,
My mind with loosely-hanging sails,
Lies waiting the auspicious gales.

On either side, behind, before
The ocean stretches like a floor,
A level floor of amethyst,
Crowned by a golden dome of mist.

Blow, breath of inspiration, blow!
Shake and uplift this golden glow!
And fill the canvas of the mind
With wafts of thy celestial wind.

Blow, breath of song! Until I feel
The straining sail, the lifting keel,
The life of the awakening sea,
Its motion and its mystery!

From *Becalmed* by Longfellow

It snowed again during the night and was freezing cold. By morning the men were impatiently active, ready to be on their way and at last to Burrows' Creek.

"I don mind tellin' ya t' second bes paht of being done fah t' wintah is getting some decent food," Dodson confessed, over a breakfast of corn bread, salted pork, and beans.

"Ayeh, an what be t' fahst?" Morrison asked.

"Finally bein' away from all yew men, corse."

"You'll be missin us fah we git done," McGee joshed, "nevah mind t' rest o' t'yeah."

The more winter dragged on, the more eager were

the men to get back to their families, often using humor as a defense to conceal true emotions. One of the men on the crew, Bromfell, was from away—a flatlander from the Bay Colony who was not well-liked. In general, provincials, who felt like the stepsisters of the Colony, were resentful of people from Boston. Bromfell was the driver—older than the other men, respected for his expertise, but not his origins nor his tendency for indecisiveness.

"He has so much trouble decidin' which way t' go," Jeffries insulted, "it's crossed 'is eyes."

"We can bring him abowt in time," Alistair offered.

"He do go on some," Hiram put in. "Seems t' me he's jest butt sprung else he's nothin' but hulk."

"I think *you* be widdershins. He's aw right," Remy defended. "Let the man be. If he could do bettah, he'd do it."

Leighton and Remy rounded up the oxen in the woods, unfastened and coiled the rope holding them, and led them to their yokes where the men hitched them up. Shortly after sunup they were on their way again. The mast road was particularly rough, having refrozen from a mild thaw, and they had to go slow. The oxen plodded along, their warm breath vaporizing, their shaggy coats weighing them down. The other teams of dumb oxen followed the lead team along like sheep. Bromfell may not have fit in well with the rest of the men, but knew what he was doing. The sun hung high in the sky above it all as, under his expert guidance, they made their way through another town. Their attention was focused on maneuvering around a bend in the road, sharper than most, when one of the men, Elwood, called out.

"There be t' rivah."

The glistening river snaked its way to the right, bending here and there. Swollen spring waters had pushed through fissures on the icy shores, rising high up onto the banks. The river would meander closer to the mast road in places, farther in others, until they aligned near the mill. The men grew expectant, and soon they could hear the falls above the mill as water plunged to the mill pond.

"That be smoke I smell?" Hodgkins questioned.

"Ayeh, it be smoke, aw right," Alistair returned. "We be nearah than I taught."

They all sniffed the air, confirming the smell of smoke. Chilled to the bone, just the smell of smoke provided warmth. Their destination could be readily seen ahead through bald winter trees. In the small settlement by the river, smoke rose up gray and straight from the chimneys of sparsely laid cabins. The tired oxen, sweat frozen to their necks, were prodded the last leg of the journey as most of the men rushed forward ahead of them. The transport to Burrows' Creek was typically full of surprises but had taken only nine days this time and was relatively uneventful, for which they were all grateful.

Finally at the river, the men guided the oxen to pull the mast tree alongside the store of others and twitched it into place. Leighton and Remy, along with two other men, unhitched the beasts, freeing them to roam. Unguided, they wandered, making circles and aimlessly heading back toward the woods. Trees were roped off to keep them contained so they wouldn't stray too far. They would be needed again to move the mast trees into the water. It looked like the ice was melting and the trees could soon be twitched. Once in the river, they'd have to be guided around rocks and rapids, at times pulled onto the embankment by the oxen then dragged farther downstream to calmer waters. A known obstacle was a waterfall several miles away, more like a cataract. It was not a surprise, and maneuvering it required brute strength, but the men were both experienced and capable.

At Burrows' mill men were busy sawing up lesser trees into lumber when they arrived. Two worked in the pit, using a cross saw to vertically slice the tree laid across it into boards. At one time there had been only a couple of sawmills in the region. Now there was one at the mouth of nearly every river, others at the confluence of a stream and river. Woodsmen and sawyers worked side by side, each appreciating the skills of the other.

The mill pond was full to the brim. Thin ice was visible in spots, but with river water rushing through the nearby race, hadn't much chance to thicken. Because the mill was positioned next to the embankment, the river ran past at a higher elevation—the strong current of water forcing the overshot wheel round and round.

By the time the men had completed their tasks it was twilight. Leighton and Remy saw to the oxen before settling in for the night with the rest of the men.

"You be glad t' see t' missus soon, I'll bet," Remy teased, as they secured the beasts.

"Won't be long now," Leighton responded. "I hope to leave tomorrow or the next day."

Hearing an osprey overhead as they trudged through the snow toward the lodge, his thoughts turned toward home.

Spring had arrived on the island about the same time as he had the year before. The osprey piped, hovering overhead, as he had secured his sloop and walked up the path to the cottage. He had brought with him two thumb-back slab chairs and, although the price had been dear, glass for the windows. All had looked well as he approached the island, but Genevieve wasn't there to greet him as was usual. She wasn't in the cottage either. Seeing the sachem's gear laying on the cot, his heart skipped a beat. He grew immediately concerned, wondering if their trust in the Indians was unwarranted. As he unpacked the boat, however, she came running from the woods carrying a basket of herbs with Macha at her heels. She looked exhausted and nearly as pale as the white kerchief crossed over the front of her blue wool dress. She didn't say much about it, and surely she was self-reliant, but he could tell it had been a rough winter. Her spirit had definitely been dampened.

The sheep were already sheared. Their wool lay in piles in the corner of the keeping room waiting to be untangled. With a cheerful smile, she showed him the wool she'd spun and dyed indigo with the dye pots he'd brought her the year before, the sweater she was knitting for him from the yarn to keep warm the next winter and, in the bedroom, the goose down pillows she'd made for their bed.

Askwedaid, the sachem, came from the direction of the south cliffs as Genevieve prepared dinner.

"He must have smelled your good cooking," Leighton laughed, his arms around her.

"Then you'd best let me get to it," she chastised.

Askwedaid helped him carry the chairs from the boat and set the benches under the windows—one in the keeping room, the other in the bedroom. Soon after supper he left, paddling to northward. Though it was still quite cold, Genevieve and Leighton walked the island together. She wanted to show him all that had been done in his absence. The Indians had helped her clear more land, the enlarged garden already springing to life with early plantings.

"The winter storms were fierce this year," she confided, as they stood on the cliffs staring at the sea. "If not for the Indians, I don't think I could have made it."

When the migrating birds returned, catkins bulged, the laurel bloomed pink, and the shad'blow white, her color and spirit returned. The ewes had lambed, the cows calved, all thriving under her nurturing care. Leighton worked the fields, plowing and planting. The immense garden flourished as never before. They soon forgot about the trial of a terrible winter and their days apart. Despite all the work to be done, they settled into an almost euphoric existence, oblivious as to how brief their halcyon days would be.

Before dawn the morning of May the first, he woke up to find Genevieve gone from their bed. He found her sitting in the meadow.

"What are you doing?"

"I'm collecting the first dew of May when at dawn, between night and day, the moisture appears. It is the time of Beltane, a liminal time between winter and summer."

They sat together watching the sunrise. A beautiful

spring day gladdened as they walked back to the cottage to have breakfast. During the day, Genevieve filled the cottage with flowers and hung silver and white spheres from the rafters to represent the moon, stars, and sun. It was reminiscent of May Day celebrations back in England when he was a boy. At eventide they walked to the cliffs, watching the sun set to the west, and a blue moon rise to the east. It was a magical time, she said.

By the time they walked back to the cottage, it was getting dark. Genevieve was more quiet than usual as they went inside. She had woven flowers together to form a crown which she set upon her head. The pastel flowers looked even more delicate in her raven-colored hair. Going to the mantle, she lit the candles then reached for the pewter tankards. After pouring wine into them, she handed one to Leighton, and they drank a toast to their life on the island, crossing their arms like the swords on the tankards. Then she blew out two of the candles. Lifting the third from its place on the mantle, she took his hand and led him to their bedroom.

"T's Beltane, a time of life-giving," she offered, loosening the fasteners of her shift and letting it fall to the floor.

Standing in the silver light of the full moon shining through the window, she blew out the candle.

"The moon is full, the tide is high. Come!" she whispered, drawing him to her.

Over the summer, Leighton built an oven of beach stones to make Genevieve's bread-baking easier the next winter when he would again be away, and for when the swallows returned to take up residence in the chimney. He also made a loom so she could weave the sheep's wool she'd untangled, spun, and dyed with deft fingers. From wood, he made piggins for storage and a firkin to store goat butter. The glass he'd brought from the mainland was fitted into panes for each window—three rows, two panes across. It added so much light to the rooms that it was almost like being outside.

Most days Genevieve rode one of the horses bareback across the meadow, often going to the south cliffs "to sit with the wind for a time," she would say. He didn't know what the wind was telling her and didn't ask, but each time she returned her mood was sullen. When she wasn't seeing to the animals, she tended her garden and began the process of drying herbs and roots. Wandering in the woods one day, she found a bee hive, marking its location so she could return for the honeycomb before winter. She sewed patches for the battered sails of his sloop and, from salt rushes, wove a small rug for inside the doorway of their cottage. Macha followed Genevieve everywhere as though her shadow, watching what she did and, every chance possible, sitting in her lap.

"That cat thinks she's you," Leighton teased, holding Genevieve as the cat curled around and through their legs.

"She is me," Genevieve quietly responded.

Mid-summer, he suggested they go to Stone Island to visit friends. Early the morning they were to go he found her gathering herbs from the garden to take with them. When he went to help, she said it was Litha and the gathering must only be done by her because the herbs were very powerful.

The MacKenzies were surprised but happy to see them. Usually, when the islanders got together, it was for sugaring off or corn husking, but Genevieve and Leighton had never participated. The idea of a celebration for no specific reason seemed to please everyone. Only Genevieve claimed there was good reason for celebration. It was the summer solstice, when the hours of daylight were the longest and the sun was at its zenith, before again beginning to fade to its nadir.

No one played the fiddle but that did not deter Ian MacKenzie from singing. When the meal was finished, he leaned back in his chair, folded his hands and, unaccompanied, began *Barbara Allen*. "Twas in the merry month of May, when green buds they were swell-in', Sweet William on his deathbed lay, for love of Barb'ra Allen." When he spoke the last verse instead of singing it, they knew the song was ended. "Until they tied a true lovers' knot, the red rose and the briar." Renditions of *Robin Adair* and *O Waly, Waly* followed, as all joined in singing the familiar words.

Returning to Sobagpeka that evening, the fog was as thick as gulls behind a porgy, and Leighton grew concerned about safely finding their way.

"We can make it all right with the wind behind us," Genevieve encouraged. "The fairies and elves will help us."

He was not surprised when the breeze freshened from the west, and the fog thinned enough for them to easily find their way. Macha greeted them at the shore. The fog immediately returned, a bank of it shutting them in. For days rain pelted the windows, the wind hooted and howled, and the leviathan sea roared. It was so damp that moisture beads formed on their clothing and hair. They stayed indoors most of the time. Genevieve knit or worked with her herbs while Leighton made repairs to his ropes and lines. When the sun finally came out again, it burned off the fog, and their busy lives resumed.

Late in the summer, Leighton smoothed the outside of their cottage with daub, covered it with lime wash then whitewashed it. Genevieve had not thought their cottage could be any better but was thrilled. The garden had reached its peak and harvesting began in earnest. She was quite insistent that all herbs be gathered by the August full moon, saying it was Lughnasadh, a turning point in Mother Earth's year. From the woods she also gathered roots and herbs, hanging them to dry in the storage space he'd made for her.

Early September, Leighton trapped two mink in the woods. Handing them over to Genevieve as she met him at the doorway, blood from the minks he'd strung dripped onto the stoop. She jumped back in alarm and ran into the cottage. Despite his prompting, she wouldn't explain her concern, and he had to conclude it was just another of her haunting superstitions.

For several days she seemed sullen, withdrawn. He

assumed it was because it was just about time for him to leave again and return with the mast team to the woods. When the leaves turned copper, bronze, brass, and gold slashed with red, the goldenrod bloomed, and the crickets began to chirp, a sea chill let them know their time together was coming to an end for another summer. With fall weather, the geese arrived. Genevieve gathered their eggs and Leighton went fowling. While she plucked their feathers to make a down mattress, he dried the meat. He also hollowed out gourds from the garden for water and flour ladles.

Making winter preparations, they stored up dried venison, salted fish, tubers, and a supply of flour, and cornmeal. Genevieve insisted that all the crops be in as well as the herbs culled before Samhain, saying it was a period of cosmic darkness marking the end of one year and beginning of another.

"You'll be gone by the time of Samhain, but I will cut several yew branches to hang next to the fireplace as a symbol of rebirth when we will be together again," she told him as they worked. "Do not forget the yew."

Their ability to fend for themselves bolstered their confidence in being able to manage well year round on the island in the years ahead, but it would be a lonely winter for them both. Leighton was especially concerned for Genevieve who could only look forward to an occasional visit from the Indians. Dead leaves crunched under their feet as they walked to the cliffs, the dry smell a sad reminder of all the falls they'd had to say good bye. Brown oak leaves, hanging tight to their branches, murmured in the wind as Leighton and Genevieve stood above the sea. It was then she shared her secret with him.

"I'm with child," she began, squeezing his hand.

Leighton took her into his arms and held her tight. The news was happy for him but, more than becoming a father, he wanted for her to have her heartfelt wish and become a mother at last. He kissed her long and ardently.

"Was it Beltane?"

"No—but soon after—in August. The baby will

arrive in March but not during the void moon if I can help it. The timing will be perfect," she assured him. "I'll spend the winter on the island preparing for the baby, and you'll be back in the spring before the birth. There is so much I need to do to get ready and it will keep me busy— but not too busy to miss you," she quickly added.

The sun turned flame red over the black waters to the west as they stood holding hands. Twilight hung low over the darkening horizon. It was the evening of Mabon, the autumnal equinox—the time of equal hours of daylight and dark, gradually getting darker as Samhain, the end of the pagan year, approached. Holding his Genevieve close, Leighton pledged to her that this season of being a woodsman would be his last. He was surprised when her reaction revealed less enthusiasm than expected. She was obviously happy about the baby to come, but something in her eyes told him there was something she wasn't revealing to him.

"I might be home early enough for us to go sugaring for the first time," he offered, hoping to brighten her spirit. "It will be close to the time the baby will be born so I'll get Duncan to help. You'll only need to watch. Soon after I return I'll buy more rose bushes and enough supplies and staples to see us through so we can spend the entire summer on the island. And the first thing I'll do is build a cradle for the baby. Before next winter, I'll build a bigger table, a harvest table, and outside wooden shutters to keep the cold away from our baby next winter," he promised as he held her.

"You'll be here before the baby is to be born, won't you?"

"Yes. I won't go with the mast team all the way to the landing pond, so I will be here long before the baby arrives."

"Once you're home, we can all be together here on our island, forever. I'll teach our baby from the books I've saved. We'll spend our first Christmas on the island together, just the three of us. I'll gather wintergreen and partridge berries, we'll have spice cakes and mince, and I'll fill the cottage with bayberry candles."

"Christmas Eve we'll raise our tankards of sylla-bub and toast our wonderful life."

Following a restless night, he awakened to a dull morning befitting of his mood. It was the day he was to leave. He found Genevieve standing on the doorstep with the cat, cocking her head as though listening to the wind. Hearing him stir, she turned, wiping tears from her eyes she could not hide. Despite every effort not to, every promise to herself she wouldn't, she pleaded with him not to go.

"Please don't go, Leighton. I had a dream last night that dassent sit well with me. You were walking across turbulent waters, trying to reach me."

"What happened?"

"I woke up."

"It's just a dream, Genevieve," he assured.

"No dream is just a dream, only another reality."

Walking with him to the shore as he carried his gear, she was crying. He remained resolute, mindful of her concern but knowing he had to be their strength.

"Don't worry, my dearest. I'll be home as soon as I can be. Then everything will be fine. We will be together and welcome our baby into this world."

"We will be together," she repeated, pressing a yellow jasper stone into his hand as they embraced, "of that I am sure. "Yellow jasper will prevent a man from drowning—even when he walks across roiled waters."

"I'll keep it with me always," he promised.

"Don't return at low tide, especially a low dreen tide. People die on the ebb tide."

"I promise. You'll need to make yourself a new dress this winter, Genevieve. This old threadbare indigo dress will soon be too small for you," he offered, patting her stomach. "Take great care of you—and our baby."

He fervently kissed her then, after a lingering hug, turned and waded to his boat. The painter was unwound from the boulder at the shore, and he pushed the sloop into the waves. Looking back from the boat toward shore, he saw the great concern evident on her face turn to one of resignation. A tremulous smile spread across her countenance. He'd worried about her since she'd confessed her loneliness to him, but felt consoled in knowing that she would soon have the child she so desired. Rowing out into the reach, he made ready to set sail. Looking back, her cloying smile was all the reassurance he needed, and his concerns diminished.

Standing on the shore in her worn indigo dress, watching as Leighton sailed out of sight, Genevieve was glad he couldn't see the tears that flowed from her eyes. She would like to have been able to ignore the things she knew, things the wailing wind had told her of omens, forebodings, and mystic changes, but she could not. There was a definite slump to her young shoulders as she patted her swelling stomach then strolled up the path to the cottage and went inside with Macha, closing the door to the outside world.

— CHAPTER SIXTEEN —

How the Titan, the defiant,
The self-centered, self-reliant,
Wrapped in visions and illusions,
Robs himself of life's best gifts!
Till by all the storm-winds shaken,
By the blast of fate o'ertaken,
Hopeless, helpless, and forsaken,
In the mists of his confusions
To the reefs of doom he drifts!

From *The Masque of Pandora,*
Chorus of the Fates by Longfellow

Finally they were at Burrows' Creek with the mast tree safely stowed. It was good to be out of the vast brooding forests of black growth and feel some space and light around them. The men relaxed at the lodge with enough aqua vitae to go around, looking forward to a night slept in an actual bed with reasonably clean linens.

Leighton made ready to leave the next morning, but Gorman said a thaw was due and insisted he stay to help twitch the mast trees into the water and follow them to the mast yard. Leighton's impatience was beyond measure. He explained that his contract didn't require him to complete any work beyond getting the tree to Burrows' Mill. Gorman refused to pay him unless he complied. After much argument, a compromise was reached. Gorman finally acquiesced to a degree, no longer insisting he go all the way to the mast yard, agreeing to payment if he would stay long enough to get the trees into the river.

Reluctantly, Leighton agreed. In the days that followed, waiting for a thaw, he tended the oxen and helped the men tamp down a snow pathway to the water that would make it easier to twitch the trees. Finally, a week later, it had thawed enough that a wide channel in the river opened up and they could get the trees in. It took several days. By the time they'd finished the work it was late afternoon so Leighton decided to leave the next morning, getting an early start.

Talk that night in the lodge centered on Harpswood. Though few had met him, all agreed the surveyor-general was of a dour nature. The more resistant to his authority were the millmen, the harder he came down on them. Often mills were disabled in his attacks. He had repeatedly harassed woodsmen, dragging them into court for violations, trumped up or otherwise, to intimidate them and further establish his authority. Judges, often millmen themselves, were reluctant to follow through with convictions and fines, but the torment continued.

The Act of 1729 had been enacted to strengthen the one of 1722, further riling woodsmen, landowners, and especially millmen, but left much to interpretation. It reserved all white pine trees not on private land for the Crown regardless of size. Townships no longer qualified as "private" land. This blatant extension of legislative authority added fuel to the fire, angering reduced colonists, polarizing rebels and loyalists. To call the surveyor-general's practices into question, the millmen had asked him to interpret the new act, hoping to discredit him by his explanation. The unintended result was that he tightened his control, setting licensing requirements and stiffer fines for violation. It served only to widen the growing rift between him and those he was charged with overseeing.

Recently he'd burned sixty canoes at the Falls River sawmill, claiming they were made from trees reserved for use as masts. At Beacon's Creek he seized a tree thirty-six inches in diameter that Beacon intended to turn into shingles. Hauled into court, Beacon was fined more than he could make in a year. While the case was under appeal, it did not look good. In protest, woodsmen set fires, scorching trees marked with the broad arrow, making them suitable only for lumber. In other cases, white pines were girdled by making a cut around them three or four inches deep. This made the sap unable to rise, eventually killing the trees. With no resilience, they could not be used as masts, only shingles or planking. Some woodsmen even went so far as to cut away all the smaller trees around a marked mast tree that protected it, so a heavy wind would blow it down, shattering it and rendering it useless.

Harpswood had tried to get the mast merchants or agents to buy the timber he'd seized, but they refused. His authority and motives questioned, he became even more intimidating, stepping up the frequency of his visits and seizing tons of lumber. More often than not, once he'd left the mill, the timber he'd seized at mills was shoved into a river then floated downstream, unmanned. The trees became too damaged to be usable. Other seized stores were sawed into short lengths and sent to saw mills, or burned where they stood, by colonists tired of British authority and oppression.

Because Harpswood had a large area to cover and multiple other duties, to date he had not visited Burrows' Creek mill. The forest camp at Koasek was relatively new and very remote. So far the mast teams had been able to get their masts to the water and down river without experiencing his heavy hand.

The morning Leighton was to leave, the men were awakened early by a sound that could only be the loud, thunderous voice of Surveyor-General Emanuel Harpswood. When they emerged from the lodge, he was not inspecting the mast trees that had been twitched into the river for their trip downstream. Instead, he surveyed the stock of trees brought by sleds and scoots from the clearings they'd made for the mast road, stored near the pond and waiting to be sawed into planks, shingles, and staves.

"These trees are white pine and were taken illegally from public land. Who is the owner of this mill?" Harpswood demanded, grabbing the nearest woodsman stumbling from the lodge in his flannels.

No one spoke up. Awkward moments passed.

"So you won't tell me who the owner is," Harpswood hissed and sputtered. "Have this man caned," he ordered with righteous indignation, turning to one of his deputies.

It might have been obvious that the mill at Burrows' Creek was owned by a man named Burrows, but Harpswood had no way of knowing for sure, and the men held steady, refusing to reveal the name of the owner.

"I'll show you not to thwart the authority of the Crown," he shouted, grabbing another man for the cane. "The owner of this mill will pay dearly for this act of treachery."

The woodsmen quickly scattered to escape the cane, emerging from the woods only when they knew Harpswood had left and it was again safe. Fearing reprisals, several of the men agreed to follow Harpswood to see what he planned, but lost him in the massive woods. Leighton had not witnessed before, first hand, the man his fellow cutters spoke so defiantly of, and finally understood well their grievances. Rather than leave that day, he stayed to see what would happen. When night came, the confederates gathered to discuss the issue, and he intently listened. As they plotted against the injustices of Harpswood and the British Crown, he questioned his loyalties for the first time.

"He'll be back tomorrah, t' be shurah," Alistair cautioned. "An' we'll be ready fah 'im. Let's git some sleep so weah at ahr best."

It seemed like hours before Leighton fell asleep—his mind fraught with worry over what might transpire the next morning.

— CHAPTER SEVENTEEN —

Peradventure of old,
Some bard in Ionian Island
Walking alone by the sea,
Hearing the wash of the waves,
Learned the secret from them
Of the beautiful verse elegiac,
Bringing into his song motion
And sound of the sea.

For as the wave of the sea, upheaving in
long undulations,
Plunges loud on the sands, pauses, and
turns, and retreats,
So the hexameter, rising and singing, with
cadence sonorous,
Falls; and in refluent rhythm back the
Pentameter flows.

From *Elegiac Verse I* by Longfellow

The cottage was empty when he awakened. He struggled to stand, then hobbled out the door. Emma and Nemain were no where to be seen. It was a lovely day. He limped to the shore and sat on a wet glistening boulder near the water. Warm, sunbaked stones beneath his bare feet felt soothing. The breeze fluttered blooms of alexander growing between the rocks at the water's edge. Looking to the right, he observed horses running in the pasture as though sea winds chased them. Seals rounded up out of the waves, beady-eyed gulls cried and dipped overhead, and diving shags disappeared for countless minutes under the salty water. Windswept fields of clover waved beyond the meadow where sheep and goats foraged. Apple trees hung low with fruit in an orchard interspersed with alder trees. A song sparrow sang in the distance, its melodic tune playing with his mind. The scene gave him an extreme sense of satisfaction and peace for a time. Then vague feelings of upset and dread hovered, circling like vultures, as he endeavored to keep them from descending.

Watching flotsam washing against bird rocks out from the shore, he had, on previous forays begun to piece some things together. He remembered being at sea and, from his injuries, concluded there must have been a shipwreck. But he couldn't remember where he was from, and his tattered clothes could have been those of any seaman. *What kind of ship was I on and where was it going?* he repeatedly asked himself. Logically, if he was a sailor, unless it was a very small ship, he wouldn't have been able to sail it alone. If there were others, where were they? In answer to his many questions, Emma had told him only that she had found him on a rocky ledge by the seashore of the island and there were no others.

It had often occurred to him that he might be dead or living in dreams—surprised it made no difference to him. Having spent so much time asleep, when awake, he was happy just to be alive. Dead or alive, he was completely content, and the only thing that mattered anymore was that Emma was near. Over time, he began remembering more bits and pieces of his past, resurrected from the dark corners of memory. He remembered his name and the name of his ship, knew that he'd captained a ship bound for America, but answers as to the whereabouts of his crew, how he'd gotten to the island, or where he had been before, continued to elude him. Eventually the questions no longer mattered and he quit asking them.

"Come, Lanyon," Emma called, appearing from the meadow with an armload of catkins. "I dug clams in the flats this morning when the tide was low. We can shuck them and I'll make a boil for our supper."

"I'm coming," he called out, as he hobbled to the cottage, dragging his bum leg to the side.

While he shucked the clams, she prepared the other ingredients. When all was ready, she hung the pot on the hob and swung it out over the fire.

"Today we take off that splint," she announced, standing akimbo before him.

After pushing the cat off a chair and helping Lanyon to sit, she knelt before him, carefully loosening the leather thongs that held the splint in place. It was a relief to finally have it off. Patiently, she rubbed his leg with ointment and massaged it. When she'd finished, he stood up and tried the leg, walking slowly around the room.

"I think the only thing holding me back was that splint. My leg feels fine. Thank you for all you've done for me."

"T's nothing. I think it's the fresh air that has done you the most good."

"It's so nice to be outside again for longer periods of time—to feel and smell the sea breezes. But please don't diminish your role in my healing."

He watched her intently as she stood near the fire preparing their meal. Whenever she moved close to him, he became guarded, trying earnestly to hide his involuntary response. Sitting across the table from her, he made only cursory glances, certain his feelings would be evident if he gazed at her too long. The clam boil was delicious and he ate two bowls full. She had made bread as well, and he enjoyed the grainy herbal flavor.

"Do you feel up to a walk?" she asked, once they'd finished eating.

"Yes. It's time to try my leg."

Together they walked out into the flickering sunlight, Nemain trailing behind them. In the dooryard, Emma slipped her arm in his as naturally as if they'd known each other forever. She made the gesture with ease, but he felt jolted. Forbidden feelings surfaced, and he pushed them away, disallowing them from intruding on the intense joy he felt at her touch.

Her beauty was beyond measure. Thick-lashed, dark, ancient, and mysterious eyes adorned her face. Her hair was black as night and her smile, enigmatic and engaging. More than any other of her attributes, it was the scent of her that most captivated him—a pomander of fresh air, the salty smell of the sea, and the herbs she gathered, especially mint. He inhaled her scent with each breath, never able to draw it in deeply enough. It had a narcotic effect on him. Close to her, it seemed like his being expanded into hers, joining them together into a merged, composite being. *Eternal love cannot be eclipsed by distance because eternity knows no distance*, his mind inexplicably echoed.

She had never touched him beyond that necessary for ministrations, until that evening when she linked her arm in his. Walking to the south end of the island with her, he felt a peace and calm settle over him like a gentle wisp of fog, euphorically happy for reasons far beyond his understanding.

As they stood on the cliffs together, Emma talked about the importance of the sea, the wind, the earth, and fire, saying they worked in union, and contrived to provide everything needed. *The elementals*, she called them, were building blocks for all else. Reaching for the stars that hung as big as life in the sky, she talked of other dimensions, other realities. At first he was so distracted by the nearness of her, he couldn't listen. To concentrate, he focused on her eyes, disturbed in seeing in them a deep sadness. Fearing he had offended her by not listening, he endeavored to do so. She spoke of the suspension of time—*no time*, she called it. *Love cannot be measured in time because it belongs to eternity and eternity has no time,* his thoughts answered. When she described their time together as *no time,* at some level he understood because it was how being with her felt.

Nemain came from the woods to stand between them, rubbing up against their ankles.

"Nemain will have answers for you," Emma predicted, "if you remain open to them."

He wasn't sure what she meant but somehow it didn't matter—all that mattered was her presence. After gazing at the moon for some time, they returned to the cottage, her arm again linked in his. By firelight, they sat enjoying each other until very late. Sometimes they spoke briefly but, most of the time, they lingered in silence in avoidance of words they were both reluctant to utter. Alone in his cot, watching silvery moonlight shine through the window panes, he grew anxious. He desperately wanted to sort out the angst he felt about things he couldn't remember from the intense joy while with Emma, but didn't know where to begin. Struggling with remote yet familiar feelings, sensations remembered and forgotten, he slipped again into that shadowy world of the past.

— CHAPTER EIGHTEEN —

A lovely morning, without the glare of the
Sun, the sea in great commotion, chafing
    and foaming.
So from the bosom of darkness our days
    come roaring and gleaming,
Chafe and break into foam, sink into
    darkness again.
But on the shores of Time each leaves some
    trace of its passage,
Though the succeeding wave washes it
    out from the sand.

From *Fragments* by Longfellow

Fearing difficulties in his seizure of logs, Harpswood sent an advance party to check things out while he remained safely behind. It was nighttime when they arrived at Burrows' Creek. Most of the woodsmen were asleep in the lodge. When the scouts saw that all was calm in the settlement, they thought everything was all right. Their orders were for some of the men to stay in the settlement, keeping an eye on things, while others returned to present a full report. A couple of the woodsmen, still awake, realized what was happening and rousted the others. Leighton joined in the fray as the woodsmen and millmen set upon Harpswood's men, beating them and driving them into the woods. Thinking the matter settled, they then returned to the lodge, went to their bunks, and again slept.

It had been Harpswood's intention to return to the settlement the next morning with a seizure order from the vice-admiralty. With him would be his deputies, a marshal, and some hired hands—loyalists all. He had even engaged a unit of the provincial guard to help. When the men who had been beaten returned, reporting what had happened, Harpswood, now quite exercised, immediately returned with them to Burrows' Creek in a surprise attack.

Harpswood had the beaten men identify their assailants, who were dragged from their beds and caned. Next, he attacked the mill with an iron bar, ruining the blades. By this time, the woodsmen had reorganized, and they set upon Harpswood and his men with a vengeance. The provincial guardsmen never showed up to assist Harpswood because they'd been detained by some of the woodsmen, so the surveyor-general was greatly outnumbered. Recognizing this, when the woodsmen fired shots, Harpswood and his fellow intruders ran from the settlement. Luckily, no one was killed. To make sure that was the end of it, some of the woodsmen and millmen were posted as guards, and Leighton willingly served first duty. It was when he discovered that, in the fracas, he'd lost the jasper stone Genevieve had given him.

The next day Burrows met with the woodsmen. He convinced them that, while he appreciated their help in defense of him and his mill, rebellion was not the answer.

"Enough of *backwoods anarchy*! There's any numbah of ways t' deal with this besides violence. T' idea 'at t' British could hold all of New England as a reserve fah masts is absurd and will come back t' haunt 'em."

He had met with lawyers in Waban who had advised him of a loophole in the 1729 Act that would allow land owners to charge the officials of the Crown with trespass. Ignorant of life in New England or the timbering process, from their armchairs in England the Board of Trade had overlooked a detail that would completely frustrate their policy. Legislation reserved all white pine for the Crown but said nothing about all the trees that had to be felled in order to remove them from private land. Lawsuits could be brought against Crown officials, mast merchants, and agents, for all other timber destroyed in the process of creating roads for hauling the mast trees out or clearing an area for felling them. They would need to pay land owners for these extraneous felled trees or be charged with trespass. It was a victory that would resound throughout the New England forests and make it difficult for the Royal Navy to obtain masts in the future.

"We'll use the courts, which ah sympathetic t' us, t' defeat their intent," Burrows advised. "And a little mischief and hahrassment will go a long way, if I do say. They wah fools t' think they could enforce a policy 'at kept men from earnin' a livin'."

Leighton went to bed that night a different man, no longer a confirmed loyalist but sympathetic to the cause of freedom from British rule.

— CHAPTER NINETEEN —

Tell me not in mournful numbers,
Life is but an empty dream!
For the soul is dead that slumbers,
And things are not what they seem.

Life is real! Life is earnest!
And the grave is not its goal;
Dust thou art, to dust returned,
Was not spoken of the soul.

Not enjoyment, and not sorrow,
Is our destined end or way;
But to act, that each tom-morrow
Find us better than today.

From *A Psalm of Life* by Longfellow

Hearing Emma come bounding into the cottage, Lanyon awakened to another day on the island. She carried a basket of culch, so he knew she'd been in the woods or gathering herbs. Her hair, bound at the neck by a scarlet ribbon, was in disarray. It hung down her slender back, swinging from side to side as she flounced across the room toward him, her eyes bright and smiling. Nemain was at her heels, mewling.

"Hush now," she admonished the cat. "You can hardly be starving. A good cat would show more patience. How you be this beautiful morning, Lanyon?"

Lanyon sat at the edge of the cot, rubbing his eyes to hurry wakefulness. He looked to the ewer of fresh roses he found each morning on the small table beside his cot, inhaling their wonderful scent in the hope of centering his mind.

"I'll fix us something to eat," Emma offered, going to the hearth as Lanyon got up from the cot and walked to the open door.

He had slept longer than usual and awakened grog-gy. The sun was barely up over the horizon but already bright enough to begin clearing the mist that had settled on the island overnight.

In their island days together he had grown progres-sively more vital. Though needing to rest often, and una-ble to retrieve his memory full, he felt healthy again and knew it was solely to the credit of the woman who had rescued him from the sea's grasp. His feelings for her had evolved into more than gratitude but, not wanting to risk offending, he did his best not to show it. Some vague loy-alty honorably bound him. Sometimes he wondered if it was for Genevieve, the woman in his dreams. Emma's beauty was so extraordinary he couldn't help but gaze in her direction. Sometimes he got the feeling that if he stared too long or perchance held her, he would dissolve into the mists of time she spoke about. The thought brought him a troubling sense of bliss and comfort.

Besides the perplexity of Emma, there were other confusing aspects to his life on the island. It felt as though time had stopped or was suspended somehow. The crops, flowers, and trees completed subtle, almost imperceptible seasonal cycles but, except for an occasional shower, eve-ry day was the same—beautiful. Scattered between the days of inexhaustible spring, the flowers bloomed then their bare stems stood tall. Within days they again bloomed. There were other things that didn't make sense—the rosy-colored light that surrounded everything, where Emma had come from, why she lived alone on the island, why they never saw anyone. Even the Indian, Askwedaid, had disappeared. Lanyon refused to question any of it for fear his life would be altered, and he would have to find a way to do without Emma. They lived in complete peace and harmony, within a familiarity that felt as though they had always known each other, had always been together. Yet a barrier stood between them like some unspoken ban.

When Emma was busy with her spinning or weaving, he would venture out into the fresh air without her. He admired the rose bushes that skirted the cottage. The fragrance of their lovely red flowers filled the air. When the blooms had expired and only the robust crabapple-sized orange hips remained, he harvested them, hanging them by their stems in the storeroom to dry, knowing she would want them for making tea, and counting on her nod of approval. In the dooryard, chickens ranged free, clucking and fussing as they pecked at the ground. Near the meadow was a bountiful garden. In addition to vegetables that were constantly ripe, a vast assortment of herbs thrived. He had asked Emma their names and learned she had made some of them into the ointments and salves used to heal him.

As his vigor increased, he helped Emma where and when he could with chores. Some days they trapped shad and alewives, overhauling nets that should have been unable to hold them all. The herring ran thick, their iridescent bodies flashing in the black water before being caught, strung, and dried with Emma's blessings said over them. At her request, he built shutters for outside the windows that could be closed against the rain and incessant wind. Game animals abounded in the woods—silver-gray fox, moose, deer, squirrels, mink, and rabbits. Emma was very particular as to how the animals were to be hunted. He had watched in awe as she cast her spell, putting the animals into a trance so they would not suffer when killed. After the hunt, as they were being prepared for eating, like the fish, and fowl, she thanked their souls for the nourishment they provided.

Some days she went to the woods alone, and he was left to explore the island on his own. It was a lush and fruitful place, with windswept fields full of rich growth. On the north end, at low tide, seals sunned themselves on rocks breaching the water while, nearby, cormorants dried their wings. Sheep and goats grazed on ladino clover beyond the meadow where the horses stamped and chewed.

He located the tidal flats on the western shore from which Emma had dug mussels and clams. Under rockweed, he found lobster trapped at low tide, pulling several out before the flood tide facilitated their escape. At the fresh water pond inland, he found otter, beaver and, in the nearby bog where catkins grew in abundance, cranberries. The geese trumpeted their arrival at dusk, settling their fat, downy bodies in the fresh water until dawn when they loudly honked to signal their departure. Wherever he went on the island, if Emma wasn't with him, Nemain was always at his side.

Life took on an ethereal quality as he went about everyday activities. Tentative feelings emerged, familiar yet forbidden—haunting in a strangely positive way. He no longer questioned his existence, no longer searched his memory for answers that refused to surface, or tried to sort out reality from dreams, past from present. It was enough to merely be living on the island with Emma.

When they walked along the eastern shore together, she showed him the runic figures carved onto ledges among the accumulation of shells, rocks, and sand. Deciphering their meaning, she told him that strong, mysterious winds would blow changes difficult to handle, but the future would bring him great happiness and relief if he believed and allowed it. Picking up tawny stones, she stuffed them in the pocket of her dress. Later he would find her fingering them and mumbling strange words—the meaning lost to him.

Early morning and late afternoon, a smir of fog shrouded the island and the sun peaked through when it could. At night he dreamed of Genevieve, pulled into a life with her he didn't want to leave once there. The dreams began haunting him, telling him things didn't end well. Sometimes he dreamed of another woman. She seemed to be known to him, but remained mysteriously in the distance hidden by the mists, as though observing him. Then he would awaken to find Emma and their endless days together. He grew increasingly reluctant to go to his dreams, staying up late each night in avoidance. More and more he desired only to linger in the moist air of the sea smoke, riding the currents of a present he hoped would never end. He didn't realize it was really the future he was living. The beauty of the island, and his life with Emma, was so serene that there were days he grew convinced that, through no credit to him, he had landed in heaven.

He watched Emma closely as she worked at her weaving, silhouetted against the rosy light that always surrounded her. Her hands magically completed tasks without effort, her look was other-worldly, her form at times slightly amorphous, out of focus. None of it did he find the least bit strange, blaming his eyesight or continued confusion of mind. When she came near, her fresh minty scent lingered long after she had moved from him.

For reasons he couldn't explain, her mysterious ways did not alarm but enchant him. Once he saw her pass a willow branch over a ewe that wouldn't accept her lamb. The next day the lamb and ewe were inseparable. She heard voices in the relentless winds that blew over the island with messages just for her. The eternal brume, thinned by her hand, erased the barriers of space, suspended time, telling her of things that would come to pass or possibilities that existed in the realm of creation. In time, he grew eager to share these awarenesses with her.

They spent their days blissfully together, admiring each other from a distance yet somehow knowing the space between them was a chasm that could not be spanned. Evenings they dined on fresh fish, mussels or lobster. Sometimes, she made clam boil. Always there were tubers from the garden and fresh greens. At night they'd walk to the cliffs at the south end of the island and she'd point out the constellations and stars in the heavens. She knew them all—read the sky like a book.

Snow had fallen one morning as he arose to find Emma wasn't in the cottage. Looking out the door, he saw that it had snowed—saw only the tracks of the cat leading toward the woods. It was a lovely spring day and, as he followed the tracks, the snow melted, erasing them. He found Emma in the woods picking herbs. Together they carried her culch back to the cottage through a flowering meadow.

"I need your help this morning if you be willing," Emma inserted, as they finished eating breakfast.

"Yes, of course," Lanyon replied, always happy to do what he could for her. The day did not seem to him in any way unusual or different from any other, but he would be wrong.

After their meal they set off for the salt marsh where they spent the morning working. He cut marsh hay with a scythe while she bundled it, then they carried the shocks to the crude clapboard shed near the woods. While she fixed their noon meal, he chopped cord wood, stacking it by the fireplace and jealously thinking of the Indian he'd thought was her husband.

In the afternoon, chickadees sang nearby as he and Emma picked berries alongside the woods. Emma thanked each and every bush for their bounty. It was growing dark, and a moon rose in the east as they walked back to the cottage. Tired from a hard day of work, they went to their beds soon after the evening meal.

Just before midnight, Lanyon awakened with a strong breeze lapping at his face. The door was open. Moonlight streamed through the window, casting its silvery light throughout the room. The cat sat, illuminated, on the sill. When he got up, the cat jumped down and ran out the door, compelling him to follow. The freshening wind felt bewitched as he trailed Nemain, as the cat scampered ahead of him. He was unable to keep up and lost sight of her in the meadow. Arriving at the south end of the island, he found Emma standing at the precipitous cliff edge.

"T'is a Hunter's Moon," she offered, in an uncharacteristically sad voice, as he approached.

"Why are you sad?" he asked, standing beside her.

"It is the moon of Samhain, the end of the year, when the veil between the worlds is at its thinnest. All must be revealed now or all will be lost."

There was something very foreboding in her voice as she spoke, and he felt a loss he couldn't explain—a grieving for what could be, what should be, but hadn't yet manifested into his awareness. He had often seen thoughtfulness, mystery, even love on Emma's face, sometimes sadness, but never before had such sorrow whirled like eddies in her sparkling coffee-colored eyes. Then, as the wispy gray sea smoke slowly rolled in, enveloping them and creating its distortions, her eyes became veiled from him. He became suddenly fearful that all he loved, all that had grown dear to him, was about to vanish into those mists. *Do not let your devotion destroy you, love again*, his mind echoed. Fearing he'd lose her and, not knowing how else to defend against it, he broke the unspoken taboo between them and grasped a hold of her hands.

With the touch of her, he felt himself transcended, merging with her, his illusory Soul free falling into an abyss of unanswered desire. Drawing her close, he held her, fulfilling endless days of longing. She did not resist or retreat. Lifting her face to his, he kissed her lips. She held him close, returning his ardent kiss. For a time it seemed as though they were swirling with the mists, lost from the world and rising above it. Then their feet again touched the earth.

"Do you know what my name means—what Emma means?"

"No," he answered, breathless with passion.

"It means wholeness. We are now whole, as one. I've enrolled the goddess to help us be together. I will never leave you, have never left you, have always been by your side," she whispered. "The future is ours and ours alone."

He cared not to understand her words, only to hold her. Words, utterances, had no meaning to him so overcome was he with passion for her. A brume rolled over them, and they walked slowly, dreamily, back to the cottage as in a dream. At the door, sitting on a woven mat, Nemain greeted them. Emma pulled a sprig of mint from her apron pocket and laid it on the doorstep beside the cat.

"This will tell you all you need to know," she advised, as they stepped into the cottage, "and you will remember."

In the keeping room, she lit a candle, picked up its holder and carried it into the bedroom, indicating for him to follow. A captive of his passion, he willingly obeyed. Standing in the moonlight, she let her threadbare shift fall to the floor. Her black silken hair glistened as she let it down to fall across her bare, ivory shoulders, and reached for him. He took her into his arms, enveloping her in an embrace, kissing her, his hands exploring her willing body. Her skin was soft as satin, her downy neck warm and inviting, her breath sweet and fresh. Lost in her ebony eyes, he succumbed to a passion long held in abeyance. In their union, they experienced pleasure beyond all human sensations, merging with the emotions of eternal love and trust—lost in the mists of time.

— CHAPTER TWENTY —

Art is long, and Time is fleeting,
And our hearts, though stout and brave,
Still, like muffled drums, are beating
Funeral marches to the grave.

In the world's broad field of battle,
In the bivouac of Life,
Be not like dumb, driven cattle!
Be a hero in the strife!

Trust no Future, howe'er pleasant!
Let the dead Past bury its dead!
Act, act in the living Present!
Heart within, and God o'erhead!

From *A Psalm of Life* by Longfellow

It was late March by the time Leighton was able to leave. The weather was unseasonably raw and uncertain. He caught a flatboat at Burrows' Creek and rode down the Elbow River to his destiny. The day was cold, but the sun shone brightly and he basked in it, relieved that his woodsman experience was behind him, and he could finally go home to stay on the island. Steam, drawn by the sun's warmth, oozed from the dark pine trunks along the river's edge. He'd gotten a later start that morning than he would have liked and was exhausted from all the commotion at the camp. By the time he got to Foggy Harbor, the tide had nearly turned and it would have been a favorable time to sail out, but it was growing dark. A cold wind blew as he snugged his boat in. Drawing his coat tighter around his blue woolen sweater, he looked toward threatening clouds hanging over the hills silhouetted against the dim light to the west, deciding to spend the night at a tavern in port. He would get an early start the next morning to catch the tide going out. It would be a neap tide—at low ebb, higher than usual. Something he forgot to take into consideration.

A chill ran through him in noting the moonless night. *Is it the void moon or an eclipse,* he asked, recalling mention of it by one of the men at the mill. *A lunar eclipse would mean the moon goddess can't be counted on for protection,* he thought, remembering Genevieve's words. *Do I need her protection?* Through the thickening fog, he saw lights on shore. Grabbing his gear, he headed for the inn. Wooden commercial buildings lined the shorefront street, most housing sail or block makers, counting houses or taverns. A fishmonger's wagon, drawn by a team of horses, crossed his path as he stepped into the dirt street, splashing him with mud from a puddle left by a morning rain. Avoiding a passing dray, he approached the inn's front door and ducked under the low lintel to go inside. Several men were gathered, drinking, in the low-ceilinged main room of the inn as he made for the stairs.

"Hey Leighton," someone called out.

It was his old friend Duncan, sitting with some friends over in the corner of the tavern. Leighton ambled over to the table. He didn't recognize the other men.

"What's doing?" Duncan asked.

"Just in for the night. I'll head out in the morning."

"I heerd foul weather's comin' thissa way," one of Duncan's friends warned. "The line storm's about due."

"I dassent think you'll be findin' anything keepin' him from his lady," Duncan put in. "Have a drink with us."

"I'll do, but just one, I'm warning," Leighton advised.

He sat next to Duncan who introduced him to the others. They had heard about the rebellion at the sawmill and were curious about events. After ordering an ale, Leighton filled them in on the details, downplaying the dramatics as best he could. As a loyalist, he had tried to keep his politics to himself and remain neutral. Nothing had changed in that regard. Despite new leanings, he endeavored to see all sides of the issue and was not proud to have become embroiled in the rebellion. He emphasized to the men the non-violent solution Burrows had suggested rather than the conflict. When he'd finished his ale, and his story, he excused himself to go to his room.

"You be cahful tomorrah," Duncan cautioned. "I be shur Genevieve dassant want no broken man comin' home."

"Ayeh. I'll be careful."

"So you should."

He was exhausted but, instead of sleeping well, tossed and turned through the night, drifting through dreams.

A woman stands on the shore of an island, a gray cat at her side. She takes off her tattered and worn indigo dress, donning instead one of golden silk. Jewels bedeck her soft, white neck. Her hair and eyes are the color of ebony. At first she looks like Genevieve then someone else. He tries not to look at her but cannot stop himself from staring. She is beautiful beyond all others. When she beckons, he rows toward her through churning waters. When he finally gets to the island, only the gray cat is there, staring at him from the shore.

It was still dark when he walked to the harbor the next morning. It was Friday—another detail that had escaped his notice. All but the brightest of the cold stars were obscured by mist and useless as guideposts. Seeing no ice in the harbor bolstered him. There was a knot in the painter of the tender, frustrating him before he ever got started. By the time it was undone, a red sun peaked up over the rim, smearing long fingers of orange and amber light across the eastern horizon. He rowed out to the mooring where his sloop was tied, shooed a crow off the rime-streaked bow, and climbed aboard. Glancing to the west, he yanked the frozen line to crack the coating of ice, and pulled it in. Through the mist and early light, he noted banks of lee-set clouds resting low on the horizon. It didn't bode well, but he remained undaunted—his reunion with Genevieve the only thing on his mind.

He thought about what Duncan's friend had said about the line storm being due, recalling other years when a late storm marking the turn of winter had hit. Each year he'd still been at the lumber camp when it came, bringing snow, sleet, high winds, and sometimes hail. But, as when he'd worked at the rope house and lived inland, the storm had always been moderated by the shelter of trees. He had never experienced the ugly sea during a line storm, underplaying its dangers.

As the sun brightened, a parhelion appeared through wisps of fog to the east, giving him an eerie sense. The prime season for fog was beginning. Preparing to set sail, he had misgivings. More than once he thought of staying ashore. The tide had hit slack and was ebbing. It made going with the current easier, but the wind had died. It was cold, of that there could be no doubt. By the time he'd stowed his gear, a wall of fog was slipping toward shore from the east, obscuring the sun and shrouding the islands. His single-minded thoughts were of Genevieve. Now only a stretch of sea kept them apart, and he took on the challenge, eager to conquer it and be home. There were known risks, but he felt helpless to choose otherwise. His inner spirit hummed an indefinable dirge, grieving for reasons he couldn't explain.

It was three miles to the first island. Never had he considered the trip out to the island more like a passage. Never had the sea felt so lonely nor had his thoughts so strongly turned toward home and his Genevieve. Their days together had been happy, their union strong, and now a baby was to be added to their joy. He could think of nothing else. In just hours they would be together, and the bliss felt in that realization lifted his gray spirit and carried him over the gently rounding waves.

As the fog thickened, he skirted close to shore on the lee side of the island. Seeing ice floating at the edges, it occurred to him to snug up in the nearest bight and wait for a brighter day or perhaps return to the mainland. Instead, like a dog on a bone, he slacked the sail and bore to eastward.

His thoughts turned inward, breaking the bounds of awareness. With yearning desire, he stared at the sallow sea, thinking of the next winter when he and Genevieve could go ice fishing near the snug harbor of the island, hunt in the woods or gun for brant, black ducks, coots, and eiders with the Indians. Recalling the taste of Genevieve's coot stew strengthened his resolve. *I know the way like the back of my hand,* he confirmed, as he steered through slate-colored waters and dense fog, oblivious to clues that should have given him pause.

Skirting around the second island, now almost completely obscured by fog, his hopes dimmed. The tides, varying twelve feet with extreme undertows, had broken up the ice then refrozen into rough piles along the shoreline. It forced him out farther than he would have liked. The ice rumbled and snapped from the pressure of the tides and currents, forming ridges, here and there opening narrow leads of water. He thought about following one of the leads and snugging his boat into a safe harbor but didn't know how close to shore he could get. Leaving his boat and walking to shore was not an option. Salt ice couldn't be trusted to hold him.

Sea smoke hung about him in icy fringes. Straining to catch a glimpse of Gull Island, through the dense fog, he lost track of where he was. Instead of heading for the Bitawba Reach and Sobagpeka, he unknowingly turned toward open water.

A light breeze suddenly came up from the east, making progress more difficult. *I'll have to row the rest of the way,* he concluded. He furled the puffy sail and sculled the oars. Waves started building and the sea rolled bleak and threatening. Tugging at the oars, bending to the task, he pulled hard against the chop. On he struggled, his strength completely enervated. When the wind intensified, pushing the brume leeward, he realized he was nowhere near the islands. His melancholy mind grew heavy, his thoughts circling like birds of prey. He understood that without being able to get square, he was adrift in a seething sea and in for a hard chance. Not knowing what else to do, he continued rowing, refusing to acknowledge that he couldn't make it.

Strong winds turned the boat broadside and the waves rolled and pitched as a cold rain poured down. He battled on through the day, refusing to give up. In white water, crushing chunks of ice, torn loose from the shore, battered the boat. The hull lay over in the water farther and farther as virulent waves crashed against the bow. A damp cold like nothing he'd experienced gripped him. It felt like his flesh was rotting and sliding from his bones, and he couldn't feel his fingers and toes. The violent sea sent icy salt water spraying over the gunwale and a spate of sleet, sharp as a knife, stabbed at him as his unquiet heart realized he wouldn't make it.

"Am I to die in solitude then?" he questioned aloud. "What penances have I left unpaid?"

There would be no refuge—no assistance from an indifferent universe. Realizing this, he quit rowing and sat on the middle board, watching as waves climbed over the boat, furiously tossing it. Amid murmurs of solitude, his mind reviewed the tranquil years with Genevieve—the first time he'd seen her, their wedding day, her arrival on the island, her joy in seeing for the first time their house and the roses he'd planted for her, the love in her eyes when telling him she was with child.

With the next wave, the oars were ripped from their wooden tholes and sent adrift on the sea. Distracted by a light coming from behind him, he turned. The setting sun turned rosy then golden, and he heard a song sparrow sing. Confusion descended. His mind, swirling like the wind, played tricks on him and he could no longer make sense of things. The next frigid wave hit with force, capsizing his boat, and violently hurling his effete body from the thwarts. If anyone had been within hearing distance, they would have heard him cry out as he plunged into the icy cold water. Staring up at the mysterious sheaves of light streaming toward him through black water, distant memories rose slowly from the ashes of his mind. Momentarily lucid, he understood that he would never hold his baby nor would he ever see Genevieve again. It had all been a dream. His life with her was only a remembrance, a dredging of the past. Flaying his arms, he surfaced for a brief moment, but the struggle was useless. His chest felt squeezed like it was in a vise and there was no breath to take. A wall of water broke over him, washing down his back, his heavy boots pulled him under, and he sank beneath the waves. His circling thoughts ceased, his eyes closed, and darkness consumed him. In the lonely silence, a voice beckoned.

— CHAPTER TWENTY ONE —

Lives of great men all remind us
We can make our lives sublime,
And, departing, leave behind us
Footprints in the sands of time.

Footprints, that perhaps another,
Sailing o'er life's solemn main,
A forlorn and shipwrecked brother,
Seeing, shall take heart again.

Let us, then, be up and doing,
With a heart for any fate;
Still achieving, still pursuing,
Learn to labor and to wait.

From *A Psalm of Life* by Longfellow

"There ya be," a voice summoned, as from a great distance.

Lanyon opened his eyes, surprised to find himself in another world. Dunnage and the bodies of his crew were scattered across the beach. Like him they had been swept from the sea and deposited amid rockweed at the tidemark. The ship, driven ashore and dashed onto the ledges, lay broken to pieces on the rocks at low tide. Flotsam littered the shore. A mild breeze blew and the day was bright. Patches of fog hovered above the water, drifting leeward.

A man cradled Lanyon's head in his lap, carefully wrapping a bandage around it—his rough beard and hands presumably those of a fisherman. Lanyon's waistcoat was off. Dread gripped him as he reached for his vest pocket. The leather pouch holding Kayna's letter was gone. His tortured and broken body reclaimed his attention as he tried to move, and screamed out.

"Yer leg be broken. Try not ta move," the man advised.

Glancing around, he saw some of his crew being carried up onto the embankment and away from the rocky shore. Among them was the limp body of Dr. Soadey. The wind carried the sounds of moans and cries across the beach. Awbrey, lying near him, groaned. Beyond him, two other seamen squirmed and writhed.

"You be the captain, I heah," the man stated.

"Yes," Lanyon weakly answered.

"Some of the men sed your ship was caught in the hurricane then the line stahm. *Mordonn* was her name?"

Lanyon could only nod as recent events came flooding back into memory. His head throbbed with pain.

"How many were lost?"

"It's true not all made it but lucky any of ya did. Judging from the look of yoah ship, it's a miracle any sahvived a stahm like that. You been lying heah fah some time it appeah. If we hadn't been blowed off course fishin the shoals, weda nevah found ya."

"Where's the woman?" Lanyon questioned.

"There be no women, only men. Some badly injured, most dead, I'm afeared," he offered, gesturing to the right.

Lanyon glanced up the slope toward where the man had indicated. Several bodies lay in a pile. Surveying the beach, he saw a man lying about twenty feet away from him raise his head and reach out his hand then fall back down on the sand. It was Ennis. Two of the rescuers picked up his body, carried him up the slope, and deposited him with the others in a tangle of pea-vines near the cottage. Past the dead, Lanyon could see a lovely orchard choked in alders, the garden overgrown with vines, yellow buttercups struggling against the weeds. Remnants of bronze, gold, and copper-colored leaves clung to trees in the woods beyond the meadow. Gone were the sheep, goats, horses, and cows. Gone were the well-cared for fields, the outdoor spit, and racks of drying fish—gone was eternal spring. It was again fall.

The cottage was being digested by nature. The vertically planked door had rotted, the iron hinges rusted, the shutters hung askew, the beach stone chimney had crumbled, and the glass window panes were broken. The weather-beaten roof of wattle, shredded by the wind, was full of holes, allowing the elements in. He could only guess at the condition of the interior, imagining the disarray. Rose bushes, once so carefully pruned and tended, nearly overgrew the house. Orange hips pendulously hung from thorny branches, and fallen red petals were strewn thick across the tall, browning grass. Lilac bushes to the north of the house had become trees, their leaves yellowed and dying. Wild flowers, spreading all the way to the woods, had taken over the meadow, garden, and fields. Beyond the meadow, he saw a pile of boards—remnants of the clapboard shed, blackened with weather.

"Where's the woman?" Lanyon repeated.

"I told you thahr's…"

"No, the woman who lives in this cottage. Where is she?"

"There hasn't been anyone living in that cottage fah a hundred yeahrs. Stahms and hahricanes have taken their toll with it but still it stands—a haunting sight to all those who have passed by this island. It's a mahcy we came upon you at all."

"What happened to her?"

"The woman? How do you know abowt hah?"

"I've heard things," he lied, trying to disentangle events in his netted mind from the revelations he was hearing.

"She was a witch they say—lahned how to cuahr the sick and raise the dead. The Indians taught hah to be a shaman. Thah's still evidence, though only the cleahring remains, of whah she grew herbs to make potions. She appahrently got hah roots from them woods ovah on the lee side of the island by that circle of stones. It's told hah husband was a coastah in the summah, slooping cobblestones to Boston, sometimes cahd-wood. In wintah he was a woodsman on the mainland, cutting masts fah the

Royal Navy. Story goes he'd cut his last tree fah the mast agent that wintah and, in the spring, planned on retahning to the island for good. T'is a well knowd stahry heah bowts.

"She fended fah hahself so much the wintahs he was gone, she'd growd ruggedly independent out of the need of it an' staying cleah of all social contact but from hah husband and the Indians. She was with child when he left in t' fall, they say. It's nevah been knowd if he knew abowt the child. Rumah has it he did, and that was why he'd quit masting ehly in the spring—so he'd be home befah the baby was bahn. Wintah ran late that yeah. Making his way back to the island, he was caught in the line stahm. The stahries of its treachery as famous today as then. Nevah been anothah like it since.

"He nevah retahned, was nevah fownd. This island is the most remote of the Ahchipelago. Though islandahs often visited one another, most didn't venchah way out heah. The Indians came to hunt and fish but few othahs. In addition to weathah preventing passage in the stahm, the reach iced ovah that spring it's told. There was still fahrwood at the hahth and owt in the shed, still food in the stahroom, so that wahn't the problem. Speculation has it that when the stahm hit, the same one that caught hah husband and dragged him down into the sea, she went into labah and had a hahd time of it. It's not known if it was the stahm, the cold or childbahth that done hah in that night. Could 'a been all three. An itinahate fishahman in a packet boat blowd off cahs, as we wah today, found them just befah the thaw. Frozen togethah, they were. Thah was blood a plenty and the mothah clutched hah baby in hah ahrms. It were still attached to hah by the cahrd. The crew buried 'em both togethah above the cliffs at the south end of the island."

"It was all so beautiful."

"What was?"

"All of it. Sobagpeka."

"What is Sobagpeka?"

"The island, this island. Sea Smoke Island."

"This island be called Foggy Island."

"But do you know its Indian name?"

"No. People call it Foggy Island cuz you kin rarely see it fer fog. Not many Indians hereabowts now. You been heah afore?"

"What is the date today?" Lanyon asked, ignoring the question, suspicions suddenly coming into focus.

"November fahst."

"So last night was Ancestor night," he involuntarily offered. "Samhain."

"What?"

"Halloween. Last night was Allhallow's Eve."

"Ayeh. T'is a foul wind that blows on Allhallow's Eve. Many a ship is wrecked on Allhallow's Eve."

"So today is All Saints' Day."

"If you say so."

Two fishermen moved Lanyon further up onto the shore as the tide turned to flood and began slowly crawling up the beach.

"Where's my waistcoat," Lanyon blurted, thinking he might have stuffed the leather pouch into one of those pockets instead of his vest.

"Dunno but t'is shuah to be wet. This blanket will keep you wahm," he said, wrapping a blanket around Lanyon's shoulders. "Lay heah now and be still and rest. I'll be back."

Lanyon cared little for the loss of the waistcoat, but the knowledge that his letter from Kayna was gone, rolled over him like a crushing breaker. The leather pouch and letter was all he held dear in the world. Memories of Kayna descended on him and he again felt the pain of his loss, his loneliness, his never-ending grief. Sighing, despondent, he lay still. Aches and pains tore at his body, indistinguishable as to their specific location. As night came on, the fishermen built a fire and made a makeshift shelter for the survivors then went to their boat, moored in the cove, to sleep. It was a mild night despite the lateness of the season. A ceiling of clouds hung low, but a bright and full moon flashed through them as they drifted past. Lanyon's thoughts briefly turned to Lamorna, wondering what was to become of her. Against his will, he finally slept. At morning light, he was awakened by the activity of fishermen on the beach.

The bodies of the dead were loaded into the boat, carried out to sea, and unceremoniously dumped into the reach. On shore, the wounds of the few to survive were tended. They were only Awbrey, Smitts, Chegwin, and two other seamen. Several others had died during the night. When the fishermen returned from delivering the last of the dead to the sea, the remaining crew were carried to the boat. Captain Penberthy was to be put on last. Fog rolled in from the sea as one of the fishermen helped him to stand, supporting his weight as he struggled toward the water.

"That leg a yahs must be set. We'll see to it once weah on shah. The only wood we have heah is driftwood and I doubt it would do the job," the fisherman helping Lanyon explained.

"C'mon," the captain urged. " We need to get across the reach before the fog."

Lanyon's mind was teeming with questions and he felt suddenly compelled to turn for one last look at the cottage, trying to make himself believe what he'd seen. Wisps of fog enveloped the cottage, nearly obscuring it. On the stone stoop in front of the dilapidated door sat a gray cat.

"Where did that cat come from?"

"Don't know," a disinterested voice near him answered. "I seen it heah one summah, las time we come by heah a cupla yeahs past. Don't know how it sahvives. Lots of stahries bowt cats and witches on this island here abowts."

"I want to see the cat," Lanyon stated matter-of-factly, breaking loose from the men helping him and turning toward the cottage.

"We need to go afore the tide turns agin," the sea captain instructed from the shore. "Fog's already gatherin."

"Just give me a moment, please."

Hobbling up the well-worn path, dragging his broken leg, Lanyon slowly made his way toward the cottage.

"That cat'll not come to you," the captain yelled after him. "Tis as fahral as the wind that blows across this island."

In that moment Lanyon cared not whether he was to be rescued or if the boat waited for him. It was like a spell had come over him, urging him toward the cat—urging him to see if what his heart was telling him could possibly be true. When at the cottage, he bent over and talked to the cat.

"Are you Morrigan, Macha, Nemain?"

The cat came to him, touching his hand and purring as he scooped it into the curve of his arm. Love and protection immediately surrounded and embraced him. Looking into the cat's eyes, he found the confirmation he was seeking. One eye was blue, the other, dun-colored.

On the stoop where the cat had sat, he saw that the woven mat was like new. Next to it lay a sprig of wild mint, a jasper stone, and a small leather pouch. He picked up the items one by one, examining each. The sprig of mint was fresh and fragrant, as though it had just been picked. Looking at the unique markings on the jasper stone, he knew it could only be the same one Genevieve had given him. The leather pouch held two neatly folded letters. They fit perfectly inside and were in restored condition, like they'd just been put there. In the distance, a song sparrow sang its melodic tune. Then, in a suspended moment, time stood still, events slashed through his pragmatic mind, and he remembered—remembered it all.

"Emma, my love. You are my life, my future, my forever," he cooed. "I know now that you are my Kayna and my Genevieve. I'll never leave you again. You once fixed my broken leg and healed my wounds. Now you must heal my broken heart. That can only be if we are together," he spoke, stuffing the stone, mint, and leather pouch into his pocket. "We'll fix the cottage and build a boat to get us to the mainland when needed. We'll resurrect the gardens and fields, eat fish and all the wild resources of the island to survive. We will be together."

Glancing toward the woods, a stag stared at him before turning to disappear into the dark growth. Still carrying the cat in his arm, he turned toward the ruined cottage, ready to go inside. Hearing a voice behind him, he paused for a moment.

"Well, I'll be," the captain exclaimed, standing near him. "I didn't think that wild thing would have none of us."

"I appreciate all your help, but I want you to leave me here," Lanyon pronounced, with a strength he couldn't have predicted.

"Leave you heah? That gash in yer head has made you daft?" the captain spurt. "You be in no condition to stay heah, especially with a broken leg and all yer cuts and bruises."

"If I leave, I must take the cat."

"Come, man. We've no time fah bahthahin with cats."

"Please, it's my only request. I must take the cat with me."

"Ya must leave the cat," the captain insisted, a deep scowl forming on his weathered face.

"I won't leave without the cat."

"Vahry well. Dixon," the captain roared. "Come and get him."

Lanyon could see the fishermen holding the boat in the shallows just offshore. One of their burliest was wading through the waves. As Dixon strode up the embankment toward him, Lanyon recognized defeat.

Nuzzling his face into the downy neck of the cat, he whispered promises into her ear. Then, setting her gently down on the step, he turned to face the captain and Dixon, resigned for the moment.

"Come on then," Dixon commanded.

Before Lanyon could further resist, Dixon slung

him over his shoulder like a sack of grain and headed for the beach with the captain following close behind. Slashing his powerful legs through the waves to the boat, he deposited his charge over the gunwale. On the crowded deck, Lanyon joined what remained of his crew, nestling into the sternsheets alongside of them. He was given a blanket, made as comfortable as possible, and given fresh water to drink. The boat reeked of fish but none minded—all but Lanyon grateful for the rescue.

He bore his physical pain, uncomplaining, as he looked shoreward. His only conscious ache was a deep longing to stay with Emma. Focused on their pain and misery, his crew didn't notice his despair. His was not a physical pain, but emotional, even spiritual. *A leg will mend, but what of a heart*, he questioned within. Only the captain knew of his desire to stay on the island or take the cat with him. Occupied with getting them underway and, concluding the bizarre request had emerged from Lanyon's addled mind, he gave it no further thought or concern.

The crew of the fishing vessel weighed anchor as Lanyon stared back at the cottage with a deep sense of frustration and loss. The cat continued to sit for a time, staring his direction as though aware of his reluctance to leave. A calmness settled on Lanyon with this awareness, and he understood that when he returned to the island, his Forever and One True Love would be there waiting for him. The door to the cottage, which had been closed, opened slightly and, as if to convey her resolve to reclaim their island home and wait for him, the cat turned and walked into the cottage.

"Ready we go," the captain yelled.

The men rowed into the waves. Once past the ledges, the boat was turned to flow with the tide. The captain ordered the sails set, and the boat was steered around the north end of the island then into Bitawba Reach. Looking back toward Sobagpeka one last time as it receded in the distance, the cottage erased by sea smoke, Lanyon sighed and relaxed into the only truth he knew.

I'll be back and we'll be together.

EPILOGUE

According to Celtic mythology, the Etains were three sisters whose names were Morrigan, Macha, and Nemain, all of whom had connections with magic, fertility, rejuvenation, and the giving of life. (1) Often called the Three Blessed Ladies, these trinitarian fate-goddesses represent the woven threads of past, present and future, the cycles of which are "intertwined... an integral and sacred part of the web of life and the spiral of time." (2) Other triunes they represent are the daughter, mother, and grandmother, the maiden, matron, and crone, the body, mind, and spirit, our intellectual, creative, and spiritual aspects, (3) the phases of the moon.

The waxing, full, and waning phases of the silver moon represent the rhythmic "patterns of transformation and the eternal promise of renewal." (2) The moon goes into darkness for three days, waxes toward a full moon, and wanes to a new moon, cycling through its phases of life, death, and rebirth over and over again. Its phases show us that time is not linear but circular and "no event is irreversible, no transformation final, no ending a true death." (2)

Water symbolizes the emotions, the sacred feminine, and the threshold between worlds. It is during Samhain, when the veil is thinnest, that the limitation of time can be seen as the illusion it is.

Epilogue References:
(1) The Secrets of the Tarot by Barbara G. Walker
(2) *Queen of the Night* by Sharynne MacLeod Nic-MHACHA
(3) *Women in Celtic Myth* by Moyra Caldecott

About the Author

Miriam Nesset is originally from Wisconsin. She currently lives in Maine where she continues to write. She is a Ragdale Fellow and a member of the Maine Writers and Publishers Alliance.

Other Books by Miriam:

Captured

Dream Legend: Facing the Condor

Georgie Blake and the Bushie Sisters

Murder in Between

Left of the Moon

To learn more, visit her website at www.miriamnesset.com